The Mermaid of Lake Superior

The Mermaid of Lake Superior

a novel

Aurora Lothbrok

Beaver's Pond Press
St. Paul, Minnesota

Beaver's Pond Press is committed to turning interesting people into independent authors. In that spirit, we are proud to offer this book to our readers; however, the story, the experiences, and the words are the author's alone.

Edited by Paige Polinsky
Cover and interior illustrations by Jill Myer
Book design and typesetting by Laura Drew

ISBN 13: 978-1-64343-677-7
Library of Congress Catalog Number: 2023911265
Printed in the United States of America
First Edition: 2023
27 26 25 24 23 5 4 3 2 1

Beaver's Pond Press
939 West Seventh Street
Saint Paul, MN 55102
(952) 829-8818
www.BeaversPondPress.com

To order, visit www.auroralothbrok.com.

Contact the author at www.auroralothbrok.com for school visits, speaking engagements, book club discussions, and interviews.

For my husband—
Is this proof yet that I was actually writing
and not online shopping?

For Arabelle, my beloved Samalama, and
for tortured pharmacists everywhere.

In loving memory of Speed in Spenard and George the Poodle.

Author's Note

THE WATERS OF LAKE SUPERIOR are saturated with hidden archives of the past. The greatest lake of all time blesses us with life as well as takes it. Acknowledging the water as final resting place of many souls and ships, we must pay our respects to those who have lost their lives in her tumultuous waters.

Accounts of shipwrecks portrayed in this voyage through the waters are based on true stories and historical events. Names of those lost have been borrowed and frozen in the hourglass of time, reminiscent of a former era, but the characters are lovingly fabricated. In some instances, the characters' pasts are based on history, but the names have been changed. Grateful for the historical slice of life that the lost souls of the lake have gifted us, this work of fiction honors their legacy by making them an important part of our journey through the waters. Those who found themselves at the mercy of the sea and perished in the deep will never be forgotten.

As rich in history as she is deep, Lake Superior has seen many events unfurl before her splashing waves. Prior to colonization, the lands surrounding the lake were home to the Anishinaabe people. Places included in the story, such as those now known as Isle Royale and the Apostle Islands, were important spiritual lands for the Ojibwe. The significant history of these lands is included in our mermaid's journey to honor the Indigenous, both gone and still living, the first to grace the waters of our beloved lake. The pristine waters not only provided nourishment to the body but also the spirit.

Tidbits of Ojibwe culture and mythology are included this modern-day tale because the story of the lake may have started with melting glaciers, but it ultimately began with her relationship to the Indigenous people. Spirit beings have been borrowed from the Anishinaabe to solidify their importance in the history of the lake. This mermaid tale is forged with the utmost respect for the Anishinaabe cultures and is a tribute to their importance. To paddle the waters of Gitchi-Gami with the Ojibwe is a gift. May it inspire one to be thirsty for a tall glass of Lake Superior's history, including that of her original residents.

As for the adventure at hand, it is time to send one last acknowledgement to the realm of Norse mythology. The stories of the Norse Gods have inspired many mortals, as the Gods have had their likenesses in pop culture for some time. Deities of the ancient Norse religion bless the pages of this story with humble respect for those who practice the Old Norse religion to this very day. The Norse myths are beautiful and intricate with dynamic Gods, and I hope to do justice to the mention of their names.

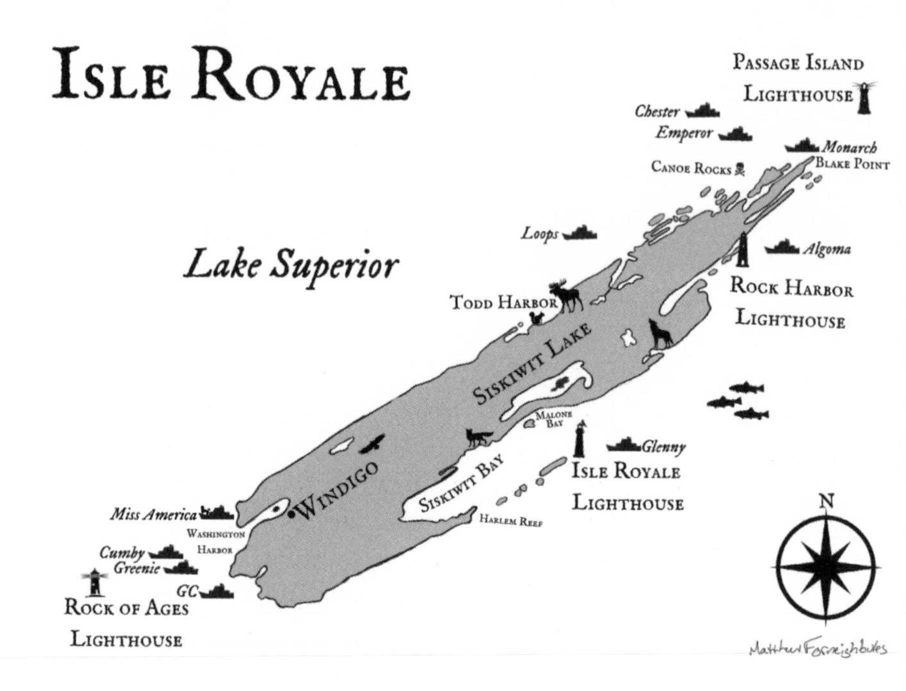
Isle Royale
Passage Island Lighthouse
Chester
Emperor
Monarch
Blake Point
Canoe Rocks
Loops
Algoma
Lake Superior
Todd Harbor
Rock Harbor Lighthouse
Siskiwit Lake
Malone Bay
Glenny
Windigo
Siskiwit Bay
Isle Royale Lighthouse
Miss America
Washington Harbor
Harlem Reef
Cumby
Greenie
GC
Rock of Ages Lighthouse
N
Matthew Fosneighbors

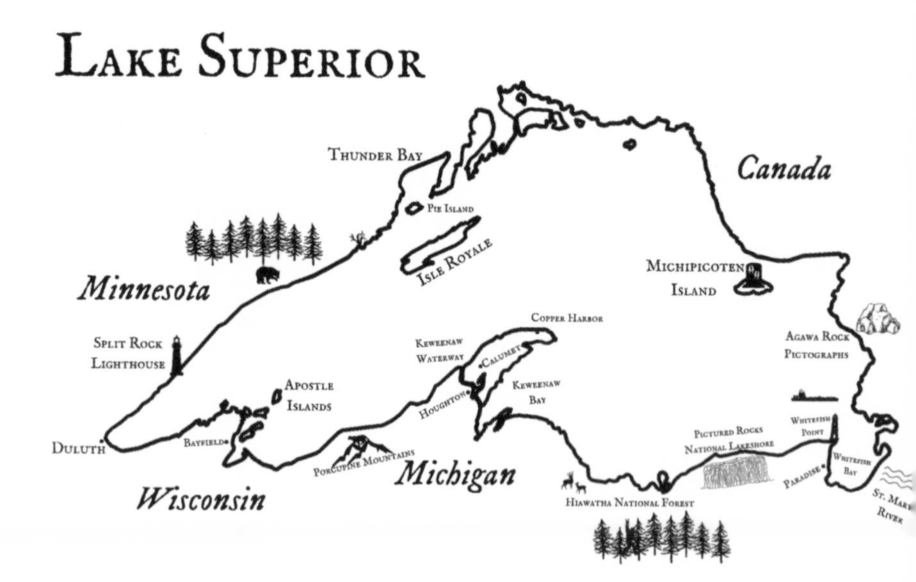
Lake Superior
Thunder Bay
Canada
Pie Island
Isle Royale
Michipicoten Island
Minnesota
Copper Harbor
Keweenaw Waterway
Calumet
Agawa Rock Pictographs
Split Rock Lighthouse
Apostle Islands
Houghton
Keweenaw Bay
Whitefish Point
Pictured Rocks National Lakeshore
Whitefish Bay
Duluth
Bayfield
Paradise
Porcupine Mountains
Michigan
Wisconsin
Hiawatha National Forest

Foreword

Greetings, fellow underwater explorer.

It is my delight to accompany you on this magical journey through mystical depths of Lake Superior. I'm here to clarify the murky waters by providing bits and pieces of pertinent information along the way. Back in my day, I was a volunteer for the historical society.

You go ahead. I'm going to sit for just a minute and finish my tea while the ball game wraps up. Oh–that reminds me! Please do not consume bananas while reading this book.

Warm regards and good fishing,

Shirley

Prologue

A WAVE ROARED AND TRANSFORMED into a myriad of disintegrating white bubbles after colliding with a battered and smooth gray rock cliff. Despite the water's relentless ventures, the north shore of Minnesota persisted with timeless beauty. The rocky shoreline of Lake Superior went on for miles, lined with lush mosses, menacing rocks, and spunky green conifers. Another wave splashed as though reaching for the land, keeping time with a strong sense of duty. The waves, a mere portion of a powerful and dynamic dancing body of water, constantly grasped for earth from the depths of the great omnipotent lake.[1]

A sleek, brown body fluttered across the rugged sand, face twitching with curiosity. The gentle pitter-patter of his toe beans was hastened by the sight of his best friend lying motionless in the rocks. It was unusual for Nigig's beloved mermaid to look so

[1] Let's be honest, folks. Those waves had nowhere else to go with all that momentum. Crash and splash!

haphazardly washed ashore, and today she resembled something the raccoon dragged in and abandoned. Her body rocked to the rhythm of every incoming wave, and her gorgeous locks wrapped across her body in a splay of tangles. He placed a gentle paw on her pale arm. The white noise broke when his voice, heavy with enthusiasm squealed, "Hey, H, hey!"

H brushed her long, dark hair out of weary ice-blue eyes, skin dripping with cold water droplets.

"Nigig?" she answered, voice meek with exhaustion.

The inquisitive river otter's long whiskers tickled her hand upon the beach.

Nigig propped his front paws up on her arm and tilted his head sideways as he read her appearance.

"Oh, girl," he sputtered in a high-pitched frenzy. "Shish-ke-nards! You don't look so good."

H blinked her weary eyelids and looked up at the fluffy, maniacal spring clouds overhead. The mighty sun tried to peek out behind the bank of fluff, but the clouds prevailed, splashing just a whisper of sunbeam around them. Her rosy cheeks were sullen, and she flipped her raven locks to the side as she sat up in the shallow water.

"Good gravy!"

She winced and arched her back like a Halloween cat, revealing a large round burning-red sore nestled right below her right shoulder blade. Concentric scarlet dots lined the interior of her inflamed skin, so red it was almost maroon. The swollen area had a small blister, which oozed a glorious yellowish-green pus.

"Do you even know what gravy is?" Nigig giggled, preening his dense chocolate-brown fur. "What makes it good? Broth? Spices?"

"Yes," H answered. "One of the sailors told me all about it! They put it on pasties and on smashed potatoes. Lou never stops talking about human food, and, of course, I've done my share of sampling in the galley."

Nigig wriggled closer to his friend. "Oh, you and your ghostly sea voyagers. They've got you talking like a sailor," he responded, clasping together his front paws and peering over her shoulder.

She hadn't even mentioned the gleaming silver pop can that was gently tinkling against the shoreline. If litter couldn't fire her up, something was certainly out of sorts. Nigig's nostrils flared, and his beady eyes suddenly burned with the glowing tenacity of the harvest moon. The fur on his neck ruffled up and he took a step back, navigating the rocky unsalted coast with finesse and ease.[2]

"I think you need to see a healer. I mean, I could lick your wound for you, but you smell like barnacle balls."

H pointed to her gleaming silver tail, which she wriggled with a snarky little splash of defiance. She had never interacted with humans—well, alive ones at least. All her human friends were ghosts, and not just regular ghosts. These were the men and women who had lost their lives to the waters of Gitchi-Gami.[3] The spirits of the deep had always fascinated H, as they bestowed upon her their knowledge and stories of life on land.

"You need a veterinarian—like my cousin Horace had to visit once, when he almost got taken away by that rude-ass eagle—or maybe a real human doctor? I don't really know . . . you're, like, half scaled and half biped. I shall ask the Gods[4] for guidance."

His adorable pleading eyes hit H right in the feels. Nigig had been her best friend for as long as she could remember. Her visits to the remote and rocky shores were the highlight of her day, but a dense fog was rising through her brain, and she couldn't focus. Something was very, very wrong. She felt hot and clammy—in the human sense, not like a molluskan. Moments like this made her yearn for family . . . if she even had one. Being a wild merlady with a BFF otter was fun and all, but knowing where she came from would be nice, especially when fighting for her life out in the deep blue nowhere.

[2] The muscular tail of a river otter helps them with balancing and grappling on uneven terrain. The swole (as the kids these days say) appendage also comes in handy when they swim.

[3] Gitchi-Gami, Lake Superior's name from the Ojibwe, translates to "big sea."

[4] Many creatures believe in the existence of a higher deity—be it the Norse or Greek gods, an ambiguous Creator, the earth herself (Mother Nature), or the Christian God.

Chapter One

"THAT'S HOTTER THAN A FRIED bologna sandwich!" Lou exclaimed as his harem of sailor friends shook with belly chuckles.

His eyes twinkled as he turned his gaze to H, her pale skin glowing in the water.

"Anyway, you should have seen the *Algoma* in her glory days. We had quite the time navigating that canal."[5]

H nestled in on her barstool with hopes that Lou would tell the entire story of the wreck. To prod him along, she chimed in with her best impersonation: "The lake unleashed so much fury that thousands of pounds of railroad materials and supplies were violently thrown into the freshwater sea! It's such a mess that even the curious divers don't visit."[6]

[5] The *Algoma* was too large to navigate the Welland Canal to Lake Superior. They cut her in half, put her on pontoons, and reassembled her in New York. One might wonder, "Why not just build her in America?"

[6] Buried by underwater currents and covered in algae, present-day Algoma wreckage is discombobulated, slimy, and only mildly identifiable. Parts of the wreck remain undiscovered by humans.

H looked around and realized she had captured the room's attention. She raised her fist in the air and continued.

"The engine was recovered and given the rare second chance at life that everybody deserves! Recycling is good business, for the pocketbook and planet alike."

Lou looked up as if watching his past unfold before his eyes.

"It was a frigid November morning. The year was 1885. The two-year-old SS *Algoma* tragically perished in a hurricane-force blizzard when she ran aground near Isle Royale.[7] You bet your bottom we didn't go down without a fight!"

His mustache danced as he reminisced with affection.

"If I could go back, I'd still choose the ship over land. If the waters didn't getcha, the smallpox would have!" Lou put his hand over his heart. "Forty-five brave souls went down with the ship, all before their time."

A moment of silence fell across the crowd as the men bowed their heads. Over 260 feet long, the ghost of the *Algoma* sparkled with a white haze. She looked freshly constructed, straight out of the Glasgow shipyard, with sails erect. Ropes hung from the mast, which also supported an array of flags that waved gently with the currents of the water. Those same ropes and riggings were what white-knuckled crewmen had hung onto for dear life when the astronomical storm hit. The lake was so cold and deep that many vessels that didn't fall to pieces like the *Algoma* rested in the waters perfectly preserved. At some depths, the bodies of men were essentially frozen in time. Even painted wood maintained its bright color.

"Isle Royale's rocky shoreline has garnered many a victim, you know," Lou continued, wide-eyed with passion. "Grand ships are no match for a grand storm. Many seek refuge behind the island and use her as a shield from the wind and waves; but between the rocks, reefs, and low visibility, the island has a built-in ship catcher. Voyaging on Lake Superior is not for the faint of heart."

"Thank God for the electricity, because I would have never

[7] Isle Royale is the largest island on the lake, deemed a national park in 1940.

boarded this vessel otherwise. Luxury is modern technology, you know."

A hand gloved in white lace pointed to the faceted crystal chandelier in the middle of the room as Genevieve Frost joined the conversation, her bustled Victorian dress billowing in the water.

"You're just lucky, Lou, that one of those sea sirens didn't lure you to your untimely death first!"

She looked at H with a smile and wink. Time hadn't changed her one bit: she sported her favorite ruffled plum frock, regal pearl earrings, and shoes with a modest heel. Even in the afterlife, she looked like the socialite of the season.

H met Mrs. Frost's gaze and smiled.

"Frosty, you know I'm the only mermaid in this giant mess of water—and for that matter, I've never taken a sailor for sport!"

In H's simmering blue eyes, *siren* implied an evil temptress living in that half-human, half-fish body. She despised the stereotype of preying on humans but tolerated the term begrudgingly. H had never met a human, ghost or otherwise, that she didn't like and therefore had no reason to become a murder-maid.[8]

Frosty draped a perfectly tailored arm around H.

"Oh, you know what I mean, my dear. You're the beautiful mer-daughter I never had and always desired."

H took the liberty to pluck the flower-adorned hat from Frosty's head, placing it on her own noggin and twirling around to model the vintage bonnet. The yellow flower danced in the underwater current as if it were alive in the wind.

"Oh, honey, that doesn't quite go with your outfit!" Frosty said with a grin.

Between sailors teaching her every knot known to man and her friend Vera giving her knitting lessons aboard the SS *Kamloops*, H had compiled pale, old ropes into an intricate crop top decked in decorative knots. It fastened securely around her neck, and ropes crisscrossed the back like a Victorian corset (a detail Frosty had insisted upon).

[8] That's a bit of a stretch; H isn't a huge fan of Stanley. There we go being midwestern nice about it again.

"I'm still dressed to perfection, thanks to your help," said H with a jingle of galvanized steel chain—the hot technology of the 1830s—adorned with smooth brown agates.

"Indeed," answered Frosty with a little hesitation. "You still look a bit like a vagabond, though. Don't take it personally."

Frosty slipped behind H to straighten her corset straps.

"I'm just glad you have something to protect your breasts from getting a nasty sunburn when you visit Nigig on shore. You know, my dear, pale skin was once a sign of wealth and social status."

"Nowadays, being pale is merely a sign of melanin deficiency," replied H. "I'm clearly meant to be a deep-water fish. It is evolution at work."

"You should bring us some of those science books from the other vessels," said Lou. "I get bored with my 1800s knowledge and need a snide reply when you say things like that."

"The best book I read was actually on land. Nigig knocked it off a rock while some college students were drinking beer and studying. He pushed it to the water's edge so I could enjoy it later," H said with a laugh.

The souls of the *Algoma* gathered frequently on the vast promenade deck to socialize and dance. Below sat the main saloon, where Lou served liquor, hot meals, and insults. As if recreating their ship days, the ghosts would congregate there for daily meals.[9] Round wooden tables filled the room, each surrounded by carved wooden chairs occupied by the murmurs and laughter of afterlife banter. It was thought by the ghosts that the ship itself had a soul of her own, and she could feel the love the sailors had for her and reciprocated the sentiment from the afterlife.

"There's no place like home-a on the *Algoma*!" Lou cheered.

Lou lifted a pint of ale behind the bar.

"We've got the modern amenities and *spirits* to get you through the worst of times—pun intended."

He flicked a switch, illuminating small lightbulbs in iron wall fixtures behind the bar.

[9] Ghosts don't actually need to eat. They do it because food is good and it's fun.

Lou continued, "You won't need a primitive lantern in your room tonight. We've got electricity!"

Modest shelves lit up Lou's pride and joy: handblown glass bottles filled with aged Scottish whiskey. A barrel of wheat ale sat against the wall, and a couple of bottles of red wine sat on the counter in front of them. The wall, papered in gaudy burgundy and mauve, featured a colorful oil painting of a lighthouse at sunset.

"Electricity was invented by nature, not man," H pointed out with a shrug. "It could have been Mother Nature, Zeus, or Thor throwing temper tantrums. We'll never know. But lightning has existed since the beginning of time. I'd toss a few bolts if given the chance."

"Aye," Lou responded. "The Gods don't mess around, especially with the weather on this lake. Neither does Thomas Edison when it comes to inventive science, so says the newspaper."

Lou slammed a green wine bottle down on the counter and looked at Frosty and H.

"Would you ladies like a fresh beverage this evening?" The wine bottle danced in Lou's hands as he showed off the vintage.

"Don't tell me you just want water. There's no money in water!" His eyebrows lowered as he tried to fake a serious demeanor.

Frosty chimed, "I'll take a whiskey on the rocks today."

Lou promptly picked up a glass, dropped a few agates into it, and poured a hefty shot of whiskey while holding back a smirk. Much like the spirits and the ship itself, the joke never got old.

"Oh, you're such a royal troll, Lou!" Frosty exclaimed, lifting the glass delicately to her thin pink lips (pinky up, of course). "At one point in my life, I would have yelled at you for putting filthy rocks in my drink!"

The hours of her afterlife spent conversing with sailors became quite apparent when Frosty joked around with Lou, yet she managed to maintain her class and poise while throwing in a sailor word or two.

"What's on the menu for dinner this fine evening?" Frosty asked.

"I've managed to cook up something really delicious for the likes of you. We'll be feasting on red potato and leek soup with a bit of lake trout covered in my special garlic herb buttery breadcrumbs. The world's best wild blueberry cobbler will be served for dessert."

Lou pronounced the word *blueberry* like a seductive and magical thing. He floated off momentarily to stir the giant pot of soup on his stove, then flipped some hearty fish fillets on the grill. He wiped his hands on his white cloth apron and floated back to join the ladies.

H's eyes lit up at the words *blueberry cobbler.*

"I'm gonna pass on the trout, as that would be half-cannibalistic of me," she said with a shudder.

"Big fish eat little fish all the time, honey," responded Lou. "It's the circle of life, the vortex of existence, survival of the shittiest . . ." His voice trailed off into a whisper, "Some mothers eat their young. The horror!"

With a wink, Lou plopped a warm bowl of blueberry cobbler down on the counter. H squealed with delight and slid the scalloped white china bowl toward her, grabbing the gleaming silver spoon and taking a moment to admire the decorative vines etched into the handle.

H shoveled a heaping spoonful of cobbler into her mouth. She couldn't explain why she could see ghosts, talk to ghosts, or eat ghost food. She could speak to animals—both ghost and living—as well. She knew she had to be some sort of special hybrid, like a tiger muskellunge.[10] Weird genetic traits could occur when crossbreeding species. H had lungs and gills, allowing her to breathe air and water alike. Her gills were small and tucked behind her ears; with her long black hair flowing and draping over them, they were like the hidden prize on a game show behind door number two.

Before Frosty could take a delicate bite of soup, H had already finished her dessert. "Life is uncertain; eat your dessert first," she said.

[10] A northern pike and muskellunge can breed to make a tiger muskie. They have traits of both fish and grow faster, but they are sterile. Tiger muskies like to eat northern pike—and thank God someone does! I've always considered them too bony.

Frosty gave H a nudge of approval.

"I sure as hell wish I would have!"

"Are we really sure there is a hell?" asked Lou. "I mean, you did end up here for all eternity."

H stifled a snort, laughing from her belly up as Frosty giggled.

"Oh, Lou. That was delicious, and the cobbler was good too! Best I've had yet," H said, her hand making a chef's kiss from her lips.

The room grew silent. That's how you knew Lou was a good cook—nobody ever managed to speak a peep once their plate hit the table.

"Perfectly cooked meals like this make me wish my corset weren't so damn tight," added Frosty.

Just then, Mr. Beau Frost and their eight-year-old son, Henry, rushed into the dining area, as though the most horrible thing they could do was be late for dinner.

"Apologies, Lou. The crewmen were showing Henry how to run the steam engines! We had to clean ourselves up a bit."

Beau, ever the gentleman, wore a long button-up black coat, dark gray trousers, and collared dress shirt. A pair of maroon suspenders and matching bow tie spiced up the ensemble. He removed the black bowler hat from his head in preparation for a proper meal.

"Mother dearest!" exclaimed Henry. "There was no mischief to be seen. All we did was work today. What's for dinner, Sir Lou?"

Lou sat a beautifully plated spread in front of the Frost men as they each grabbed a stool at the counter.

"Next time, it'll cost you extra for me to keep it warm and waiting for you scallywags."

He flashed a smile at young Henry.

Waiters floated about the saloon in simple black-and-white uniforms, dishing up second helpings and dessert as Frosty caught up with her family. Young Henry dreamed of being a ship captain someday, so much so that even dying at sea hadn't crushed his dreams. One of the waiters made the rounds pouring tall helpings of ale to anyone with an empty mug, including Lou. The room started to come alive again.

The post-dinner festivities were H's favorite part of the evening. Men gathered around tables and played cards, people sang and danced, and ghosts told stories by the fireplace. They looked so classy, with their dark coats, crisp white shirts, and pleated trousers. These were the type of men who wore leather shoes and took the time to shine them, who wore bow ties—some even had silver or gold cuff links or pocket watches.

The crewmen wore thick navy blue wool pants to keep warm while working the deck. Some even sported hand-sewn sailcloth shirts beneath their jackets. A lot of the men sported Aran jumpers[11] as an extra layer. Lake Superior was pretty freaking cold in the middle of November. The hats of the crew were sun battered and worn by the wind, and many of them grew beards because they claimed it kept their faces warmer.

As the liquor flowed through their dead veins, the songs of the sea came alive. H could listen to the men sing their shanties all night. Those from Scotland had the best accents and delightful songs. You'd think they were trained vocalists with the three- and four-part harmonies they were throwing down. An American sailor named Butch was H's favorite singer of them all. A swallow, an anchor, and a nautical star decorated his tattooed arms, and he expertly played pretty melodies on a scraped and scratched wooden guitar.[12]

The first time H met Butch, he'd asked about her "tattoo." She'd just gone along with it, explaining it was the roots of a cedar tree. That's what she and Nigig saw in it, anyway. When asked what it meant, H had bullshitted about the symbolism of her unending exploration of water.

The Buck Brothers locked elbows and danced in a circle as they sang harmonies, careful not to slosh the beer out of their mugs. The next song was meant to honor the ship, and every voice passionately sang the song of the *Algoma*. Not a soul on that ship was silent.

[11] Traditional chunky hand-knit wool sweaters, also known as "the fisherman sweater," originating in Ireland (and a joy to knit).

[12] Each swallow means the sailor traveled 5,000 nautical miles (5,753 regular miles). An anchor meant the sailor had crossed the Atlantic Ocean. A nautical star was tattooed so the sailor could always find his way home.

There once was a ship called the Algoma
Her sisters, the Alberta, Athabasca
Made with strong human hands
Steel from other foreign lands
Set sail from faraway Scotland
Broke in half on her way to Canada
Put together, all better, now through the canal
Ready to haul you all through the waters of Hell
There's no place like home-a on the Algoma
Storm-torn, weatherworn, nice to know ya
Take a knee, pray for me, on the Algoma
November gales, waves and ales, hurricane snow
Run aground, thrown around, many drowned
Tossed to sea, Heaven's plea, sweet Algoma.

H sang along at the top of her lungs and gills. A few songs later, she grew weary and said her goodnights. A long hallway served as an artery from the main saloon hall to the living quarters. Black-and-white photographs of prestigious and serious-looking men, displayed in ornate iron frames, speckled the walls between doorways. Tapestry rugs sprawled across the polished wooden floors. The residents of the Algoma had made H her very own stateroom, where she loved to curl up under soft down blankets and white cotton sheets. She loved to trace her fingers along the iron lamp and stained-glass lampshade details, imagining the hands that had worked the raw materials into a work of art.[13]

H nestled into bed with a contented sigh and contemplated where the morning would take her. Lake Superior boasted hundreds of shipwrecks, and she could swim anywhere she wanted to visit the quirky and fascinating souls of the deep. H routinely made her rounds north from Duluth, up the shore of Minnesota to visit Nigig, and then out to sea toward Isle Royale, one of her favorite areas to visit.

[13] With enough luxurious first-class rooms for 240 people, the ship had accommodations to spare. Tufted velvet sofas, hand-carved wooden tables on curved legs, and floral wallpaper adorned the rooms. After all, they had to do something special to compete with the railways for passengers. Standard rooms could host another 500 people.

As she dozed off to sleep, H thought about her gray wolf friends Rolf and Ma'iingan, and wondered how their litter of pups was faring on the island. Perhaps it was time to seek a safe place near shore and pay a visit to her frisky, feral canine friends. The pack was finally growing, and H couldn't wait to hear how family life was going.

H awoke in the middle of the night with a feeling that she was missing something spectacular. She quietly swung open her door and peeked down the long corridor. The ghosts were still resting.[14]

With a thrust of her shimmering tail and a wave of her muscular arms, H propelled herself down the corridor and twirled up the stairway to the deck. She looked upward in the darkness and, wanting a look at the world, swam straight up, almost one hundred feet, until her head poked out of the water. The clear black sky twinkled with thousands of stars. Not a living human soul was anywhere nearby, so H took the liberty of swimming on the surface.

"Good evening, diamonds of the sky," cooed H. "I've missed you, even though we all know that stars still shine behind the clouds. Are you keeping the secrets of the sky safe?"

She wiggled her tail and leapt upward in the moonlight, water splashing off her long, wet locks. She took a moment to part her hair and quickly braid it into pigtails. With another bolt of her tail, H neared the abandoned lighthouse in Rock Harbor. Her body skipped like a rock along the surface. When she lifted her head and looked north, her eyes lit up like Lou's chandelier.

"Wow," H marveled. "The more secrets you keep, the brighter you twinkle. Is that how it works?"

The northern lights danced across the darkness. No longer did the sky appear pitch black; it was now a dark blue illuminated by bright green, edged with sprigs of bright pink. The sea was calm. H rested her arms on a rock near the shore and tilted her head skyward to take it all in. She lifted her tail and the colors of the aurora reflected off her shimmering silver scales. Even the stars were speechless.

[14] Ghosts don't need to sleep but generally keep a schedule, resting at night for a semblance of normalcy.

"In the beauty of the night, one must remember: what lurks in the shadows never sleeps," a familiar voice croaked. "One best be on the lookout for paths that lead to evil."

H looked around, startled. "Revna? Is that you?" She lifted her gaze upward in hopes of spotting the infamous raven. She thought for a moment she heard the subtle brush of wings flapping in the darkness, but only silence followed.

After an hour of enjoying a front-row seat to the best performance the night sky had ever given her, H elegantly dove back to the depths of the sea. It would still be a few hours until the sun rose and the ghosts woke for their morning coffee, so H snuggled back into her nest of a cozy, warm bed.

In a hazy dreamland state, H dreamt of a winter where the lake didn't freeze over but burned. Black flames crept from east to west like a virus and slowly halted travel for aquatic species, leaving a trail of devastation. Entire schools burned trying to outswim the wrath of the underwater flames. Ships sent their strongest to extinguish a pathway for cargo, but to no avail. Mass migration to the western shores created chaos for all sea life. H tried to find her favorite fish families and spread the word to migrate riverward. She yelled at the top of her gills, yet nobody heard her. Silence filled the burning seas. She swam to land, where the river met the sea, and prayed to the Gods for a miracle. As her body began to burn, a raven flew overhead.

Chapter Two

"RISE AND SHINE, FOLKS! IT's daylight in the swamp!" Crewman Bert beat his wooden spoon on an empty pot repeatedly. He clanged shamelessly through the corridor in a red onesie, toward the saloon. "I need coffee!" he exclaimed, with the vigor of someone who definitely didn't need coffee.

The smell of bacon and syrup drifted down the hallway. H sat up and rubbed her eyelids, bothered by her nightmare but excited for a new day. She peeked out of her quarters and, seeing an empty hallway, took the opportunity to flip her tail and swim as fast as she could toward the saloon.

"Aww, did you really miss me that much?" asked Lou as H zoomed to her seat at the bar.

"Of course," she answered.

"Lies. You only want me for my cooking," Lou wailed. "I suppose you're here for the griddle cakes, and if I don't produce 'em hot and fresh, you're gonna beat the shit out of me."

H laughed, flexing her biceps. "Yeah! Where's my breakfast, hooligan?" She tried to sound mean, but her giggles held all the menace of a fluffy baby bunny. Lou floated toward the grill and returned with three perfectly round pancakes topped with blueberries and drizzled in birch syrup. As he poured her a cup of tea, she massacred the stack with a flick of her fork. She paused to add a teaspoon of sugar to her tea and stirred it gently.

Between bites, H began, "I can't help but think about the unusual gray boat I saw fishing near Duluth. For one, they were actually catching fish. Second, the boat had no name. Who doesn't take the time to name a boat?"

"Downright heathens," answered Lou. "Using a rod and reel successfully in this day and age? They might be witches! If they had that electronic device that detects fish life, I'd also consider them cheaters!"

H snorted, almost spewing pancakes. "There's a point to my story, Lou!"

"There always is," he chuckled. "You just have to find it first."

"So, there was this adorable brown dog on the nameless boat. She smiled, wagged, and got all the good-girl pets," said H. "We really do owe nature our gratitude for modern-day dogs, wolves specifically. Without their descendants, the world would be a sadder, more dismal place."

"I'll believe it when you bring me a puppy," said Lou.

"We have a lot to thank the wolves for." H grew serious. "They target slow and dying animals, and they lessen the spread of disease. It could be said they perform a public service by putting the sick out of their misery. They are sometimes painted as the bad guy, but they deserve love! Population control is important." H was sure that all wolves went to heaven in the afterlife, as being nature's grim reaper was often a thankless job. She was just glad it wasn't her standing there with the scythe.

"Ah, yes," sighed Lou. "The majestic carnivore is more than a murderer. Why the pensive analysis on wolves today? Were you up howling at the moon last night?"

"There was no howling," replied H. "However, I did see an amazing display of aurora borealis. I'm going to visit the wolves today."

"Be sure to give those good old wild dogs some pets from me. If they were here, I'd always drop them my leftovers." Lou picked up the white rag he used to wipe down the counter, released his grip, and watched it slowly drop through the water.

"By the way, Lou! The pancakes taste like shit," she joked. "Most dreadfully dreary breakfast ever. Alert the papers!"

Lou poured more tea into her delicate china cup. "I get by merely on my good looks," he answered, rubbing his head. "Do you want some worms with that? Some leeches? Maybe a watercress sandwich, hold the cress?"

"I'll pass on the fish food, Lou. I hate to eat and swim, but the trials and tribulations of the wild outdoors await." She very much enjoyed the company on the *Algoma* but wanted to get a fresh start on the day and catch up with her island friends.

"Nature can be brutal indeed. Hopefully your carnivorous chums haven't eaten everybody," said Lou. "It's not about *what's* for lunch; it's about *who's* for lunch!"

"Where's Frosty this morning, Lou?" asked H. "I hoped to bid her adieu."

"She's having one of her emotional relapses," said Lou. "She lost a shoe again.[15] It will pass."

H smiled at the memory of Frosty's shoe quip, set her cup down, and floated off her stool to give Lou a hug. "Goodbye, old friend. Until we eat again!"

[15] Heed the advice to never ask Frosty about her shoes. One was misplaced in the wreck, and she did not rest until her custom cobbler-made leather heel was reunited with her delicate foot. H once asked about human foot anatomy: "Why are your shoes so pointy if your toes aren't shaped that way, Frosty?" "So I can kick rowdy men in the shins if they get out of line!" Frosty answered with confidence. Obviously, ghosts don't need shoes to traverse the water, but style has an afterlife too.

"Is that *old* as in age or *old* as in duration of friendship?" Lou harrumphed in faux affront. "You know I'll never be a geriatric. I'm stuck in the middle ages for all eternity!"

Lou waved goodbye as H swam out. She stopped for a moment to examine one of the black-and-white photos on the wall. A young, bearded man with carefully parted hair stared back at her. He had a crisp white shirt, black necktie, and impeccable black coat. He wore no smile, and his intense, determined eyes spoke volumes. She squinted to read the faded cursive caption. All she could make out was *James Pryor*.

H wondered what his life became and if he knew his likeness was at the bottom of a lake, preserved for all eternity in a ghost ship. Maybe he was a ghost somewhere too. When the face in the picture turned his head and looked at her, H jumped back and screamed. Ice crystallized in the bottom corner, where she had touched the frame, and crept across the entire glass. "That's not creepy at all," she muttered as she swam away. "Just when I thought I had ghosts figured out, they pull my tail with something new."

H decided to head west, following the shoreline to the area of the island her wolf friends frequently occupied. She briefly looked around for human life but determined it was too early in the season for tourists. Isle Royale was one of the least visited national parks for a reason, only accessible via boat or seaplane. Swimming to shore gracefully in the still morning waters, H propped herself up on a rock with her strong arms. She lifted a hand to her mouth, tilted her head upward, closed her gills, and filled her human lungs with air.

"Awooooo! Ow-ow-awooo!" Her howls carried through the woods.

A few minutes passed. H watched a bald eagle fly overhead and squinted in the morning sunshine, trying to tell if it was her friend Arne, but the bird was just a speck in the sky, too far away to know for sure. She looked to shore, trying to detect movement in the bushes. H heard a few tiny voices yelp with excitement and couldn't help but grin as wide as the island itself. Rolf emerged from the tall brush first, leading the way with his long legs and large paws. Ma' followed closely behind, nudging three fluffy little pups bumbling along on stubby legs.

"It is my pleasure to introduce you to Ulf, Hilda, and Blizzard," barked Rolf proudly, his strong chest held high and bushy tail wagging. Ulf's cold blue eyes looked H up and down. He was a miniature version of his father, with gray and white coloring. Hilda, the only female, was completely black, like the suit of a dapper businessperson. Blizzard was the exact opposite, aptly named for his fluffy, snow-white fur. Ma' used her snoot to push the three little ones toward H's outstretched hand before crossing her paws and laying down behind them.

H let out an excited little squeal. She picked up Blizzard and couldn't help but hug the little love nugget in her arms. Ear rubs and chin scratches quickly earned his trust. He took out his tiny pink tongue and started to reciprocate the affection right on her face.

"That tickles!" H giggled, enamored. She plopped him down and took a turn with Ulf and Hilda, who soon squirmed away to tug on opposite ends of a stick while Blizzard opted for more pets. Rolf waited for the cuddle fest to end before talking shop.

"As you are well aware, H, the wolves migrated to the island in the late 1940s. We've done our best to observe our impact on the ecosystem, especially the moose populations, ever since." Rolf usually began his annual spring report with a brief island history. He cared about the land as though it were a living being—which, in the grand scheme of things, it was. "The humans are doing their own research, oblivious to the fact that we have it completely under control."[16]

"They just want to catch a peek because you're such a beautiful specimen," said H.

"Flattery will get you nowhere, dear mermaid." Rolf winked and smiled. A sunbeam twinkled on his bright canine teeth. "Wolf

[16] The world's longest predator-prey study, the wolves and moose of Isle Royale have been observed since 1958. Current studies are conducted by the young intellectuals at Michigan Tech, when they aren't stuck in giant snowbanks.

song records indicate that Isle Royale had the largest concentration of wolves in the entire world in the 1980s, which was well before my time. After the great decline, there were only twelve of us." His voice exuded pain at the loss. "I crossed the ice bridge from Minnesota years ago with my parents, who grew too old to have pups. Our population was in danger, but I could not abandon family to find a mate. We needed numbers to hunt, so we waited, hoping a new pack would venture forth."

Just over a year ago, with human intervention, a new crop of wolves had arrived on the island. Ma'iingan was one of the newcomers, dazed and confused by the journey. When Rolf's dark blue eyes met hers, he knew: She was the one he would howl at the moon with for the rest of his life, the one he'd share a moose flank with. He'd even let her play with the antlers afterward. That's true love.

To get to the point of the spring report, H asked, "How did this winter treat everyone?"

"You'll be happy to hear that the majority of the moose herd survived the bleak winter and has been blessed with many spring calves." Rolf spoke like a radio news anchor. "There are many mamas in hostile moose mode caring for their young, and we have respectfully allowed them that opportunity. Those who perished of natural causes were dealt with accordingly."

"Translation: Nobody wants a hoof to the head," responded H. The pups smiled, nodded in agreement, and bounced up and down.

Ma' added, "Our pack has grown, and it is our duty to teach our young the proper culling of the herd and wildlife management. The strong survive, and the weak will nourish the souls and bodies of the greater species as well as the land itself. We also pay gratitude toward the land in whose bounty we feast. If our moose population grows to excess, the land will suffer." Ma' looked down at her pups lovingly.

"Translation," H continued, directed toward the pups, "Don't be a prickly porcupine, don't kill and eat more than can fill your belly, and appreciate the gifts Mother Nature gives you in return for your wolfly duties. Awwooooo!"

"Awooo!" The three pups yelped wholeheartedly in unison, noses pointing skyward.

Rolf continued. "We anticipate the majority of the visiting humans on the far east side of the island this year, as well as the ranger station on the west side. Our pack has designated an area on each side that will keep our exploits contained away from the biped drama."

"Bipeds!" Hilda chimed in. "That's like our friend Bigfoot!"

"Yes, my pup," said Ma'. "He's been outrunning the human paparazzi for years!"

"Is that why his legs are so long? For all that running?" asked Ulf.

"What role does Bigfoot play in conservation?" asked Blizzard before his parents could answer the previous question.

"Is Bigfoot just a human who doesn't know how to shave?" added Hilda. "Is there a gene for being a hairy human? Is a human just a naked bigfoot that doesn't eat raw chicken?"

The pups peppered their elders with questions:

"Does Bigfoot poop in the woods?"

"Are there really ground-up bones of children in Bigfoot's poops?!"

"What noise do Bigfoot's farts make?"

"Does he pee standing up, or does he lift one leg?"

"Now, now," Rolf chuckled. "It's not yet time for today's biology lesson. We shall discuss evolution and family trees in much detail when you're older. For the time being, you can enjoy your imagination running amuck."

"Running in muck!" giggled Blizzard.

"Sounds like the recipe for a bath," said Ma'.

H looked at Rolf and asked, "How's Delbert?"

"Spry as ever, hungry for fresh foliage, and large and in charge." As the leaders of their respective species, Rolf and Delbert occasionally met to discuss and resolve issues. There was an unspoken respect between them, and neither would admit they were actually very good friends who could potentially fight in *Wild America*'s version of *Celebrity Deathmatch*. Both Rolf and Delbert were in their prime and quite formidable. Together they could probably take over the world, or at least the upper Midwest.

"Glad to hear that," said H. "I'm sure quite a few of those fresh moose calves will be calling him Papa D!"

"Good thing he doesn't have to pay for college!" added Ma' with a howling laugh.

Rolf turned back to serious business. "In other news, I talked to Arne the other day. He reports seeing just a few zebra mussels on the park ranger boat. I know how you like to snack on them like popcorn. I won't judge your diet, especially when it rids us of an invasive species."

"Zebra mussels all the way out here again? Those slimy bastards. I thought we had resolved that issue years ago! I have a hard time believing the rangers would have missed them. They are always so careful; the mussels must have hidden themselves very well." H had despised the species for as long as she could remember, and they'd hit Duluth back in the 80s. In an attempt to rid the lake of them, she'd decided to pop one in her mouth like an apex predator. With a loud crunch she'd found irresistibly satisfying, her favorite snack was serendipitously discovered. "The boats being launched are thoroughly checked and even rinsed before they touch the water, so they must have hitchhiked out from another source!"

"We're afraid of the water composition changes out here," replied Ma'. "The way they filter and feed creates clearer water and more algae, altering the natural microscopic biome of the waters.[17] In turn, it could bring botulism to our island. Poisoned fish will only transfer the disease up the food web, maybe even to us." Ma' cast a concerned glance at her pups, who were now sitting obediently in a row like baby ducks.

[17] Zebra mussels filter water so well that native species like plankton starve in the process, which creates a ripple effect across the ecosystem's food chain. They multiply as fast as the snowshoe hare.

"It's bad enough that we have to deal with ticks and their vile blood-borne diseases," said Rolf. "We had to put a moose down last fall. Nobody wanted to rip that flesh. He had scratched himself raw on the trees, dealing with the irritation. This past winter was cold enough that hopefully the ticks will be minimal this year."

"I'd bribe a robin to check me for ticks before ever getting that beat-up." H contributed to the conversation. "A wild turkey would probably do it for free. I could even get a little help from that giant rooster in Two Harbors everyone talks about."

"Valid response," assessed Rolf. "Every creature has a predator: furred, scaled, winged, or microscopic."

"I'll have to swim through Windigo tonight to rid the boat of those vile mussels," H vowed. "I won't give those suckers a fighting chance." She chomped her sharp teeth and smiled at Rolf.

"We appreciate your efforts to keep our ecosystem and food web safe," said Ma'.

A fishing vessel appeared on the horizon, and H knew it was time to bid her canine friends adieu. "I suppose that's my signal to keep moving. The fat robin is officially chirping," H sighed. "Come here, little ones. Boop, boop, boop!" H used a pointer finger to tap their little wet noses, then she gave each pup a kiss on the forehead. Rolf and Ma' came over for their hugs and a pat on the head. "All my love, formidable island wolves! Awooo!" H flipped her tail and was quickly underwater and out of sight.

Being spring, it was still early in the season for inquisitive students and khaki-clad tourists to be romping around the island, so H decided to head inland for a bit. She followed the shoreline up the Siskiwit River, where she navigated gentle bubbling falls up toward the lake. Her industrious beaver friends had built the Glensheen Mansion[18] of beaver dams on Siskiwit Lake, clearly claiming it as beaver territory. Nobody messed with an angry beaver—not even Rolf. Howard routinely diverted human foot traffic by flooding trails, creating perfectly engineered pools of water.

[18] Glensheen Mansion is a large, exquisite estate on the shore of Lake Superior in Duluth, well known for beautiful craftsmanship and scandalous murders.

"Howaaaaaard!" H sang to the sky. "Where's my favorite busy, busy beaver?"

A round dark-brown head popped out of the water with a small splash. "H! Are you here for construction season? The ice is gone for good, and spring is here! We're engineering a reinforced wall. Now that we have Amikbelle, we want to keep our home as safe and sturdy as the Gods of Lumber will allow. Did you see our work on the west side of the island to help control minor flooding?" Howard excitedly jibber-jabbered, eyelashes dancing above his dark eyes.

A kit poked her head above the calm water of the lake. "Dad? Did you say my name?" Even the water couldn't hide her fluff.

Howard's mate, Jillbjorr, swam over to them. Baby Amikbelle followed her mother, trying to mimic every little paddle and tail swish.

Howard glanced back at his approaching family and continued chatting. "We've perfected our tree selection and now create uniform pieces, even though it may be more work for our teeth." He smiled, revealing his perfectly straight and orange chompers.[19] "And then there's the mixture of the mud. We've found that a 70 percent—"

Jillbjorr interrupted the technical talk with a gleeful squeal and a smack of her strong tail, which ricocheted water off her sandy-brown body. "H! Seeing your face makes my day. Don't let the dam engineering talk bore you. Tell us about the outside world."

"Boring?" spluttered Howard. "We're making groundbreaking structural breakthroughs! This is exciting stuff. We've even been counting how many support—"

"You lived with your mother until you were thirty beaver-years old. Anything is exciting," Jillbjorr pointed out, cutting him off again.

"Yes, and you should see the geometric designs in the dam she resides in."

H giggled. Beavers were always so proud of their dams. "You definitely got all the brains, Howard. I got all the looks. When the Gods go in, they go all in." She tossed a long dark braid over her

[19] Iron in the enamel makes for a strong tooth with a pumpkin hue.

shoulder. "I'm surprised you haven't gone broke from paying so much attention to detail."

"Very funny," spouted Howard. "I may be a perfectionist, but I'm also ready for just about anything!"

"Oh, no, Howard," gasped H. "Are you hoarding again?"

Jillbjorr laughed. "We have a whole room full of coins, bottle caps, rope, plastic cartons, fishing line, torn fabric . . ."

"There are more treasures in there than just that. You forgot the plastic turtle with the red eye scarf!" Amikbelle added. "The stuff lines the walls taller than I am."

"I collect anything and everything I find. You never know what you will need to solve a problem. Nature's gifts are plentiful, but humans make things with unique properties," answered Howard, whose eyes lit up. "Speaking of detail, H, I found something for you. You're gonna love it!" He plunged under the water for a moment, then bobbed victoriously to the surface, grasping a slender tan leather pouch. "With your humanoid hands, this should do you quite well."

H opened the pouch and pulled out a multitool knife. She rotated the tool open and revealed a set of pliers; a smooth, pointy knife; a serrated knife; a nail file; and even tiny scissors!

"Thank you, Howard!" H squealed. She had always wanted her own but could never find one quite the right size. H rotated the tool to expose the serrated blade. "Do you need some help with any of those trees? I might be able to take one down for you, but it will take a day and a half!" The beavers laughed, revealing their orange grins. With a little manipulation of her woven crop top, H was able to conceal and secure the pouch under her armpit and out of the way. Monofilament fishing line always came in handy.

"Mama," Amikbelle spoke up. "Can we swim with H out to the island and show her our fort?"

"Of course, honey, but only if H has the time!" Jillbjorr answered, looking at H for confirmation. H gave them the thumbs-up and followed the beaver trio into the cold, clear waters of Siskiwit

Lake. They paddled joyfully toward the largest island, splashing and chatting in the spring sunshine. When they reached shore, Amikbelle hopped and frolicked her way inland to a giant puddle. [20]

"This is my fort! I made it all by myself, with only a little help from Mom and Papa. I named it Moose Island!" Amikbelle stood proudly next to a mound of dirt lined with twigs built up into a perfect dome. She climbed on top and danced in a circle while her parents walked at regular beaver speed over to join her.

"We decided to start her training early," said Howard. "This fort helped hone her building skills. She whittled down the sticks into a uniform length and used triangular supports for structural integrity. Greatness clearly runs in the family."

"She'll have a place away from prying human eyes to play with her cousins Josie and Mila this summer! And next year, she'll take it down and rebuild the fort, modifying her design after calculating the necessary improvements," Jillbjorr beamed.

"The best part is that it confuses the humans!" Amikbelle chirped. "They think the mound of dirt is an island. An island on a lake in an island on a lake in another a lot bigger island on a lake! And when we move the fort a little bit next year, they will be baffled!" Amikbelle bent over in belly laughs, her whole body bouncing. Not many people actually ventured out across the lake to the island, so they relied on aerial photos and what they could see from shore. "It's like Dad always says: If you can't dazzle them with brilliance, baffle them with bull-moose!"

"Language!" scolded Jillbjorr with a delicately stern wag of her front paw. H snorted.

"Sorry, Mama," Amikbelle shrugged. "Bull-moose!" She fell over in another fit of giggles. Howard beamed at his intuitive progeny, basking in pride and sunlight.

"Why did you name it Moose Island?" inquired H. "There are no moose on this tiny island—unless they swim out here!"

Amikbelle gleefully answered, "Because it's round like the fat

[20] Classification of this puddle is debatable. It may also be considered a seasonal pond.

belly of a moose . . . and when the humans think it's an island, they're going to be moose-staken!" With a giggle, she added, "Ungulates look funny."

H's face hurt from smiling. Even Delbert would have appreciated that one. This cute little fluffball had just stolen her whole heart. To see the world through the innocent eyes of a kit was truly a blessing. She spent an hour or so floating in the lake, playing with Amikbelle. The hours of daylight were limited, so H kissed the beavers goodbye and continued her journey around the island to make the best of her time.

"I'll miss your sweet face," she said to Amikbelle.

"Come visit me again soon, Auntie H! We're never too busy for you," Amikbelle replied, waving her tiny paw goodbye.

Chapter Three

NOT EVERY SUNKEN VESSEL AT the bottom of the lake claimed lives in their wreckage. On her way around the island, H took a detour by the SS *Glenlyon*, whose physical remains were scattered on the seafloor like dandelion seeds on the wind.[21] Its ghost rested untouched and uninhabited by the souls of the dead.

"Glenny!" H called out, "How is my favorite powerful metal beast doing? You are such a beautiful brontosaurus! Did your triple-expansion engines miss me? I know they beat with affection only for yours truly. It was love at first tail."

H switched gears, turning on her dramatic radio reporter voice: "Dastardly waves as tall as mountains devoured the *Glenlyon* on a stormy November morning.[22] She ran aground on a scraggy reef near Menagerie Island. Luckily, those onboard in distress were

[21] The SS *Glenlyon* was built in 1893 with a big heart and a large cargo hold, perfect for moving freight. She met her demise on November 1, 1924.

[22] "November is not a good time to set sail."— The SS *Algoma*

able to scram, courtesy of nearby ships. Rescue efforts to salvage the ship were unsuccessful, and she fell to pieces like Patsy Cline." H broke character. "Glenny, have you heard that song? It's a bit after your time."

H entered the vessel through the main deck and swam down the hallway to the cargo area. She put her hand on the ghost ship wall and said, "You've still got your cargo safe and sound,[23] my beauty. Wait, what is that?"

The ship couldn't answer, so H swam over for a closer look. It appeared that a bushel in the back had been knocked over, the burlap bag ripped, and wheat berries scattered on the floor. "Maybe the cargo is not so safe. Did somebody else visit you, Glenny? Maybe a ghost from another ship . . . Someone with a hankering for homemade pancakes?"

The view looked different from the back of the cargo hold. The bags were not plump with kernels, nor were they in perfect alignment anymore. Each bag had sunken a bit, lopsided and bulging. "I have no good explanation for this, Glenny. Something was on top of these burlap bags; the kernels have been displaced. Did the ghost of a drunken sailor take a nap on them? They'd make a decent pillow." Confused, H propped the torn bag upright with the rest.

With a swish of her shimmering tail, she headed to the engine[24] room, hoping to find it untouched.

"You've still got a grand heart, Glenny. You are a strong and capable mama black bear! Too bad your captain failed you. If only I could hear your engines roar like the good old days . . ." H marveled at the ship's masterfully built power source, envisioning the cylinders churning and purring strongly.

H considered the wreck a product of human error. After all, the ship had been renamed, not once but twice![25] No human token of luck could undo the unforgiveable. Even if the *Glenlyon* had carried bushels of four-leaf clovers and rabbit-feet, her fate was sealed. H hoped Glenny, at least, was at peace with her rocky past. She left a

[23] Glenny was hauling somewhere between 145,000-318,000 bushels of wheat. The papers couldn't agree on a number. A portion of the wheat was salvaged during rescue efforts.

[24] Glenny had a 1,200-horsepower engine. That's like fifty-four 1973 Ski-Doos!

[25] "What's in a name?" Shakespeare famously wrote. Renaming a ship is a recipe for disaster. (Nicknames were completely acceptable—"Glenny" was a term of endearment.) Bad karma, juju, luck—all equally and effectively describe the consequences of violating nautical nomenclature.

kiss on the door of the engine room. "I'll be back to visit again soon, Glenny. I'm not sure why anyone would touch your wheat after all these years. You're still a magnificent badass, and you don't look a day over one hundred. See you in the funny papers, kiddo!"

H swam gracefully around Long Island, following the shoreline toward her next destination. She sensed the presence of another being and paused to look around and listen. A school of glistening silver lake trout were headed right for her. H immediately recognized this posse. They were a brave bunch of misfits with an appetite for mischief, even aiming to misbehave on occasion.

Malcolm, the largest and loudest, flicked his tail toward H, pausing about a foot away. "Lady H! I swear by my pretty pink gills that we haven't seen the likes of you around these parts in ages."

"I'm making my rounds, getting the dirt on you guys," H smiled, gills flaring. "I'm surprised you haven't needed me to bail you out of fish jail yet!"

"Well, my dear, the day is young," responded Malcolm with a twitch of his fins.

Jayne, Kaylee, Zoe, and River surrounded H, their shiny scales reflecting what little light the depths of the water afforded. Their large gleaming pupils focused on H as they happily swam a little circle around her. Counting her pelagic friends, H looked to Malcolm and asked, "Where's the rest of your crew hiding?"

"Oh, you know. Simon is out watching and feeding with the parr near the Windigo shallows. They grow so slowly; it's about as exciting as watching water freeze."

"For the record, I like watching water freeze!" interjected H. "The ice crystals are beautiful, and I pretend that I can control them like puppets."

"Inara and Hoban went on a reconnaissance mission to the northwest side of the island," Malcolm confidently continued. "She's always been a bit of a picky eater, plus we need to maintain interspecies alliances. We had to touch base with some nasty whitefish about a bounty on intruders being offered by the almighty Council of Fins. Hoban and Inara seemed like the delegate types, as we renegades tend to avoid Council business altogether."

Jayne added, "There's rumors of uninvited guests causing a ruckus. They hang out near Harlem Reef, so we've not-so-lovingly been calling them *Reefers*. If the wretched whitefish are scared, we have reason to be concerned."

"Harlem Reef? That's nearby," exclaimed H. "The Council of Fins needs a good representative from each species in this lake. I hope our friends return with more information."

"The Reefers aren't from around here," Zoe chimed in, "and their appetite for our limited resources will put a strain on native communities. They're inciting fear and chaos amongst other schooling fish. Manipulation via exploitation seems to be their strategy. Our freedom is important—isn't that right, sir? We won't be scared into submission." Malcolm nodded in agreement.

"What do they look like?" H asked.

Kaylee swam forward, "The whitefish mafia claims they look like 'Satan's snakes,' so we're thinking some sort of eel or lamprey. We're going to have to deal with these outside threats in our territory, if the global warming doesn't eventually boil the sea and us in it." Her cheerful tone softened the gloom and doom.

"Look at you all squirming at the thought of being in hot water," observed H. "Those sound like formidable foes, but you are a resourceful crew. Together, we can fight for survival."

"If the Reefers are too big to eat, we'll just have River use that magnificent brain of hers to end them," Malcolm said. "We're too pretty for the Gods of Nature to let us die."

"We rely heavily on the food chain of command," added Jayne. "We also love our ice-cold water. It helps us thrive, ya know?"

"Fair point, Jayne," said H. "Without food, we would all die, and when we die, we become the food. Thank goodness I'm an omnivore with no known predators, so I don't have to watch my dorsal fin. I just saw a fishing vessel on the horizon, so your biggest immediate risk is getting stuck on a hook!"

"Oh, how I despise sportfishing. I can spot a trap a mile away," Jayne boasted. "Treasures that are too good to be true will ensnare the gullible."

"Two by two, ships of blue,"[26] whispered River solemnly. "When they come, we know the hooks are in the water."

Kaylee added, "When the food is too shiny, we know it's not real. Stay away! Stay far, far away!"

"Just don't ask Jayne about the time he had that hideous orange-and-yellow lure stuck to his head," Zoe snickered. Jayne scowled.

"I'm so glad the ghosts cook me hot, delicious dinners, free from potential lip rings and traps," boasted H in a voice so sweet it put sugar to shame.

"The mermaid life is a rough life indeed," remarked Malcolm. "Besides your leisurely swim, what's on the social agenda for you today?"

"Oh, you know. I was going to head to the SS *America*, say hello, visit with George . . . then sneak into Windigo for some late-night snacks." H waggled her eyebrows on the last word.

"We just finished our morning feeding and would be honored to accompany you on your voyage. Right, sir?" commented Zoe with a look toward Malcolm.

"That sounds like a mighty fine idea. We'd best keep an eye out for divers," Malcolm said.

"As long as someone keeps watch for stone-cold eagles when we hit the shallows," snarked Jayne. "Or someone could just tell their flying friends not to eat us; we're poisonous!" Jayne smiled his sparsely toothed yet cunning fish grin at H.

H smiled at her little silver-scaled friends. "I'm always willing to spare some of my rare but genuine thrilling heroics for the likes of you. Onward, Captain!" H cheered. With a pump of her toned

[26] River was referring to two charter fishing vessels that traveled together around the island, notorious for victimizing local trout populations and never throwing anyone back.

arm, H led the way forward through the dimly lit waters. Slender fish bodies swam in unison alongside her, their movements in stride with her much larger and more powerful tail half. H didn't need to use her arms to swim, but it made her feel more hydrodynamic and powerful.

They swam in silence, taking in the cool fresh water of the dark depths, letting the liquid massage their fins as they propelled forward. The wistful serenity of swimming in a school swept over H. Comrades in exploration made her feel invincible.

The posse slowed near the site of the SS *America*.[27] Part of the wreck was just a few feet underwater, marked with a white buoy as a warning. H emerged from the depths to check for approaching vessels and, finding none, proceeded onward, surrounded by her shiny, scaled friends. Shallow water tickled the broken bow of the corporeal ship, dancing on the lake-battered steel, easily visible from the surface.

H turned to her fish friends. "Human divers visit the remains of Miss America so often that they are actually cognizant of her deterioration by currents, ice floes, and the hands of time. They've made sure the carcass maintains its structural stability."

Kaylee asked, "Did they ever try to raise her out of the water? I've heard stories of salvage missions and seen ships missing parts."

H nodded. "Yes, but the salvage was sabotaged by a man who loved to dive. He knew in his heart that Miss America would be a convenient vessel to explore. The audacity of that self-serving, sinister man!"

"Humans are so confusing," said River.

"I've heard of these men before. I think he was what the humans call a politician," said Jayne.

The mermaid and her fish friends had finally reached the ghost ship. "George!" H bellowed. "My favorite best good boy? Or should I say Spike Theodore Brutus the Third?"[28]

A white poodle ran up the stairs to the main deck. Underwater, it appeared as though his violently wagging tail propelled his movement, although he was really just moving like a normal dog aboard a doomed ghost ship.

[27] Even in death, Miss America is one of Isle Royale's most popular vessels. Divers marvel at the bones of the Model T, explore her bunks, and admire the painted American flag that still flies with pride on the engine.

[28] George, papered and registered with an official American Kennel Club name, gets called by his nickname the majority of the time.

"H!" barked George. He could hardly contain his excitement but was taught to have manners, so he put on his biggest dog smile, pink tongue lolling, and nudged H's hand with his head.

"Hello, handsome." H petted his soft, curly fur and rubbed behind his ears. George sat on the deck and leaned into the affection. "What have you been up to, buddy? Watching divers?"

"It's just the beginning of dive season, and you bet your tail fin I'll be watching them! We've got the perfect digs, being positioned square across from the wreck bones. Gotta make sure they don't swim off with anything belonging to Miss. It is my given duty." George could forgive and forget, but H held a sizable grudge regarding the circumstances of his preventable death.[29] Call it a character flaw, but H couldn't accept injustice to a sweet, innocent doggo.

Malcolm turned to H. "Is he always this happy? That thing on his behind—does it ever stop?"

"He's happy even when he's sad," answered H. "Thus goes the life of a dog and the ever-wagging butt appendage known as a tail."

H continued by giving George some necessary belly rubs as her fish friends joined the reunion. In the presence of H, George could see and converse with the fish. She was like an interspecies translator for both living and dead.

"How come you never rub me like that?" asked Malcolm with a smirk.

"Are you a good boy?" asked George, with an inquisitive head tilt and a smile.

"I'd never use that term to describe the likes of him," said Jayne. "Maybe we could settle on *mediocre* boy." The whole posse made funny bubbling noises as they laughed.

H's stomach growled. Kaylee looked at her and said, "I believe we are here in search of snacks."

"Snacks?! Oh, sweet, slurpy heavens, I've got snacks. Follow me!" George bounded down the stairs to the cargo hold. "Feast your eyes on these!"

[29] Poor George, the only casualty of the SS *America*, was tied to the stern while its human passengers escaped safely in five lifeboats.

"If you so much as offer me a single banana, I swear to the *America* I'm going to smack you with it," laughed H. She followed George's nose to a wooden crate, which opened to reveal cartons of fresh, ripe strawberries. "*Strawberries*?! You've been holding out on me all this time? 'Good boy,' my ass-fin!"

"You never asked for a snack before," George replied with an innocent grin.

H grabbed a handful of berries and savored every bite. "Thanks, George. I'm going to remember where you hide these. It is now locked in my vault of useful knowledge."

"I wish we could eat strawberries," Kaylee sighed. "They look like they would taste good and juicy and have a nice texture."

"If wishes were strawberries, we'd all be eating pie," stated Jayne. "From what I hear, in terms of human foods, pie is the way to go."

"Does it hurt?" River asked George. "You know, being happy all the time?"

Zoe chimed in, "I think she meant to ask if your face hurts from smiling."

George looked pensive for a moment, then replied, "Nope! I just love smiling. Smiling's my very best favorite."

Malcolm had grown distracted and was swimming around the cargo hold, inspecting the goods. "What is it with these humans and bananas?" he asked, mostly to himself but ready for a sarcastic response from the crew if anyone had one.

"Funny you should mention it," started H, horrified. "Unwritten maritime guidelines deem bananas bad luck on a boat. Miss America frequently had fruit in her cargo hold. Before her demise, she smacked into a pier multiple times, hit another boat, got coated in a thick layer of ice, and ran aground—with *what* item aboard each time?"

"Bananas!" George cheered.

In unison, Zoe and River shouted, "Men!" River's nares fizzed with bubbles.

"This story is bananas," said Jayne. "Superstitions have no real-life consequences. I'd call it a coincidence."

"Serious foreshadowing there," said Malcolm. "She sank with them aboard, so I'd call it a proven theory."

H grabbed another strawberry and raised it high to emphasize her story. "Serious foreshadowing indeed! Fresh fruit washed up on shore for weeks after the wreck. I have another theory that this is how moose discovered they like bananas. Delbert could have inherited the craving from his ancestors."

Zoe asked, "What're all those brown boxes?"

"Stacked in the crates? Packages for delivery by the U.S. Postal Service, the recipients of which are all long gone by now."[30]

"Why not open them and see what else was on board?" Jayne asked. "Maybe you'd find a sunken treasure."

"Never bothered," H shrugged. "I like the mystery."

"Speaking of mystery, how did this ship sink so close to the island?" Malcolm asked.

"She used to transport folks to island resorts and cabins. Even had the honor of bringing over lighthouse keepers. She took the long and scenic route to failure thanks to her poor drivers. Picture an adequate June day with a rookie first mate at the helm. He clipped a reef as the ship left harbor, and Lake Superior pulled Miss America into her cemetery."

"It sounds like negligent driving caused all of Miss America's problems," Kaylee noted.

"The man either had no sense of direction, no depth perception, or no prescription lenses," responded H. "I've always thought that with a woman at the helm, this shit wouldn't have happened in the first place."

"Sailor language," George yipped with a wag. "Did you know that the humans wanted to make Miss bigger after they constructed her? They added twenty feet to her length! More staterooms too. People really wanted her to be best in show."

[30] Miss America brought joy to many people from Minnesota to Canada in the form of US mail until the day she sank in 1928.

H swam over to the Model T parked on the far side of the room. She sat her tail on the driver's seat, gripped the steering wheel, and pretended to drive like a human. George hopped up into the passenger seat, embracing his basic dog instinct. H ran her hand over the truck's buttons and gauges in admiration.

"Modern cars are much bigger and more brightly colored. I sometimes watch them drive the scenic highway up the North Shore. This right here is an extinct relic." H climbed out of the truck and looked to George. "Show me to your best staterooms, the aftermarket modifications of which you spoke, good sir!"

They swam out of the cargo hold, down a maze of white hallways, and up one level. George followed a corridor to a hallway lined with doors. He nudged one open, revealing a room with cream wallpaper; floral carpet in deep blues and pinks; and a coveted port window. A wooden table and tapestry-cushioned chairs sat in the corner, with an iron lamp on top. On the table sat a rosary, an iron, and a man's pocket watch—a combination of items that puzzled H.[31]

H plopped down on the iron-post bed and nestled in the woven cotton blankets. She picked up a book from the bedside table about a man named Dr. Dolittle and began reading aloud to her small audience. George jumped on the bed and cuddled right in, nestling his sweet poodle head on her lap. H stroked George's head with one hand and held the book with the other.

H read for hours, until she and her audience eventually dozed off. Nothing feeds the soul like a good nap. She awoke to a snoring poodle and a posse of fish creepily sleeping with eyes wide open. H's movement woke George and in turn alerted the trout that naptime had ended.

"You're a Dr. Dolittle of sorts yourself, H!" exclaimed Kaylee. "Being that you talk to animals and all."

"Maybe it's a nonfiction story after all," added Jayne. "Your father could be Dr. Dolittle."

[31] It makes perfect sense to me: You pray for safe passage across the waters, watch the time, and iron your clothes near arrival so you don't look unkempt.

"I am your father," seriously proclaimed Malcolm in a deep voice with a flip of his tail. Laughter bubbled around the room.

"I sense that daylight is fading," Zoe pointed out, "and the protection of nightfall you seek will be here soon. We best voyage on to Windigo." Zoe twirled around in a circle. She always yearned for adventure.

"You're absolutely right. George, my love, we need to continue our mission toward land. I might run into Delbert later, so I'm gonna steal one of your unlucky bananas on the way out." H bent her human half over and kissed George on the forehead. "You really are the best good boy."

"Aw, shucks. You're my favorite mermaid, H," answered George.

"I'm the only mermaid, buddy."

"Still means you're my favorite," said George with a giant dog smile.

"You could always join us, you know," said H.

"I can't leave Miss behind," said George knowingly. "She deserves to be looked after, and I don't want her to feel forgotten."

With an embrace around his entire poodle body, H promised she'd return for another visit soon. The fishy band of misfits swam up to the main deck, passing the actual ship's skeleton, and headed toward Windigo. H waved to George as he watched them go. Leaving him always made her a little sad.

Chapter Four

NIGHTTIME ENVELOPED THE LAKE, SPRINKLING her glittering map of stars across the sky with the delicate precision of the Gods. H looked up to find her favorite constellation—Ursa Major, the great Greek she-bear—watching over her. For some strange reason, those seven stars always gave her comfort; H felt like the she-bear was her kindred spirit. "Good evening, star bear of the north," H whispered. "You and your friends look dazzling tonight, as always." Away from cities with excess light, one could experience the unaltered world Mother Nature intended. Pure darkness devoured the island, making the stars shine even brighter.

Gentle sounds carried through the stillness of the night: Waves lapped the shore, splashing on rocks in a soothing and hypnotic rhythm. A loon sang for its beloved mate, a chilling yet beautiful call, so pure that even a human could translate the message. A wolf howled soulfully in the distance, making the hairs on the back of H's neck stand up. She wondered if it was Rolf. (He was known to sing one hell of an opera from time to time.) Trees rustled peacefully in the wind, leaves keeping time for nature's rhapsody. A beaver tail thwapped against the water's surface, echoing in the night.

As H and her trout comrades neared shore, they came upon the weathered wooden dock near the visitor center where the park ranger vessel was parked. An incandescent light bulb worthy of the *Algoma* glowed further inland, as though it was engaged in a solo battle against the night, providing meager visual guidance for humans with their inferior night vision.

"The ranger boats always stand out," said H. "They have a distinct brown stripe and emblem near the stern."

"I've always been told the rangers have more antennae than a cloud of mayflies," said Kaylee.

"Yes," chuckled H. "They use them to communicate over longer distances."

River whispered, "Does this one have a name?"

H swiftly popped up and back down again. "This aluminum workhorse of a boat is called *Great Scott*. She's built for speed and function: a large outboard motor plus a cabin to protect people from the elements."

"I don't get it," said River. "Who is Scott?"

"Here comes the moment of truth," announced Malcolm as H ducked under the stern. "Or not."

"Affirmative not, sir. I see no truths in this moment. There are no zebra mussels on this boat." Zoe succinctly assessed the situation.

"I don't understand," said H. "What did Arne see that we don't?"

"Predictable," Jayne huffed. "This boat never visits other waters. The mussels would have to be local hitchhikers. Plus, birds of prey are lying sacks of feathers."

"There's another boat docked across the way, on Beaver Island," Kaylee reported. "I swam a little out while you were looking. Perhaps we should inspect that one instead."

"Ah, yes, Beaver Island: home to friendly hares and campers," said H. "I've never seen an actual beaver there."

"Onward to Hare Island!" commanded Malcolm. "It's not far, so swim lightly. Keep an eye out for ranger danger."

"You know, I expected these shallow waters to feel much warmer," observed River. "They seem just as cool and refreshing as the deep."

"I hadn't noticed," answered H. "All water feels the same to me."

"Well, what do ya know," said Jayne, approaching the boat. "This here boat is brown, just like Scott."

"Great," said River.

"I'll be beaver-damned," exclaimed Malcolm. "I see just a few mussels down by the motor."

Zoe swooshed, "Yes, sir. Clingy little suckers."

"Silly Arne, not just rangers have brown boats," said Malcolm.

"Does this boat have a name?" asked River.

"It's the *Fake* Scott," Kaylee snickered.

"Well, I'm due for a snack." H carefully scraped the sharp mussels off the boat with her new knife tool and ate them by the handful. "They're crunchy and delicious. Are you sure you don't want some?" It sounded like she was chewing on nails.

"We'll pass on the main course tonight," Jayne responded for the whole crew.

"What better way to rid the lake of invasive species than to eat them?" H asked with her mouth full. "They could use a good roasting and maybe a little salt, but they're fine raw."

"And we appreciate your dutiful service to the lake and its denizens alike," Malcolm replied. "Unfortunately, our imposter, the Fake

Scotty, doesn't know how many parasitic stowaways it taxied to this neck of the lake. If the rangers saw this, they'd be undone . . . especially that loud one they call 'Karen.'"

"You just *had* to say her name," Jayne complained. "We can hear her incessant bitching from the depths of Washington Harbor."

"Hyperbole." River giggled. "The zebra mussel has no natural predator in North America, except the elusive mermaid."

"I'm not elusive—I just don't associate with people!" H grinned.

When the Fake Scotty was good and clean, H gave the boat one final inspection. Upon passing said inspection with a gold star, she and her trout brethren made a loop around the bay. Simon was nearby, teaching the small fry basic survival skills.

"Yo, Simon! Where you at?" Jayne called. "Come out, come out, wherever you are!"

"Hey! I'm over here," Simon answered. "And shh! The younglings are asleep."

"Hi, honey! How are our offspring? Smart and beautiful, I presume." Kaylee nudged her mate.

"Oh, they've got potential. They could grow up to be engine mechanics on a great ship or even doctors someday," said Simon.

"Good luck getting them up to speed alongside the progeny of myself and Hoban," Zoe said, "bearers of the genetic predisposition for greatness!"

"How is the babysitting going?" Malcolm wanted the full report.

"Oh, you know," replied Simon. "Educate them about the dangers of shallow water. Educate them about the dangers of deep water. 'Birds could eat you, fish could swallow you whole, and humans have hooks hidden in everything!' It's a lot to take in. That's why they literally call it *school*."

"Make no mistake, Simon, those that reach maturity will have you to thank for the wisdom that got them there," said H as she looked at her most intellectual fish friend. Survival rates for large litters of fish weren't exactly high. In fact, a ship setting sail in November probably had better or equal luck.

The dim white glow of a ghostly figure on the surface caught H off guard. She lifted her head out of the water, droplets slowly dripping down her forehead in the moonlight. Everything in her living world came to a stop as she watched two Ojibwe men rhythmically paddle a birchbark canoe.

They approached the shoreline gently and quietly, climbing out in their beaded bashkwegin moccasins.[32] Animal pelts and a birchbark basket rested in the middle of the canoe between where the men had been sitting. H marveled at their smooth hand-carved paddles and the intricate craftsmanship holding the canoe together. She wondered if they were explorers or maybe traders seeking beads or European steel. Furthermore, she wondered why she had never before encountered these spirits while making her rounds of Minong. In fact, she'd never seen *any* ghost vessel travel the lake, let alone on the water's surface.

The men started to walk toward the forest, and H shyly emerged from the water. "Hello, *nanaboozhoo*," she said. H didn't know much Anishinaabemowin, but at least she knew a standard greeting. The men turned, eyes wide at the sight of the woman-fish in the water.

"*Manitou*," said one of the men.[33]

"Oh no, no," sputtered H. "I am not a God—just a mermaid." She cringed and wondered if *mermaid* was a word they'd recognize.

"Mishipeshu sent you?" the other man asked, slowly stepping closer to the water's edge.

H shook her head. She had only heard legends of the great underwater lynx.[34]

"The elders will guide your journey," the first man solemnly said, nodding his head. "The mighty *animikii* shall show your strength, the *gaagaagi* speaks truth, and *makwa* save you. *Giga-waabamin minawaa*."[35] With that, the men silently pivoted into the woods. Behind

[32] The Anishinaabe include the Ojibwe who came to Minong (Isle Royale) to hunt, fish, trap, forage, and find copper before the park existed. Bashkwegin refers to leather or hide.

[33] Manitou generally refers to God, or a great spirit being.

[34] Mishipeshu, mighty copper protector, lives near Michipicoten Island and has vertebral spikes, antlers, and scales. It can conjure a storm with the swipe of a paw.

[35] This translates to "I'll see you again," predecessor to the long midwestern goodbye.

them, a falling star promenaded across the sky as though it longed to be closer to the earth.

H slunk back into the shallows without making a wish, frazzled by the encounter.[36] Maybe the sky was sending her a sign and she should have made the wish to understand.

"Didja see something shiny up there?" Jayne asked with a smile. "If it's shiny, it's probably a trap."

"Shiny distractions are the best kind," added Kaylee. "They're fun to look at. If you recognize the shiny trap, it means you've done a smart."

"Maybe there was a squirrel? A rare, bushy-tailed squirrel?" Zoe interrogated.

H giggled. "I do love me a good, shiny squirrel." Her tone grew more serious. "I saw the ghosts of two Ojibwe men in a birchbark canoe. I said hello, they asked if I was a God, then strolled into the woods." H simmered on the interaction for a moment. "Have any of you ever seen Mishipeshu?"

"A missed—what? Sushi?" Jayne asked. "We always eat fish raw."

"Mishipeshu," H enunciated. "The powerful lake monster from a centuries-old myth? It can control the water."

"Negative," said Malcolm. "I've not seen the likes of any unusual creature besides you."

"Sounds fictional," Zoe speculated. "Nobody controls Lake Superior."

"If it really does live here, it is probably a retired geriatric beast sipping on surface water," added Jayne.

"Maybe Mishipeshu caused some of these shipwrecks," H mused. "The men should have placated the beast for safe travels by sending a gift."

"Makes a heck of a lot more sense than your goofy banana theory," snarked Jayne.

"That's a long time to patrol the seas, let alone hold a grudge," said Malcolm.

[36] Falling stars were considered an act of the Gods—a product of when they spy on the mortal realm—according to Greek astronomer Ptolemy. The Gods were more likely to grant a wish as the stars fall. They're actually meteors.

"I'm not even sure I should say the name, out of respect," H continued, "but they said the T-bird[37]—and I hope you know what I mean—would show my strength."

"The guidance of a mighty raptor would be a gift," said Kaylee.

"A gift I'd return," Jayne scoffed. "I don't want no birds following me around, shitting on me from above."

"Show your strength?" Malcolm inquired. "Are you swimming into a burning building to save us? If so, you're a true friend."

"Was that the entirety of their message?" asked Zoe.

"The *gaagaagi*, or raven, speaks the truth. The *makwa*, which means bear, will save me," said H. "I haven't heard from sassy old Revna in ages, and there have never been bears on Isle Royale."

River chimed in, "You do have bear friends, right?"

"Yes, but not many. I know a family of bears that live up the North Shore."

"It is unadvisable to try to befriend a bear," said Jayne. "They will eat you, or even me. I'm a tasty snack."

Kaylee snorted. "Tasty snack," she echoed with a sassy tail wiggle.

Malcolm speculated, "I believe what they gave you was a standard parting blessing. It's like when a ranger says, 'Safe travels.'"

"Or 'May the forest be with you,'" added Zoe.

"I didn't realize you could talk to ghosts on land," said Kaylee. "Do you do that often?"

"No, this was the first time," said H thoughtfully.

"You are a ghost whisperer of all locations, then," said River pensively. "You could kill someone and then talk to them about it."

"Now that's a bit dark and disturbing," said Simon with a shimmery shudder.

"Overthinking is a dangerous pastime," warned Zoe. "Overall, it sounds like a pleasant encounter."

"Avast, ye mateys," said Malcolm trying to sound like a pirate. "What say ye about venturing onward? The night is young."

Clearly, the afternoon power nap had the whole school of fish

[37] Legend says the Thunderbird, or animikii, was created to fight underwater spirits and have conflicts with Mishipeshu for all eternity. They are the most powerful spirit being, sacred and approached cautiously out of respect.

ready for more interaction with their fabulous mermaid tour guide. "In our haste to get my sun-ripened snack, we passed a few ship beauties I still must pay my utmost respect to," replied H.

"Lead the way to the shipwrecks, and we'll see you later Simon, honey!" said Kaylee as she passed Simon and the offspring on her departure from the bay.

"To the SS *Cumberland*!" H exclaimed. With a few mighty tail thrusts, H led their exit from the Windigo inlet and set a straight course for the next ship.

"I know this boat," squealed Kaylee. "She's from Canada, right?"

"Yes," answered H. "She mostly hauled goods for shipping companies and the railroad. Sometimes her passengers were even livestock."

"She's got the big wooden paddle wheelies," said Kaylee. "They're about fifteen fish wide!" [38]

"Yes! Her life was a series of awkward moments," explained H. "One time she was immobilized by ice and her occupants suffered frostbite. The water actually froze her into the ice."

"That sounds . . . *cool?*" said Jayne.

"Now that's the kind of freezing water that is fun to watch," Malcolm remarked.

"One time, she ran aground in a thunder blizzard," H continued. "Another time she ran aground, the captain broke both of his legs! And then they scuttled her!"[39]

"Intentionally? To swim with the fishes? Now that's really messed up," Zoe scowled. "Human logic is wild."

"In 1874, she got caught in a storm so wretched that the caulking adhering her wooden bones lost grip. In a futile attempt to counteract the ship taking on so much water, they threw the cattle overboard. To this very day, one may randomly encounter the ghost of Betsy the rogue cow in the depths of the lake."

"Just Betsy?" Malcolm asked. "I'd assume there are others roaming about."

[38] Comparing size to fish length is not unusual for fish but varies amongst species. The average trout length of twenty-four inches would put the paddle wheels at thirty feet in diameter. It gets confusing because we have fish like Malcolm, who are above average.

[39] Scuttled refers to sinking a ship on purpose.

"Not all that die here choose the lake for afterlife," imparted H. "I've never met Betsy, for the record. But the rare encounter with her is said to be good luck."

"Did tossing the cows save the ship?" Kaylee wondered.

"Yes, but she sank three years later. She was going too fast and hit the Rock of Ages reef with enough velocity to ground her. It was her final rodeo," lamented H.

"Oh, that's so sad," whimpered River.

"The humans survived thanks to the efficient rescue operations of nearby ships. A few steamers tried to pull her off the rocks, but her fate was sealed like a finely aged whiskey. She broke in half and sank into the depths of the lake for all eternity."

"This feels like a tall tale. If you haven't met Betsy, she doesn't exist. Pure whitefish fodder," grumbled Jayne.

"You never know," H shrugged. "I almost forgot—before the ship sank, the humans had time to salvage its valuables. They were sold at auction."

"What is it with humans and money?" Malcolm asked as they neared the Cumby.

"They really milked this ship for all she had," H stated. "Cumby, do you like puns? I'm referring to the humans ridding you of valuables." She swam over to the ghost ship and proceeded to spin one of the paddle wheels like it was a challenge on a game show. "That will never get old," she said, swimming aboard the expansive main deck. "This is where cows, sheep, and horses used to travel!"

"Imagine the smell," Jayne shuddered. "All that mammalian excrement . . . I reckon they deserved to be chucked overboard."

"I wonder if the humans considered it an animal sacrifice," Malcolm speculated. "It clearly did not appease the powers that be, your Mishipeshu included."

"The more important issue at hand is if our ancestors ate steak," Jayne thought out loud.

"You speak from your stomach but make a valid point nonetheless. Did livestock know how to swim? Did they all drown in the frigid waters, beyond the depths of bacteria that could decompose their bodies? Did they die in the shallows, where fish could gnaw on their bodies? Are there more ghosts of livestock past grazing the deep than just legendary Betsy?" Zoe rattled off questions that couldn't be answered.

"Maybe if the Cumby coulda just held her horses, she wouldn't have gotten into this predicament," Jayne tutted.

"She doesn't seem like the type of vessel to act sheepishly," River mused. "I wonder if the paddles and open water spooked the livestock. Did they get their sea legs faster than humans since they had four of them to stabilize?"

"What a horrible way to die, to see all your brethren dropped in the drink with a definitive splash of doom," spoke Kaylee sadly.

"Now, now. Don't have a cow." Zoe dropped the punch line like an anchor. "The nautical life bears the cross of heartbreak and death. It's just a fact. And many a man has enjoyed a bittersweet affair with the lake we call home."

H shifted gears. "Let's pay a visit to my favorite spot aboard." She led the way down one level to a luxurious sitting room. Sofas and settees in various floral prints lined the eggshell walls near the windows. Oil paintings of forests and lakes in ornate golden frames added to the ambiance. A cart used to serve tea and delicacies sat in the back corner.

"As long as the smell of manure didn't travel downward, this would have been the perfect place to enjoy a voyage at sea," remarked Jayne.

River swam to the back of the room and gazed at her reflection in a large gilt mirror.[40] Gold-painted iron workings framed the mirror with scrolling, winding designs that tapered to a curved point. "Little trout, big pond," she said quietly.

"Only the biggest of ponds," said Kaylee. "The biggest and best

[40] Decorators love mirrors because they create the illusion of a larger space.

of all the freshwater ponds in Northern America." Fish really had an appreciation for the water in which they called their home. H was similarly enamored, not only with the lake, but the ships, ghosts, and living creatures within the confines of the cold-water reservoir.

"Oh, *Cumby*. You are an absolute queen of the water," complimented H, stroking the soft crimson velvet couch with her tattooed hand. "You did the dirty work and were very much loved, even in tumultuous circumstances." H looked closer at the cushion. "Cumby, why are the velvet fibers all askew?" She rose and swam to the golden velvet couch.

"What's that?" Malcolm inquired.

"Something rubbed the velvet against the grain. See how the fabric changes based on the direction you touch it?" H stroked the cushions, demonstrating. "The fibers are erect—like something slithered across his whole couch, leaving a trail."

"The differences are subtle yet notable," agreed Zoe.

H looked up and asked, "What happened, Cumby? Was it a visitor or just a fluke current?"

"She's not gonna answer you," Jayne scoffed. "Best leave the sleuthing to the professionals. What we have here is a mystery: The Case of the Secret Sitter. Every couch in this room looks like something was dragged across it."

"I don't see how any of this is relevant," argued Malcolm. "We would need more clues to know for sure."

H lit up. "The wheat bags on the Glenny were tampered with! Well, it looked like something had been laying on them. One was knocked over and torn open!"

"Sounds like drunken sailor shenanigans. This is probably more of the same," Jayne concluded.

"Now, now. Let's not dismiss our observant mer-friend. Keep an open mind as we travel onward," suggested Malcolm.

With the flick of her silver tail, H rose from her seat and proceeded to the door. She paused in the doorway, hand on the frame, and said, "Constructed of the best timber, you were, my dear; and you're still lovely as ever. If someone is messing up your chairs, you must tell me somehow!" This was the signal that the group was figuratively jumping ship to the next vessel.

"Where to, m'erlady?" asked Jayne.

"We're headed to the *Chisholm*, another victim of the Rock of Ages reef," H answered.

"Ooh, I know this one! It's the iconic green freighter," River shared.

"Indeed it is," replied H. "Everyone recognized her meticulous green paint. She was the largest wooden steam barge of her time, made from trees that gave their lives for the glory of architectural transportation pursuits."

"So, basically, just like trees in any other wooden vessel," pointed out Zoe.

"That sounds much less poetic, but yes," admitted H. "A master carpenter engineered the ship with steel reinforcements.[41] She could tow more than any other vessel on the lake—even managed towing two ships at once. The power made her perfect for hauling goods, and her inanimate passengers often included iron ore, grain, and coal. No cows here."

Jayne chimed in, "She was more than just a pretty face, then?"

"Oh, she was an absolute nautical beast, flexing her muscles at the whim of humans wanting to move goods," beamed H. "But her size challenged the navigational competency of the captain and the laws of physics.[42] She was a bit banged up here and there."

"Aren't we all," said Malcolm.

"On her maiden voyage in 1880, she ran aground in the Chicago River[43] and was freed by six tugboats, then grounded again in the Ogden Canal," H commented. "Two years later in the Chicago River, same thing. It took a train and a few tugboats to help pull her free."[44]

"Humans sure do make a mess of things," said Jayne.

"Greenie was so powerful that when she ferociously hit the

[41] The namesake of the *Chisholm* was a steel industry icon. Iron beams surrounded the engine like a rib cage, and iron casing protected her like a shield.

[42] Steering components could have been more responsive with chain instead of wire.

[43] Greenie blocked the Chicago Avenue Bridge and had to ditch 250 tons of coal to get her to budge.

[44] Now that's a sight I'd pay to see—a train pulling a boat!

Rock of Ages reef, her hull was too smashed to attempt saving. She was hauling barley and had been towing another boat, which had gotten loose during a large, explosive gale.[45] So much for multitasking. At least the passengers were spared."

H approached the ghost of the USS *Henry Chisholm* at the middle of three masts, grabbing a hanging rope and twirling down the mast, winding the rope as she dropped down to a hover above the main deck. She made a beeline for the doorway leading to the lower decks, fish in tow. H's favorite part of Greenie was her glorious heart, the engine room, a mechanical sight to behold.

"Hello, my beautiful, bionic thrust-worthy engine," said H, blue eyes ablaze. "What wonders do you hold for us today?" She patted the wall lovingly.

"Wow," marveled Kaylee. "This is the most fantastic engine I've seen so far. If I had hands instead of short, stumpy fins, I'd tinker with her for sure."

"Humans sure do come up with some interesting metal doodads," remarked Jayne. "Though I'd rather they make engines instead of fishhooks. I've always thought guns were cool too. Engines and guns, win-win."

"She's got over 1,700 horsepower!" exclaimed H with a fist pump and a bicep flex.

"How much is that in fishpower?" asked Malcolm with a smirk.

"Depends on the fish," said Jayne. "A big one, like yours truly? Or a little one, like River over here?"

"Hey, now, even a little fish has a lot of fight," Zoe contended. "It's not always the size of a creature that designates greatness."

"Which explains why you love Hoban so much," Jayne fired back.

"Twin boilers!" Kaylee gushed. "She's a big and strong beauty indeed, and she powered that single screw like a champion." Kaylee swam up and down, admiring the human handiwork.

[45] The real tragedy was all the wasted barley that ended up in Lake Superior instead of fine ale.

"I'd say the *Chisholm* herself was single screwed in this endeavor," added Zoe. "If you don't wanna swim with the fishes, learn how to maneuver your vessel in the wide-open sea." Zoe was quoting Hoban, who frequently made fun of human error in unsuccessful water navigations.

"Greenie transported human barbarians who would have loved to slap your butter-basted belly on a dinner plate," stated Malcolm without hesitation.

"Are you trying to tell me you've never eaten a smaller fish for dinner?" H asked, directing a snide side-eye at Malcolm. "Cannibals, the whole lot of you." H sassily placed her hand on her hip, dark braids swooshing with the movement.

"Eating little fish makes me strapping and handsome, don'tcha know," bragged Jayne.

"Don't get caught, never get bonked," River stated as she quietly inspected the lot of meticulously coiled and welded metal workings. Everyone turned and looked at the solemn non sequitur. "Why are there fish scales in the corner?" River asked.

H looked to her fish friends. "Is anyone shedding?"

"We don't routinely shed scales," answered Zoe.

"Strange. Maybe an injured fish took a rest here," suggested Kaylee. "Or they had an itch and rubbed their body against the metal gears."

"Someone had their dinner here, is more like it," said Jayne, looking closer.

"I suppose you think this is the work of your mystery couch defiler," hypothesized Malcolm.

"I don't see a correlation," stated Zoe. "It is simply strange."

"As much as I'd love to theorize about stray scales, we best be on our way." H sashayed to the engine room door and cast one last loving glance at the heart of the powerful ship. "Sweet dreams, Greenie, my friend."

The fish schooled up behind H like migrating geese, their scales shimmering in the deep, dark water. They swam in unison, making the short journey to the USS *George M. Cox*.

"What's the story on this boat?" Kaylee asked.

"The elegant GC transported humans for a living," H replied. "Her past is a bit murky."

"We like murky," revealed Jayne. "Well, unless we're trying to feed."

"GC was originally named the *Puritan* and based out of Chicago. She was the fastest boat on Lake Michigan. During World War I, she served in the navy,"[46] H said. "She didn't always have clean white paint; she was painted to camouflage her appearance after being drafted. After dutifully serving her country, she returned home to the Great Lakes."[47]

"What adventures this ship had," remarked Kaylee.

"The Great Depression halted voyages on the *Puritan*, so she was sold and purchased by a millionaire, who carelessly renamed her in his likeness.[48] The horror!" H shuddered.

River asked, "Why is renaming a boat so scary?"

"It's bad luck to rename a vessel," explained H.

"Oh, here we go again with the bad luck theories," groaned Jayne.

"This one tracks in many instances," argued H. "Anyway, lush accommodations were of utmost importance. The maiden voyage featured an eight-piece orchestra! She stopped in Houghton to show off her elegance, then headed toward Isle Royale."

Kaylee cried out, "Please don't tell us she was ruined on her first trip back as a civilian!"

H's voice became animated. "It was 1933, and GC had a need for speed. But just because you *can* doesn't mean you *should*. A thick fog enveloped the ship as she neared Isle Royale. During dinner, she ran aground the reef so hard that her hull emerged from the water! A loud thud startled her passengers, who were eating dinner . . . then a rolling buffet table shot across the dining room and crashed into their tables!"

[46] GC's top-secret duties in the navy remain a mystery. She may have transported troops, sat in a shipyard for training exercises, or traveled the English Channel. Maybe she did it all.

[47] The bow of the ship had to be severed to fit through the canal to the Atlantic Ocean. Happened a lot, it seems.

[48] GC got an extreme makeover: a fresh coat of classy paint and updates to her exquisite woodworking. She was an elegant beauty and sported electricity, which made her desirable.

"That's one way to end a dinner," said Malcolm.

"GC was tilted in the water, her hull sprawled across the rock, so they dropped lifeboats to take people to the nearby Rock of Ages Lighthouse. Her broken body rests on the seafloor to this day," relayed H with a tinge of sadness.

Jayne smirked. "How many people can they fit in a lighthouse?"

"Sardines in a can," whispered River.

"The lighthouse was cramped, but the wife of the lighthouse keeper made a mean cup of coffee. All the humans were rescued, as well as their precious luggage. Very few sustained injuries."

"That was not the swanky trip that they had signed up for," assessed Malcolm. "The old bait and switch."

River entreated, "What makes a cup of coffee *mean*?"

"Definitely the beans," divulged H. Moving forward, she approached the two decks of the GC, swishing her silver tail gleefully to visit her beautiful, sunken steel friend. "Good afternoon, GC, my fair underwater beauty," cooed H.

"Do you smell that?" Jayne bobbed his head. Everyone swam backward. "Rancid!"

Confused, H asked, "Smell what?"

"It smells like dead fish, like a straight-up rotting fish graveyard," declared Jayne.

"Oh, *that*," H stifled a gag. "Yikes! I don't see anything belly-up. Just keep swimming. It'll pass."

"Well, well, well," pondered Malcolm. "I have a feeling there's something to see here."

"Indeed, and hopefully it is not the source of that wretched smell," responded H. "We're going to the most wonderful wooden staircase and then crashing a dinner party." H led the way to the main cabin. She paused at the grand staircase. "If only I had legs and could appreciate this human convenience."

"Let me guess: The staircase leads to the dining room," Jayne said.

"Yes, and look at the intricate detailing. Each railing spindle is square at the top and bottom, tapered down, and rounded in the midsection. See down on the main posts? Those carvings are pineapples."[49] H placed her hand on the railing and traced the hand-carved embellishments with her finger. She smiled and said, "Now, I may swim up these stairs like a heathen but still appreciate the structural beauty and function of such strong carpentry."

"I'm going to take this on like an obstacle course!" Jayne swam between railing spindles, shimmying his body through the tiny openings like a slithering snake.

"I can picture humans promenading up and down in their fancy travel dresses," said Kaylee. "I imagine the perfect summer dress would be pink with ruffles and lace."

"Neon pink like a crankbait, or light pink like a wild rose?" Zoe inquired.

"Oh, definitely light pink like a rose," quickly acknowledged Kaylee. "Does anyone actually wear fire-tiger neon?"

"What a way to travel the waters," spoke Malcolm wistfully. "Just taking it easy while roaring boilers do all the work."

"The main reason I'd ride a vessel like this would be for the snacks," admitted H with an upward thrust toward the large wooden dining hall doors. She crossed the flawless wooden floors, approached a dining cart covered with treats, and snatched up a chocolate chip cookie, devouring it in three bites.

"You're lucky you have human taste buds," said Zoe. "That spread is exquisite. It would be grand not to have to hunt for every meal."

Zoe was absolutely correct. A silver platter adorned with filigree roses was covered in purple grapes and parti-color cheeses. There were crackers, salami, apple slices, and tiny muffins. A silver bowl contained a variety of olives. Much to H's delight, three types of pie—apple, strawberry-rhubarb, and lemon cream—nestled beside the snacks, just waiting to be cut. She reached for a white china dessert

[49] Pineapple is not native to the Great Lakes region. It is symbolic for hospitality; although, in my opinion, there are much friendlier types of fruit. Peaches are soft, fuzzy, and deliciously fragrant. Pineapples are feisty, with stabby stems.

plate and served herself a hefty slice of strawberry-rhubarb, found a gleaming silver fork, and went to town.

"Does that nourish your fish half as well as your human half?" Jayne questioned. "Or do you have to eat for both body types?"

H smiled, revealing her pearly white human style teeth. "I prefer the taste of human foods, more specifically desserts. I'm a firm believer that pie is the most perfect food ever created by the hands of man."

"What if we were to bake your zebra mussels into a pie?" "Then you could nourish your fish half too." Kaylee shimmied her slender body.

"I still think I'd prefer them roasted with salt, rosemary, and garlic," confessed H. "I would eat them like a bat in a swarm of insects while watching the follies of mankind." H loved to sneak into the harbor with Nigig and people watch.

"As long as nobody suggests putting fish in the pie," exclaimed Jayne. "I heard that up in Alaska, they make salmon pie!"

"Salmon choose death as a lifestyle choice. Morbid fish, really." Malcolm rolled like a torpedo as he chuckled. "If the pie were full of whitefish, you'd gorge till your guts squished your swim bladder!" Malcolm teased.

"That's fair," conferred Jayne. "You're making me hungry!"

H scraped her plate with the silver fork and licked the last bit of pie filling off. "As much as I'd love to stay in school, I've got the north side of the island on tomorrow's itinerary. Will the likes of you be joining in said adventure?"

"Negative," said Malcolm. "Feeding time is nigh, and we will feast in our hunting territory on the south side tonight."

"I'm ready for a midnight snack," confessed River. "Can I try the pie?"

"Better check for hooks," cautioned Zoe. Everyone laughed, fins flaring. "If only we could cross into the ghost world's food realm." Zoe wished.

"I'm going to bunk here tonight," said H. She yawned with a squeak. They had fit quite a bit of adventure into one evening.

"We've enjoyed your company, H!" Kaylee swam closer and H put her hand under her trouty chin, giving her a little fish pet.

"There's nobody else we'd want to explore ghost ships with," added Jayne.

"Until we meet again, Mer'lady." Malcolm dipped his head in farewell. "Onward we shall go! Set engines to hyper-dive—next stop: whitefish buffet!" Malcolm rallied.

"Goodbye, my favorite trouty bunch!" said H. The shoal shimmered in the reflection of the white ghost ship as they swished their tails and disappeared rapidly into the deep water. H swam down the hall to the premiere travel suite. She curled up in the large, down-comforter-covered bed and said, "Goodnight, GC. Thank you kindly for the delicious pie." In a moment, H was fast asleep.

Chapter Five

H AWOKE WITH THE SUN (although she'd never know it, down in the lake's depths). Enthusiastic to start her day, she grabbed a quick slice of apple pie. "I don't want you to think I'm peculiar, GC. According to Frosty of the *Algoma*, life is uncertain, and one should begin with dessert. I'm sure you can relate to the sentiment."

H sat on a tufted sofa and conversed with GC as she enjoyed her breakfast. "I apologize, GC, but I'm going to eat and swim today. I'm excited to see my friends on the *Kamloops*." H imparted, "Loops sank a mere five years before you did. I'm not sure you made it to England with the navy, but that's where she was built."[50]

H paused a moment, hoping GC was following her story. "Loops' makers thought ahead so she wouldn't have to be cut up like a slice of raspberry pie to fit in the Welland Canal. If only the men

[50] The SS *Kamloops* sank in 1927. It took humans fifty years to find her remains.

who made you and the *Algoma* had as much dimensional foresight! If that doesn't make you chuckle, I don't know what will." H gathered her thoughts. "You know, the two of you traveled similar routes. On her maiden voyage, she delivered pebbles from Denmark to a mining outfit in Calumet, Michigan. That's near where your luxury cruise journey began."

Scraping the pie filling off her plate, H continued. "How does Lake Superior like her ships?" She paused. "On the rocks!" H laughed at her own morbid joke and led into the story. "Yeah, that was bad. Anyway, I know you've seen what this ferocious body of dihydrogen monoxide is capable of in winter. It was so cold that in December, the lake trapped the Loops and three other ships in ice![51]

"Perhaps you've heard the story," said H with a tinge of sadness. "A heinous blizzard covered her with ice and froze her body. Unfortunately, a series of events left her engine powerless, but even a ship with a heart like Glenny's would have been doomed. The reckless, raging winds and waves tossed her into the rocks of Isle Royale. Unlike most of wrecks around here, she sank completely intact."

"The crew of the Loops did not fare as well as your passengers. Some made it to lifeboats, but they later froze to death. Fishermen discovered the bodies washed ashore."[52] With a somber tone, she added, "We all know Lake Superior never gives up her dead, human or ship for that matter."

H moved toward the exit, pausing in the doorway. "I hate to leave you on such a depressing note! I wish you could tag along and visit the crew with me. They're a delightful bunch—well, most of them, anyways. Until next time, goodbye, my friend!"

H proceeded onward, noticing no horrible smell on the way out, and set course across the north side of the island for the *Kamloops*.

H approached the ghost vessel, excited to see her friends once again. "Greetings from the outside world," yelled H as she neared the deck. Not a soul was stirring, which meant everyone was in the great

[51] History repeats itself yet again. Two years later, the Loops and one hundred other ships were stuck in ice! What a mess.

[52] All twenty-two crew members died in the wreck. Some of them never left the boat, and the body of a man nicknamed Old Whitey remains in the engine room to this very day, preserved by the cold water and lack of bacteria.

room either eating, congregating, or independently pursuing hobbies. H was comfortable enough to just let herself in and find the gathering.

"Oh, my goodness," a gentle voice said. "Look what the catfish dragged in!"

H turned to see the kind eyes of Wadeen looking at her, and she promptly swam over to give her a hug. Wadeen was the closest thing to an auntie H had. "I've missed you, Wadeen!" H squealed as she swam a circle around her friend, who was wearing a delightful teal drop-waist dress and leather Mary Janes.

"Keep it down out there! This is a freighter, not an elegant promenade vessel!" yelled Stanley down the hall.

"Ignore that grumpy old coot," whispered Wadeen. "You're lucky you don't have to enjoy his company for all eternity. I wish he'd just go be at peace already."[53]

H scrunched up her nose. "I would have trouble resisting the urge to throw that man overboard."

"Believe me, we did! As a stewardess, I never cared if he was comfortable. Come into the great room and sit," said Wadeen, nestling into her modest green couch.

H noticed the brothers Samuel and Dean across the room at the dining table and waved. "It's nice to see that everyone is maintaining their nonexistent routines."

Dean looked up from his newspaper. "Hello, my favorite cryptid! Nice to see you back again!"

"You should check out our latest work in the engine room," said Samuel. "We had a breakthrough and painted more red symbols to keep bad spirits away. It's right next to the sign that says *Safety First*. You can never be too careful with these matters."

"It's goddamn graffiti, you fucking miscreants!" Stanley bellowed in the distance.

"You see? It's already working—keeps Stanley at a distance," boasted Dean. "Evil spirits are no match for us." He took a bite out of his cheeseburger.

[53] Stanley was right on the freighter part. *Kamloops* carried many goods made in the United Kingdom to the British Empire of Canada back in her glory days. Unfortunately, those goods didn't include manners.

"Ever prove your theory that ghosts cannot survive in saltwater?" H queried.

"Nope," answered Samuel. "That is yet to be determined but extremely plausible."

"Maybe you can practice on Stanley," plotted H quietly. Dean held up a saltshaker and tilted it in agreement. H turned back to Wadeen.

"I've been reading the most interesting story about young Abe Lincoln," Wadeen said with a glint in her eye, motioning to the book on the pine table next to her. "He was quite the reasonable and decent man, driven by the need to make the world a better place!"

"What, did he hunt vampires and slay fire-breathing dragons?" H asked sarcastically.

"Metaphorically, yes," said Wadeen with a chuckle. "You know as a young man he worked on a riverboat on the mighty Mississippi? I'm sure he could have handled Lake Superior with long sea legs, and he certainly could aptly wield an ax."

"Was the ax for the vampires, dragons, or both?" H inquired with a snort giggle.

Wadeen smiled. "Only the trees, my darling. The tall, brilliant man also had a patent for a floatation device for boats to assist movement through shallow waters. I'm not sure it would have done us any good way out here, but commercialization and further development of the product could have led to an invention that would have saved our mortal lives."

"And if you would have lived to tell those mortal tales of modern technology, I would have never met you," H pointed out with a flick of her tail. "A bittersweet conundrum indeed."

"He was an enabled *murderer* and we have evidence that he was in fact a demon!" Samuel interjected from the back of the room.

"All men in power make deals with the devil," Dean added.

"He's not entirely wrong," H acknowledged. "From what I understand, his presidency was a bloodbath.[54] Maybe that's why there were so many vampires?"

[54] The grisly Dakota War of 1862 occurred during the Civil War and ended with thirty-eight Dakota Indians hanged per Abe's orders. That is the largest mass execution in the history of the United States, and it happened right here in Minnesota! It's a long story, but in 2021 the state government and historical society gave a portion of land back to the tribe.

Wadeen smiled. "The Civil War years were a turning point for America, albeit ugly."

"The romanticization of American history strikes again," H cheered, fist pumping upward. "He's remembered for his good deeds, and I'd wager the author took liberties with his dirt."

"I think he tried to do what was best for America at the time. You make a valid point, though. Many presidents leave a trail of casualties. Best we can do is learn from the past and hope for the future," Wadeen added somberly.

"I wish the text didn't justify every bad deed or omit them entirely—for all modern works anyway," sighed H. "I suppose the sugarcoating had to start somewhere!"

"It all depends whose side you are on," Wadeen reasoned. "America was divided in multiple ways."

"They could at least do better up there for Indigenous communities whose ancestors they killed and land they trampled. According to Athena, some of them don't even have clean water!" H exclaimed. She softened. "I'm hydrophilic, by Greek definition. Water is my love language. What's interesting in your book?"

"Lincoln was the first president ever to have a beard!" Wadeen blurted it out like it was the ripest, juiciest gossip she had ever known.

"I adore a good beard," confessed H. "Practical and handsome. I wish I had one to keep my face warm! I adore when the sailors' beards grow icicles!"

"Yes! That happened the day we sank, a bright spot in the horrid affair." Wadeen continued. "Amongst other important things, he knew sporting a beard would lead mankind in the right direction." She looked upward and placed her hands over her heart.

"We all know that John Wilkes Booth was evil by his sinister caterpillar creeper mustache," said H. "He must have gotten really jealous by the full face of hair on Abe. Perhaps there was a bit of beard envy present at the Ford's Theatre that dreadful, murderous evening." H raised an eyebrow suspiciously.

"Now, now. Thou must not judge all men by their facial hair—or lack thereof," replied Wadeen. "A man's intentions do not rest solely on the follicle content of his face." Wadeen always sounded so wise, even when H engaged in playful banter. "The man abolished slavery,[55] not sinister mustaches."

"Maybe karma is a mustache," chuckled H.

"Did I overhear something flattering about men with beards?" Bruce asked, pointing at his own well-manicured beard. He walked over in his dapper gray suit, carrying a large platter of gingersnap cookies. "Pardon my interruption. Are you having an enjoyable day, ladies?" He offered them each a cookie, which they graciously accepted.

"Of course, kind sir. The *Loops* is a wonderful place to be." H gestured across the room and curtsied with a cookie in one hand. After taking a bite, she exclaimed, "Bruce! Did Barnacle Bob make these? They're fantastic!"

"Thank you kindly," responded Bruce. "Barnacle Bob did play a role in baking them, but I helped. The secret is in the molasses. We only use the best."[56]

"Of course, it helps when the ship goes down with the best Honey Bee molasses money can buy," confided Wadeen. "We also have a lifetime supply of Life Savers candies . . . which, come to think of it, did little in the event of a true emergency to help save our lives."

Bruce gushed, "For what it's worth, I think our supply of fine British goods has made our trip through the afterlife much more enjoyable, especially the exquisite teas."

"Tea, warm homemade cookies, and a good historical nonfiction book are very much my idea of a good time," Wadeen stated. "I also enjoy haunting a nationally registered historic place for all eternity."

"I'd certainly agree with you, Wadeen," agreed Bruce. "I'd add intellectual conversation and card games with fine wines, cheeses, and gourmet dinners to the list. If only we had the theatre."

"The theatre isn't all it's cracked up to be. Just ask Abe Lincoln," said H.

[55] Fun fact: The Emancipation Proclamation freed the slaves in only ten states.

[56] Bruce would never settle for anything but top-shelf quality. He'd ended up on the doomed journey after selecting goods from England, which he wanted to personally deliver, for a wealthy friend. Despite his higher class, he took a job as a crew member to avoid boredom on the long trip to Canada.

"Shakespeare had a unique way with language and tragedy," Bruce reminisced. "Imagine what he'd write about the events on the *Titanic*, or an ice-covered ship that sank in a brutal winter storm in the greatest of freshwater lakes for that matter!"

"I'm sure the iceberg would have a melodramatic monologue about how it felt to be rammed by a bloody ship," H joked. "Dibs on that part!" H grabbed another cookie and daintily stuffed it into her mouth.

"What's that about icebergs? They're great for keeping whiskey cold, I could use one right about now!" Matthew Forneighbules entered the room, sporting tan trousers and a bright-yellow shirt. He carried an old glass bottle—presumably filled with finely aged malt liquor—and a couple of drinking glasses. "H! Is that a banana in your shirt or are you just happy to see me?"

"Fourballs! It's a banana that I smuggled off the Miss America to give to Delbert, and it matches your shirt! If I were wearing yellow, you'd never have noticed. How many bananas are you hiding in there?" H had forgotten about her banana and swam over to give her friend a high five. His last name initially confused her, so she honored him with a similar sounding nickname. "You're looking festive in that banan-o-flage. Where on earth is the missus?"

Before he could answer, Stanley yelled, "They're not actually married!"

"Just because we got hitched in the afterlife doesn't mean it is invalid," Fourballs yelled back. "Go clean the head!"[57]

"Stupid mermaid, bringing a banana to the *Kamloops*!" Stanley yelped. "Now we'll have bad luck even in death."

Vera poked her head out from behind a large easel in the corner of the room. H hadn't even noticed her over there quietly painting on her canvas. She had a wicker basket near her feet, filled with paints, yarn, a sachet of loose-leaf tea, and a tin of chocolates. The table next to her was littered with jars of paint and a delicate wild-rose-adorned teacup of carefully steeped bliss.

[57] Head is slang for a ship's toilet, a term used as far back as the 1700s.

"Vera Meyer-Fourballs," exclaimed H as though paging a ship via radio communicator. H swam to the corner and wrapped her arms around Vera in an exuberant hug that almost knocked her over. Besides painting, Vera also knit chunky wool sweaters for the crewmen. Part of H wondered if the purpose of the sweaters was so that nobody would ever freeze to death again.

"What are you painting today?" H asked.

"This is a seascape of Lake Superior's north shore, featuring the cedar Witch Tree," answered Vera. "The Witch Tree, sacred to the local American Indian people, grows out of bare rock." She turned her canvas so H could see. The tumultuous blue-green watercolors were so vivid that H could feel them. The twisted old tree perched on a rock overlooking the lake while ominous clouds loomed overhead. H had visited the tree in real life a few times and always marveled at the simple beauty she possessed.

"Wow," said H, taken aback by the detail. "You have such interesting perspective. I can feel the wisdom of the tree, and you perfectly captured her wild spirit."

Vera smiled. "Thank you. That's exactly what an artist longs to hear. It also helps to have limitless inspiration in this awesome slice of the world. Look at me, getting all deep and philosophical and shit!" Vera wiped her hands on the cloth apron that covered her purple sweater and gray slacks. She wore a pair of fancily crafted leather high-top shoes.

While H was examining Vera's masterpiece, Bruce and Fourballs had cracked open the bottle of brown liquor and were toasting to glaciers, magnificent ice monuments crafted by the hands of time.

"I was just visiting GC and telling her the story of the Loops," said H. "I feel like she was heartbroken when I told her how you made it to shore in a lifeboat but still froze to death."

Vera turned to H. "Did you mention the part where I sent a message in a glass bottle saying we were freezing and starving?"[58]

"No," answered H. "I didn't go into that much detail."

[58] The message was discovered one year later in Canada.

"It was sent in hopes of rescue, but also for my mother. One day, she saw what she referred to as 'a metal bird in the sky,' and the conspiracy theories consumed her. I needed her to know the truth about my disappearance so she wouldn't blame extraterrestrial beings or waste money on psychics," Vera explained. "In the end, our frozen bodies were found and provided closure, which would have put the kibosh on that anyway. Meanwhile, my father would have walked up mountains in a thunder blizzard carrying a bison to get me back."

"Have you ever heard of Area 51? It's where the government hides secrets about aliens. If only your mother would have lived long enough to see it," murmured H. "I've heard stories."

"She would have stormed the place and demanded to be put in charge," chuckled Vera.

"And then she would have burned her bras and spearheaded the women's liberation movement," added H.

"Sometimes people are just born in the wrong era," acknowledged Vera.

The clinking of glasses drew H and Vera out of their private conversation.

"Although the creative juices are flowing, I wholeheartedly welcome an interruption to take a snack break for a cookie," said Vera as she moved out of her arts-and-crafts corner to the middle of the room where others were socializing, bringing her delicate teacup with her. Vera sat next to Wadeen on the couch and slowly savored every bite of the scrumptious baked treat.

Fourballs confided to the ladies, "The way to Vera's heart is through her stomach."

"That's why we get along so well," H replied between bites.

Bruce turned to H, looking for all the juicy gossip about other ghost ships. "Have you talked to any other fine folks who reside in the waters deep?"

"Lou makes a mean blueberry cobbler, George has strawberries, and my favorite trout think trouble is brewing southside—a group of creatures named Reefers. In island news, Howard is busy with dam life and father duties, and Rolf has sweet baby pups. A boat near Beaver Island had a few zebra mussels, which I obliterated." Her eyes lit up as she remembered. "Has anyone left the ship lately or gone out for a drunken adventure?"

"No," said Wadeen. "Why do you ask?"

"It's probably nothing, but the bags of wheat kernel on the Glenny looked like someone had been sleeping on them. One of them was knocked over," H relayed. "I also noticed on the Cumby that someone had been on the velvet furniture."

"It wasn't us," promised Fourballs, "although I think we are all due for an outing. It is just so hard to leave home. I'm overdue for a journey around the island to finish my underwater maps, and I very much enjoy the maritime history our neighbors provide. Did you see my newest land maps on the wall?"

H turned for a quick look at the sketches, one of Lake Superior and another of just Isle Royale. "There were some fish scales in the engine room of Greenie and a DEFCON 1, skunk-emission-level nasty odor surrounding the GC as well," H reported. "I doubt any ghosts would be the source of these findings."

"Interesting findings nonetheless," Wadeen contemplated. "Sounds like you have some stinky fish on your hands."

"And the *Algoma* still provides swanky accommodations and has rowdy sing-alongs with drinks?" Bruce inquired excitedly, trying to disguise his envy.

"Yes," replied H. "It's a jolly good time once the shanties start flowing. You should go pay them a visit. I'm sure Lou would love a new face to harass and feed. What's holding you back?"

"I don't know," Bruce hesitated. "I just feel obliged to stay home and putter about. I used to leave a lot, you know. I was a socialite in my past life. I once dined with the Queen."

"I think you have a serious case of what the humans call fear-of-missing-out, abbreviated as FOMO," said H. "You love visiting other ships but don't want to miss anything exciting that happens here."

"That sums it up precisely," said Bruce. "How did you ever learn of this FOMO? It sounds like a disease."

"It is not as intriguing as you may think," answered H. "There was a boat named *FOMO* near Duluth, and I had to eavesdrop a little to figure it out."

"I wish George would jump ship and come haunt with us," said Vera. "I do so very much love the company of that wonderful poodle. Maybe I should knit him a little sweater."

"Should I be jealous?" Fourballs asked jokingly.

"Yes, you should be jealous," answered Vera. "Love for a good dog is unconditional. Fortunately, as far as you're concerned, I will tolerate your overly bright shirts and continue my wifely duties uninterrupted by the visual distraction."

"I wouldn't argue with that," said H. "George is one heck of a cuddler."

"How are the lighthouses holding up?" Wadeen inquired.

"Kissed by the weather, guarded by seabirds, and aged to perfection,"[59] reported H.

"Why the seabirds?" Fourballs asked.

"Some of the seabirds believe lighthouses were made by the will of a supreme being, much like the pyramids," explained H. "Birds that migrate talk a lot, sharing truths and mischiefs around the globe faster than any other creature. Lighthouses serve as a resting point over large bodies of water for birds carrying important messages from the Gods, with a secondary duty to guide ships when the weather turned brutal."

"Birds nowadays don't relay messages to and from the Gods, do they?" Vera's eyes widened.

"The only bird I know of that has contact with celestial beings is our raven Revna," said H. "She descended from Odin's ravens, mainly dealing with the Norse celestial beings until gaining the trust of other factions. I've heard her mention names of the archangel Michael and even Zeus in passing. However, I would assume there are more birds out there that do the same. We live in but a small piece of the world."

[59] None of the four lighthouses around the island are in service anymore, but they still attract curious visitors.

"How interesting!" Wadeen exclaimed.

"You would think, but it's a conundrum. Revna can't actually interfere with normal life. She relays warnings as cryptic messages, hoping one will figure out the correct course of action to take, and she doesn't always reveal the source of the message. I haven't seen her in quite a while, although I thought I heard her voice a couple of days ago," said H. "Usually, matters between birds and Gods are pretty serious, and honestly I think she comes to visit us sometimes just to gossip."

"That's a bird I would love to chat with," said Bruce. "Does she converse with ghosts? I am now very motivated to leave the ship!"

H laughed. "I think so, but Revna moves so much you'd be lucky to even catch a glimpse of her! Anyway, I think the lighthouses serve the purpose of helping out our flying friends when their wings grow weary regardless of if they are messengers or not."

"How delightful! If only every island could house such a historically important and mystical structure," said Wadeen wistfully.[60] "Perhaps we should name all of them first, though."[61]

Fourballs responded, "We shall start by naming the remainder of islands after yours truly." He pointed both thumbs at himself and grinned. "My mother would be so proud."

Bruce laughed. "If there were an island named Whiskey, you'd never leave it!"

"That's accurate," said Fourballs. He picked up his glass and took another sip, then spit it out in surprised laughter: Barnacle Bob had entered the room, sporting a white cloth apron and nothing else.

"Jesus, Bob! Put some clothes on!" Stanley bellowed down the hallway.

"Whatever you do, don't turn around! Or do—whatever works for you," said Bruce with a shrug.

"Nobody warned me there would be a full moon tonight," said Vera.

[60] Lake Superior has over 450 islands. It would never look dark with that many beacons blaring!

[61] Only about one hundred of these islands have been given names.

"If I were a wolf, I'd be howling! Hear that? I think Rolf is singing his heart out up on the main island!" H said through giggled bursts.

"The ocean tides are very confused right now," added Fourballs. "We may have a global catastrophe on our hands."

"That's no moon!" exclaimed Wadeen, innocently confused by the sight of Barnacle Bob's bottom.

Bob set down a tray of freshly cooked peameal bacon[62] finger sandwiches, turned around—everyone shielded their eyes and groaned—and sat his bare bottom on a tufted armchair. "Ya best eat up while it's hot, eh!" The crew didn't need an invitation; they had already started happily picking at the sandwiches.

"The spot of mustard creates a symphony in the mouth," complimented Bruce.

"I don't know if I can trust a naked chef," Wadeen admitted between bites.

"Naked chefs have the best bacon," said Barnacle Bob. "Please don't tell the rest of the world my secret."

"Your secret died with the Loops, as far *ass* I'm concerned," said H. She barely spit the pun out before bursting into laughter.

"I imagine it was too cold on the ship to ever let it all hang out in real life," said Bruce. "I never made it into the kitchen with you at the time, but I'd imagine you were bundled up like the rest of us."

Barnacle Bob answered, "I think I could manage the cold, except for my manly bits. If only Vera would knit me a sausage warmer. I mean, it's basically a woolen sock, so it should be easy."

"A very *tiny* sock," added Fourballs with a wink toward his wife. "Mine will require much more yarn."

"Why? To accommodate your four balls?" H asked jokingly while playing with her braids. The room echoed with deep belly chuckles.

"There will be no knitting of anything for the man bits, sir," said Vera firmly yet playfully with a smile.

[62] Peameal bacon is made from lean pork loin, not smoked, and rolled in ground yellow peas (nowadays they use cornmeal). An English man named William Davies, who moved to Canada in the mid-1800s, is said to have invented the dish. Much like the ship, Bob had Canadian roots and was a master of their cuisine.

"If you can't stand the heat, get naked in the kitchen!" Bob exclaimed. "In all actuality, with those scalding stoves and fires, I could have worn next to nothing and been perfectly fine."

"So, when you baked your cookies with Bruce, were you fully clothed for the occasion?" Wadeen asked, glancing at the almost empty cookie platter.

Bruce laughed. "A gentleman never tells."

H licked her fingers. "I don't care what you're wearing. As long as all the food tastes this good, I'm not going to judge you for one second!"

"You know, H, we all think you're the bee's knees. I'm pleased as punch you decided to join us on the humble Loops this evening for exquisite company and fine spirits." Bruce raised his glass in a toast. "The whiskey is good too." Everyone laughed, but he wasn't wrong.

"We know you are just passing by, like we are two ships in the night," said Fourballs. "Where wilt thou travel hence?" Fourballs tried to talk fancy when lubricated with alcohol.

"I've not thought very far ahead, but I do hope to sneak a visit to Delbert the moose. He usually resides on the north side of the island, not far from here. Sometimes he even gets close to humans because they have the best snacks to steal, mainly bananas." H lifted her eyebrows as though she knew a secret mission was in order. "I just have to steer clear of human activity. If he's not patrolling the shoreline, I can always send a bird inland to find him."

"Maybe you shouldn't bother avoiding the humans," said Bruce pensively. "Let them see a splash of your tail so they have stories of the big fish in Lake Superior. Confuse them, let them wonder. The world loves a good mystery."

"Show me the tourists that have no mega-zoom cameras or drones and we'll talk April Fools' Day pranks," said H with a smirk as her eyes met Bruce's. They giggled together somewhat evilly at the thought.

"Hey, now," said Fourballs. "Easy with the tomfoolery. I once was a wee lad who wanted to pull my father's leg. I switched the salt and sugar on the table, and he poured salt in his coffee. He blamed my poor mother because I was too afraid to get a beating for the joke. She put cilantro in his eggs the next day, and he said they tasted like soap. Her herbal assault continued for over a week until he said his apologies. My ass was spared." Fourballs raised his glass, a fleeting glint of mortal glory reminiscence in his eye. Vera lovingly rubbed his shoulder.

"One should never mess with another man's food," declared Barnacle Bob. "Trust is the most important thing that comes out of the kitchen." As he spoke, he lifted and crossed his legs without warning. His apron was a lot shorter than it looked.

Old Whitey wandered into the room, still dressed in his ragged crewman uniform. He took one look at Bob, shook his head, and sauntered back out. He had a penchant for mischief but knew when his lot would be empty.

"Grandpa Whitey, won't you stay for a beverage?" Bruce called out. The old man wandered away without turning around to respond.

"He's not the most social fellow, unless he can pull your leg for a laugh," said Fourballs.

"No fibs there," agreed Bruce. "He's always been our very own Puck—you know, from *A Midsummer Night's Dream*!"

"At least he's friendly," added Wadeen.

As if on command, Stanley screamed, "Is the abomination still here? *The mermaid is one of Satan's vile creations!*"

"It's about time for your exorcism, Stanley!" Dean yelled from the back of the room.

"What a ruckus. We do apologize, H!" said Bruce sweetly. "Back to your moose friend Delbert. Did you know there is a moose named after me?"

H giggled. "Yes, I've heard this story a million times. Bruce the Moose lives on the east side of the island. He's a dapper and social fellow who likes to block the trail to mess with the humans."

"Well, then you see the resemblance?" Bruce shrugged. "Dapper and social."

"His antlers are a wee bit bigger than yours," said H. "He's not one bit camera shy, either. He's probably been photographed more than Slate Island's caribou herds, up in Ontario! You know Bruce the Moose is the son of the infamous Delbert? He's got a strong, desirable bloodline."

Bruce nodded and lifted his hands. "See? We're one and the same."

The room erupted in laughter, and the crew decided to play a game of poker for evening entertainment. Vera was a silent killer, with plenty of spare buttons to use for pretend bets, but H tried her best anyway. The woman could use a challenge, and the game often devolved into adult Go Fish anyway. As the evening wound down, H had a bellyache from all the laughing at Fourball's antics. At the end of the night, she curled up on the couch for a gratifying snooze before her early morning trek to find her beloved moose friend.

Chapter Six

SINCE IT WAS QUICKLY BECOMING warm enough for humans to tolerate, H approached the island east of Todd Harbor.[63] Increased human activity always prompted her to avoid the ferry route, just for the sake of not having to engage her mermaid stealth mode skills. She looked up and down the rocky shore, where overgrown grass and bright-yellow dandelions painted the landscape. The delicate bouquet of springtime smells tickled her human nostrils, delighting her olfactory center. Her braids dripped with cold water, large droplets trailing down her back, reflecting the sunshine and mirroring the scenery of the shoreline like tasty pieces of a wide-angle landscape painting.

A sudden burst of loud, distant chattering caused H's human heart to run wild. "Angie, is that you?" she softly called up to the shore.

[63] "It's cooler by the lake." —Humans

Coniferous trees rustled, branches bouncing. H noticed a tree with antler scrapings carved into the bark. The sheer size of the mark confirmed this was Delbert's territory. A red squirrel bounded down the tree and pranced through the grasses, bushy tail upright. It was indeed Angie, the sweetest and sassiest red squirrel Isle Royale had ever known.

"Hello, my darling!" chattered Angie. Angie stood on her hind legs and clasped her tiny front paws together. Her dark eyes glistened in the sunlight, and her tiny nostrils flicked, making her whiskers dance in the gentle breeze. "We were just about to engage in the most sacred activity of the red squirrel clan: the bushy tail dance! Would you care to join us with your shiny, scaled hind end? A girl can still shake it, even if it's not fluffy. Actually, I have enough fluff for the both of us." Angie spun around and wiggled her little squirrel butt, wagging her flouncy tail with precision and glee. This squirrel had all the moves.

"Unfortunately, if I shake my tail, you're probably going to get a cold shower," answered H with a light mermaid tail slap that bounced the water over her scales daintily.

"Aah, I could probably use one," said Angie with a wink. She hopped about, zigzagging closer to the water's edge, and scampered into H's outstretched hands for some chin scratches and a tiny squirrel hug.

"How are the kits, and the grandkits? We all know that all you squirrels do is make more squirrels!"

"Nutty as ever." Angie smiled. "We have the highest population of any mammal on the island, so we're clearly doing something right." Angie raised her eyebrows up and down.

"A badge of honor, indeed," H solemnly cooed at her tiny friend.

"I'm actually a great-great-grandma now." She popped her hip to the left and dropped a front paw on it. "I don't look it, right?"

"You don't look a day over one litter of your own, my little love."

"Interestingly enough, we've been trying to trace our ancestors through the history in the sacred tree dens. However, the squirrel scratches have faded over the years and become harder to decipher. Anyway, it was once thought that the island's red squirrels were a unique subspecies. Now we believe our ancestors swam here and started to breed like snowshoe hares. We may have even crossed the ice bridge just like the wolves."

"Your ancestors must have been resourceful if Rolf's ancestors didn't decimate your kind," said H.

"Resourceful? Pshaw! We all know red squirrels are the evil ones," admitted Angie proudly. "We don't make for a very nutrient-dense snack, anyway. It's a lot of work catching one of us, let alone enough to satiate the hunger of an apex predator."

"Squirrel stowaways could have arrived via ship with every intention of total domination," replied H. "I don't think squirrels are completely hydrophobic, either. I've heard stories of a trained squirrel who visits conventions on the mainland in Duluth and water-skis like a human."

"I, too, have heard of the famous squirrel who does water tricks—but can she dance?" exclaimed Angie. "We are no different than our counterparts who live on the mainland in the upper Midwest."

"By 'no different,' do you mean all squirrels are just as evil?" H asked. Angie responded with giggles. "Isolation does wonderful things to genetic profiles, does it not?" H asked wistfully. She longed to study biology like the students in that building with the large windows overlooking the Portage Canal in Houghton.

"Only the strong survive, my beautiful merlady! If a dash of evil makes us stronger, I'll take it! I like to use the terms *formidable* and *cunning*. My tail-shake brings all the survival instincts to the yard—I can teach you, but I'd have to charge." Angie smiled and sang, nose twitching, as she twirled in H's hand. "You can tell who my kits are by their lush, bushy tails." She pointed to her tiny backside and floated her tail up, affectionately wrapping her short arms around it. "My grandkits have it too. Time will tell if the great-grands will be as blessed."

"I'm really glad we crossed paths, but I came here in search of Sir Delbert. I was going to send a bird to relay the message, but maybe you could help me instead?" H asked.

"You mean you didn't show up here solely for a dance party with yours truly? The nerve!" Angie jokingly squealed.

"For a thousand-pound ungulate with the widest symmetrical antler spread on the island, Delbert has a way of hiding in plain sight," H stated.

"I know what you mean," said Angie. "The boreal forest embraces that rack, and the shrubbery hides his long stick legs."

"He's so big that he eats like fifty pounds of vegetation a day. Thank Gods the island has abundant foliage, but he could be at the tree line, watching us, and we'd have no idea."

"You should see the cows trample all over the island and flock to him in mating season," said Angie, shaking her head. "At least he's become more selective with his mates over the years."

"I imagine it's easy for the moose around here to unintentionally partake in more inbreeding than biologically healthy," H speculated. "I suppose the herd has a way of finding balance between genetic perfection and variability."

"Well, he's either sneaking around in the shade watching humans, or resting in a bog somewhere," divulged Angie. "You won't find him up and about much except at dusk and dawn."

"It all depends on bananas. He loves them and will get dangerously close to humans for a taste," relayed H. "He loves the thrill of making calves almost as much as he loves eating bananas."

"He is definitely a wise and caring moose elder," Angie added. "He's never even lost a fight. The dude acts like he owns the place."

H laughed. "He certainly does his part in making sure the herd doesn't overfeed and strain the plant life of the island.

I am glad he pays attention, a moose with the munchies could wreak havoc!"

"It would be my honor to aid milady in her quest to talk to the Moose Lord. I shall conspire with the birds of my tree and get his location. Don't stray too far, my love. I will return in a bit!"

H kissed Angie gently on the forehead and set her back on shore, where she scampered off, tail ablaze with her new quest. Angie was a loveable boss bitch, and she knew how to get shit done without creating drama. Red squirrels inspired H because, much like the beavers, they worked hard for what they wanted to accomplish.

Five minutes later, Angie bounced back through the tall grass. "Good news! Athena Sparrow spotted Del this morning about a mile away. He was snacking, of course. She's sent off to request his presence, milady." Angie bowed.

"A moose snacking at the island's all-you-can-eat buffet is no surprise. I am grateful for your assistance. You know, I owe you a favor now. Just let me know when you want our official dance party to happen, and I'll be here."

"In that case, we're going to have to request Revna talk to the Gods about the date for the best aurora show of the year. Then we'll dance under the colorful moving lights and bright-white stars, as the Gods intended. The birds, insects, and frogs shall sing for us using their daytime voices, not their creepy night sounds." Angie's eyes sashayed over the tree line, and she talked as fast as she scampered. "Humans tried to recreate this mystical aurora effect, you know: disco balls and neon lights. It's a shame they don't just get outside and enjoy the planet's organic beauty. The canvas of the Gods has no competition; and in a national park, we accept no substitutes." Angie raised a fist. "Regardless, we know if the aurora is a-blazing, the Gods are burning down the house, so to speak!"

Red squirrels, known for their love of a good time, were quite passionate about creating the perfect ambiance for shaking their tails.

In H's mind, there was absolutely nothing wrong with being a nature snob. "I'm glad you accept my trade, and I am just as excited as you are! I've always wanted to learn the ways of the squirrel dance."

Angie stood on her back legs and alternated moving her front paws up and down. She started to shake her booty, and her tail followed. "I will show you the ways of the dance, young one. Just you wait."

A few minutes had passed, and a shadow from overhead closed in on the party planning. Athena swooped down and landed silently on the ground.

"H! I heard you were visiting our humble home," Athena chirped. "I am honored to be in your presence once again." She tilted her head, looking up at H. "Girl! I missed you."

"Thank you, sweet sparrow." H smiled. She always felt so loved when the creatures of the planet were happy to see her. She wished to repay the affection and helpfulness the earth always provided her.

Athena summarized the situation: "Del was about a mile up the shore. It's post-birthing season, and he's giving the herd mamas their space by running protection detail. He'll be here shortly, or however long it takes those tree-trunk legs to propel his giant body through the forest!"

"What is the velocity of an unladen moose?" H wondered aloud.

"American or Canadian?" asked Angie, squinting thoughtfully.

"Well, we all know a moose hauling ass at max speed goes about thirty-five miles per hour," answered Athena, looking at H. "It's been concluded through vigorous observational studies by sparrows on a trail course with minimal altitude changes. We may have a deal with the spring peepers to conduct timekeeping in such matters."

"Do you have any studies on the art of squirrel dancing?" H asked. Angie giggled.

"So, in theory," continued Athena, "he could be here in about two minutes. Some moose have egos as big as their antlers. They come to us to see if they can break the record! Occasionally, we indulge them and let them try."

As if on command, the ground shook with the thunder of large hooves. The trio turned inland as the booming slowed down. "H!" Delbert's baritone rumbled distinctively. "The songs of the wolf indicated the Fish Lady had returned! I knew you'd be paying me a visit."

"Wait, you speak wolf? Only wolves understand their sacred song!" Athena perched on Del's antlers and waited for an answer.

Del chuckled, shaking his large muscular chest. "When you've lived here as long as I have, the local predators are quite easy to decipher. It's a survival tactic and practical life skill."

"They sang about me?" H put her hands on her chest and gushed.

"Yeah, right, Del," Angie chimed in. "We all know you and Rolf have a bromance. Was this a secret back-trail conversation? Did it end in snuggles? Were you big spoon or little spoon?" She crossed her arms and placed a paw on her chin.

"Your presence is worthy of such tribute," answered Delbert. "After all, you are the only being who can bring news from the depths of the sea to the shores. You should have heard his pups vocalizing." Delbert's large dewlap bobbed to and fro beneath his chin.

"Aw, buddy, I love and respect you too. In fact, I love you so much that I stole you a banana off the Miss America!" H reached into her top and pulled out the banana. She put her elbows on a rock, propped her head in her hands, and looked up with adoration at her moose friend.

Del grinned. "You've got a keen memory, Fish Lady. I shall award thee as an honorary member of the Mooz of Minong herd.[64] Thank you for the treat." Del ate the entire unpeeled banana before continuing. "You know I have eyes and ears everywhere."

"Yep," said Athena. "I'm your eyes in exchange for antler rides. You're more fun to sit on than a boring branch. The trees don't talk

[64] Mooz is Anishinaabe for moose.

back—most of the time, anyway . . ." Her eyes darted from side to side as though she had said something she shouldn't have.

"Look at us! We're like a harem of hotties swooning over our mighty moose man." Angie wiggled her hips. "Don't even pretend to be humble."

Delbert looked down at the tiny squirrel, with whom he rarely talked. "I feel like you were destined to be my evil little sidekick, tiny sassy one."

"Oh, for sure," answered Angie. "My sass is as big as your . . ."

"Ass?" offered H.

"I was going to say *rack*, but OK." Angie shrugged.

"Humans would totally pay to watch your adventures," said Athena. "The antics of a squirrel and a moose together would inspire children to make better choices and appreciate their Mother Earth." Everyone looked at Athena with a bit of confusion. "When I migrate, I see things like trash in rivers," she explained, "smoke pollution, deceitful rainbows reflecting off devious oil spills. And you know what? *It makes me wanna swoop at people!* Intelligent, evolved bipeds could make smarter decisions about how their actions affect the world around them." She stopped abruptly. "Sorry. I got going and began to rant."

"Angie would dance the bad people away with a flick of her bushy tail, and Del would smash the bad guys with his rut rage!" H exclaimed. "Oh, and Angie could have a superpower like flying to make her attacks even more epic! This sounds like a bit from the funny papers!"

"Your female imaginations have really run off-kilter. Is it my pheromones or something?" Delbert asked suspiciously.

"What is the velocity of an imagination running off-kilter?" Angie looked to Athena but couldn't hold in her laughter.

"For you, twice the speed of light!" Athena answered without missing a beat.

"I do love it when you all talk nerdy to me," said Delbert,

turning the conversation back to business. "Speaking of science, interesting population developments draw more biologists here to study us."

"You always wipe out our shenanigans like your herd wiped out the caribou," said Angie.[65] "And, yes, Sir Del, the red squirrels are victoriously thriving."

"Only the strong and handsome survive." Delbert recited his answer as though he affirmed the statement daily while puffing his regal chest. "Our island is not home to many regional mammals that would compete for our food or hunt us. I mean, we have no bears, caribou, deer, or porcupines. If only the spirits of our ancestors could tell us how the flora and fauna of the north found Minong. The wolves didn't infiltrate our secret hideaway for decades."

"You don't choose island life; the island life chooses you," sang Athena. "If ya listen, Mother Nature talks."

"Maybe the island chose her inhabitants, and she sang her song to seduce a worthy predator for the moose overlords as a way of keeping them in check. In terms of developments, you're talking about the wolf pups, right?" H asked. "They're the most adorable little loves I've ever seen!"

"They're adorable all right—until they eat your face off," snarked Angie.

"Yes," replied Delbert. "Moose populations are at an all-time high. The rate at which wolves consume the herd has lessened substantially over the years due to lack of procreation. Rolf's pups may tip the scale a bit."

"You *would* be the expert on procreating," said Angie, mimicking the grunts of a moose in rut.

"I don't know, Angie. I think the squirrels have it mastered!" H said with a snort.

"With all those moose eating extreme mouthfuls of greenery on a daily basis, we might not have much of an island left!" exclaimed Athena. "Ya ungulates need to take it easy on your Mother."

[65] Caribou became extinct on Isle Royale in the early 1900s. They were most likely over-harvested, victims of wildfire, migratory, or disrupted by logging. Rumors spread over the years that the 'bou didn't coexist with moose, and the critters throw shade (not the kind moss on a fallen log thrives in). The 'bou also became scarce on the mainland, so I'd wager a bet that humans played a part.

Angie jumped up and down. "Dear wolves, eat moose! Spare the squirrels. Smooches!"

"The point at which food becomes scarce should not be tested," said Delbert. "That would not be the way of the herd. We take our population and its resource consumption quite seriously. Winter starvation is no small matter."

"So y'all are on strict diets?" Angie blurted.

"We relegate our feeding grounds to different areas of the island. To avoid depleting the resources in one spot, the herd moves frequently, giving the flora time to recover," Delbert answered seriously.

"You should see the view from up there." Athena pointed her wing toward the sky. "Fat and happy in a beaver pond is how a lot of moose here spend their days," said Athena.

Delbert continued. "The birds have also brought news of deep-water predators slaying our whitefish at alarming rates. Perhaps the trout have been filling their bellies a bit too ferociously . . . or we have a new underwater contender on our hooves. Lynneh the loon has heard whispers in the waters and similar mutterings from the gulls."

"Never trust a gull," screeched Athena. "They squawk nothing but lies, I tell ya. Tiny-brained sky rats."

"The Council of Fins is discussing the matter," said H. "They've got a few theories about rogue lamprey, eel, or some new long and skinny fish. Whatever they are, they're hanging around the outskirts of Harlem Reef, and the trout are calling them Reefers."

"What about the big, long boys? Sturgeon?" Angie asked with little confidence.

"Sturgeon are the largest fish in our sea," said H. "However, they prefer benthic feeding. *Sieve* some snacks for the rest of us, am I right?" H raised her fist in triumph.

"Ooh, they're the vacuums of the sea!" cried Angie.

Delbert held back a laugh. "Sturgeon have always been a peaceful species. They live with honor for their lost dinosaur companions and carry the weight of the earth's history and tragedy on their backs, which is why they live in such deep waters."

"So, the sturgeon suck, but we love them anyway. Got it," squealed Angie.

Athena looked down at Del. "Do moose have theories for everything?" Angie looked at her and nodded.

"The sturgeon are only dangerous when they leap out of the water with enough velocity to knock boaters out,"[66] said H.

"What is the velocity of an unladen sturgeon? Well, funny you should ask . . ." Athena started back up again. "Oh, my wings, I am just tossing waves at y'all."

Del cut her off as the ladies started to giggle, oblivious to the previous conversation about his land speed. "I'm not saying you should go looking for trouble, H, but if you could find out what is happening down there to ease the rumors, I'd much appreciate it. You know that disturbances to the ecosystem make some species quite nervous. Sturgeon are old and wise and might have some insight."

"I'd be happy to investigate the situation, Del. Unfortunately, I haven't seen Old Man Sturgeon in ages. When I round the east side of the island and head south, I'll talk to the resident whitefish. You know, I usually swim with lake trout, and my usual comrades reported similar rumors."

"The spread of misinformation is truly a vile disease," said Athena. "Blasted gossip birds. Get the truth for us, H!"

"Speaking of history, Del," started H, "have you ever seen the ghosts of a couple of Anishinaabe men walking the island?"

Del looked down at H with surprise and opened his mouth to talk but paused, furrowing his eyebrow whiskers.

"I saw them near Windigo in a birchbark canoe," continued H. "They disembarked and walked inland."

"Interesting," said Del. "Those who can see the spirits of the past have become rare in these parts. At one point, we thought the gift could be passed through our genes, but our theory was disproven

[66] This has actually happened in Florida, but would never happen here. Our sturgeon are midwestern nice.

by the time I was born. Currently, Chaos the red fox is the only mammal present with the gift, and she has not reported an observance in months. Then again, she's a bit shy. The Mooz of Minong herd has not bred a seer in decades. We thought Bruce was one, but it turned out he likes *living* people. The gift is now thought to rotate between land species: when one seer dies, another is born."

Athena looked down at Del. "Point of clarification, Del—does our girl H count as a mammal or a fish?"

"That's debatable," Del chuckled and again grew serious. "My grandmother bore the gift, and our verbal herd history has always been a bit vague on what she saw and how it led to her early demise. Her body was never found. She just disappeared into nowhere one day. The ravens said she simply walked away with ghosts." Del paused briefly to compose his thoughts.

"That's quite the legacy to behold. Perhaps she sacrificed herself for the good of the herd, Del," H said, trying to keep the old wound from seeping. Del was tough and would never show weakness, but she knew he appreciated knowing she cared. Mysteries simply drove moose crazy, which is why they had theories and took the time to analyze data which would support or decline their hypothesis. A lot of the time they just spent bull-moosing about the craziest scenarios they could create.

"Official Mooz of Minong legend states that if the heart and soul of a person becomes part of the island, they will spend the rest of their days here as one with nature. Those who die of hardship, as you know, can haunt their place of death for all eternity. The island chooses who will stay and which spirits will nourish her," Del explained. "As for your sighting, I'd suggest you give Chaos a shout. She's usually on the south side—not far from your friend Howard."

"We could be surrounded by ghosts and never even know," said Angie. "I hope they enjoy my dancing, those dirty little devils!"

"When I'm underwater with my fish companions, they can see my ghost friends as well," said H, turning to Athena. "If we were in the presence of the spirits right now, I would know, and you would see them too. It is my humble superpower."

"That's an intriguing development from our half-mammal seer," said Del, looking out toward the water. A boat had appeared in the distance, and he nodded toward the horizon. "I will take this as our cue to adjourn, but I look forward to our next conversation and shall keep my ears open for more information that applies to previously discussed topics."

"Bye, Del. It's always a pleasure." H reached up and rubbed Del's nose. As he turned and walked away, Athena waved goodbye from her perch on his left antler. She didn't look like she'd be moving any time soon, perhaps because she wanted to talk more about saving the planet.

Angie scampered over to H and hopped into her hands for one more kiss on the head. "Tell the family I said hello," said H. "Send me word via bird about our future dance extravaganza too!"

"I look forward to it!" Angie hopped down, shook her favorite appendage, and turned into the tall grass. She stopped to politely wave goodbye like a princess before quickly scampering into the privacy of the ground cover.

Chapter Seven

WITH A DELICATE SPLASH, H set a course for the SS *Chester A. Congdon.*[67] As H APPROACHED THE ship, a mysterious chill ran down her spine. She twirled around, dark braids flinging outward, and looked in all directions. But she was completely alone in the cool, deep water. Her human skin was peppered in hostile goosebumps. Perhaps her fish senses detected a danger her oblivious human half could not understand. Water pounded in her ears like a drum, and her neck gills flared rapidly.

Fighting the urge to flee, she proceeded to the site of the wreck. First, she smelled something similar to her visit to GC, the most gosh-awful rancid aroma. Then she stumbled upon what looked like a crime scene, and the shock rendered her motionless. "Is anyone here alive?" H cried across to the massacre. Hun-

[67] Originally named *Salt Lake City,* Chester sank in 1918 after running aground twice before Lake Superior finished the job with the trifecta of Canoe Rocks, ferocious seas, and opaque fog. A crewman paddled five miles to the nearest lighthouse for help after communications failed. World War I had just ended, and more grandiose historical events overshadowed her death. The loss was a huge financial catastrophe—she sank with 380,000 bushels of wheat worth $1.5 million.

dreds of whitefish were scattered across the sandy seafloor. Nobody answered. "Why are you not floating to the surface? Did this just happen?" she thought aloud.[68]

H carefully picked up a body and examined a circular wound where something sharp had attached and sucked the life out of each victim. Whatever it was had ripped almost all the way through the fish's body. She carefully set the fish back down, noticing a few white scales scattered about the mess. It was as though H had entered a hostile garden and needed to obtain a machete to cut horrifying thoughts that grew like vines and encompassed her brain.

Ice-cold tears of frustration and sadness escaped her eyes, consumed by the sea. "Evacuate the premises," said the voice in H's foggy head. She felt the undeniable urge to swim. Without making a sound, she aggressively increased her velocity using her shimmering, muscular tail. Athena would have been proud as H's mind wandered into the frivolous comparison of her underwater speed to Del's land speed. She was definitely faster, and she pushed the entertaining distraction out of her mind. H set a course for her next ghost ship and didn't crane her head around to look back into the silent, eerie dark at all. She was scared, possibly even petrified, and something about this uncomfortable situation had her literally jumping ship. Her fight-or-flight response told her to get the fuck out and never come back.

Her proximity to the SS *Emperor*, another victim of Canoe Rocks, made H feel more at ease. The glowing ghost vessel appeared in the darkness, and a wave of relief overcame H as she slowed to a comfortable, less vigorous pace. Captain Erldon, whom everyone lovingly called Speed, met her on deck as though awaiting her arrival. He was a seasoned war hero turned ship captain who often fondly reminisced about his military days.

"Welcome back to the largest ship Canada ever produced," he said cheerfully. "At the time of production, anyway!" Speed relished the *Emperor*'s claim to fame and wore navy blue denim trousers, brown leather boots, and the most ragged plaid flannel shirt H had

[68] As a fish decomposes, gases fill the body and the fish floats to the surface.

ever seen. He always wore a carved-bone beaded necklace with a black bear claw hanging as the focal point. "To be honest, you look like you've seen a ghost! Did Old Whitey get you by surprise?" He chuckled gruffly at his own joke. Apparently, Old Whitey's antics were appreciated by his fellow deep-water afterlifers. You had to give the old man credit: he had a legendary reputation.

"Speed! I was dropping by Chester for a visit and discovered a whitefish massacre. It looked like a war zone! Have you noticed anything unusual happening in the Canoe Rocks graveyard?" H blurted the question as fast as her frazzled mind could form the words.

"Nothing unusual has been haunting us here," answered Speed.[69] "We're still dealing with the same old ghosts." Noticing her uneasy body language and stress, Speed added, "Come on below and we'll have a refreshment with my sweet bride, Wendi."[70]

H nodded. Speed took H through the never-ending steel rat maze which was the *Emperor*, a simple vessel known as The Pride of Canada, built for hauling excessive loads, without the fancy amenities throughout her name would suggest.[71] The Captain's quarters, however, were decked out and swanky much like the *Algoma*. Speed had his own private deck on the bow of the ship with a private staircase up to the helm.

"Welcome back aboard our big and wild martini deck!" exclaimed Wendi at the sight of H. "Take a load off, sit. You'll see the crewmen on the main deck playing a rigorous match of curling today. Drink, dine, and overlook the scenery as the world passes by. Just like the good old days." The sights were indeed beautiful when traversing the Great Lakes from Canada. Underwater window views were a bit different.

"Soon we'll see more divers exploring the *Emperor* wreck," said Penny, their fluffy, off-white cat. "She's the most popular ship for deep-water dives around the island."

"H, may I interest you in a gin and tonic?" Wendi headed straight to her bar cart before H could answer, mixing the ingredients

[69] In 1947, Canoe Rocks claimed the Emperor after a navigational error by the first mate. Twelve lives were lost as well as 100,000 tons of iron ore.

[70] Nobody talked about how Wendi didn't go down with the ship. She said her heart lost the will to keep rhythm and she crossed into the afterlife. Some say she threw herself into the lake to join her love for eternity. We accept the mystery to avoid Speed's temper.

[71] The company named all vessels after royalty, creating an elegant-sounding cargo fleet.

and garnishing the beverage with her signature plump blackberry. "This is my proprietary recipe, my sweet," Wendi divulged. "I make my own sassy simple syrup infused with fresh blackberry and rhubarb. Give it a splash of *sassy* syrup. We don't always have citrus fruits this far north, so without a lime I had to be innovative. Today life gave me lemons, which is actually a good thing! Garnish with a slice that will make you pucker. Now, sit and stay a bit!"

H had been swimming back and forth across the room. Wendi grabbed her hand, led her to the polished black-walnut table, and placed the cocktail in front of her. Speed nestled himself into the light-brown cushioned armchair across the room, whittling away on a scrimshaw as though massaging the bone with his chisel. The man loved to carve and had been perfecting his bladework for years. Penny sat on his lap the moment he sat down. H picked an olive off a charcuterie platter and turned it in her fingers.

"Cat got your tongue, mermaid?" asked Penny. "It's me. I'm the cat."

Wendi sat across the table from H and reached for her hand. "I can sense it, dear. Something isn't quite right with you today." Her eyes looked H up and down, trying to read her like a good book. H took a sip of her gin and tonic, relishing in the tart rhubarb and blackberry essence. Nobody under the sea mixed a cocktail as well as Miss Wendi.

Speed looked up from his handiwork and said, "Tell her what you told me."

H began at the beginning and told the entire story: from the disturbed bags on Glenny to the rumors near Harlem Reef to the whitefish bodies by Chester. "Perhaps I'm overreacting," said H thoughtfully, hands wrapped around her drink. "I felt a foreboding presence and physiologically reacted in a way that confused my human half. It's as though my fish senses detected a danger, but my human body couldn't comprehend the data. And then when I saw the corpses, I just froze! I can't help but think this was caused by those Reefers everyone's talking about."

"Impending doom," said Wendi. "You could be having a heart attack. Does your arm hurt, love?"

"If she made it this far, I'd say her heart is fine," answered Speed. "Her physical heart, anyhow. The *emotional* heart of a woman, now . . . that's another story altogether." Speed winked at Wendi, who flicked an olive at his head in return.

"Did you eat something bad? Have you been with the likes of Lou? Or Barnacle Bob?" Wendi rattled. "When they call a baked good *special*, that doesn't always mean *unique*."

"I've seen both Lou and Bob," H answered, "but, no, they didn't poison me."

Wendi pivoted, focusing now on location. "The Chester is an unhaunted vessel. If lost souls found the ship, they could potentially call it home. A demon could even set up shop there—exiled demons could seek sanctuary, meet, and conspire amongst themselves. We may be dealing with beings from other realms, planets . . ." Wendi's eyes grew large. "Were there human divers nearby?"

"Honey," started Speed, "I don't know why anyone would want to live or dive in that lousy graveyard of old wheat and missed opportunities. I'd go full carnivore to avoid that shithole." Speed smiled at his own snide comment. "I think we have an old-fashioned sea monster on our hands. It sounds like 'the Reefers' are some kind of kraken or sea serpent that's come out to feed."

"Ooh, that's good!" agreed Wendi. "The theory, I mean—a monster would obviously be very bad. A big kraken could reach those tentacles into a school of unsuspecting fish, attach with its suckers, and pull the life out of them!"

"A serpent is plausible as well, dear," Speed postulated. "H's trout said it was a long and skinny invader. It matches the descriptions."

"Human ghosts make sense, though, Speed! Bitter investors who lost hundreds of thousands of dollars wander eternity looking for revenge or closure, whatever they find first." Wendi fabricated theories much like moose did. "A ship's namesake could despise the fact his legend sank instead of living on for generations. Angry ghosts give off weird vibes, and that negative energy can manifest into all sorts of different things."

"Wait," said H, "I thought most of the dead found closure after castrating their demons."

Speed spit out his drink narrowly missing his carving. "The term is actually *facing* one's demons, and I'm not sure the dead take their demons to the grave."

"Oh, I know the term," responded H. "I wouldn't want to face them or even bother looking them in the eye. I'd grab them by the balls and make them suffer for their crimes. My beaver—"

Wendi interrupted wide-eyed. "Whoa, honey. Where is this going?"

"My beaver *friend* Howard gifted me this handy knife." H emphasized every word while pulling the shiny tool out of her secret pocket, opening it to reveal the scissors. "If I ever find my demons, they're going to be in for a real surprise. I would be happy to castrate your demons for you as well, Miss Wendi."

"That's our girl," cheered Wendi. "We strong women must relish and protect each other until the end. To slay the demon of a friend is the act of a true comrade with a pure heart indeed! A friend like that is worth more than pure gold and as rare as the albino wolverine. To straightening the crown of a fellow queen!" Wendi held up her glass.

"Let me see that blade," said Speed as H flipped through her tool options. She closed it and tossed it over. Speed felt the knife carefully with his thumb. "Just as I suspected. It's a bit dull, but—lucky for you—I can fix that." Speed snatched a whetstone off his side table and began to work on the tiny blade, making short scraping noises as he worked methodically.

"Speed can fix anything dull," Wendi whispered across the table. The women burst out in fits of giggles.

"What was that, honey?" Speed looked up for a moment.

"Nothing, dear. Just mixing our sweet merlady another beverage." Wendi popped up to her bar cart and masterfully concocted her signature cocktail, red high heels tapping daintily on the floor. The extravagantly beveled decanter of gin made a loud clink.

"Wow, we really saw Angie and got off topic," said H.

"Angie?" Wendi furrowed her brow as though it would help her place the name. She looked like the black-and-white photo hanging on the wall: a Scottish woman with resting bitch face.

"Angie," said H. "Angie the red squirrel with the infamous tail."

Wendi nodded. "Squirrel sighting confirmed! Distractions are always welcome on the big wild martini deck." She lifted her drink in toast to the squirrel, adjusted her rose-printed shirtdress, and sat back down.

"Let me reel this in like a trophy pike," said Speed. "Regarding Chester and the haunting, ladies, rational thinking does not always join one's body in the afterlife. We've seen men go cuckoo before." He looked thoughtfully at H as he paused his sharpening. "A pissed-off spirit, scorned and distraught, can bring nasty stuff to multiple realms. Maybe what you found was an animal sacrifice. God help us."

"The only person who would want to live there would be a baker," answered H. "All that wheat—imagine the pies, cakes, and pastries!" Wendi's eyes met Speed's gaze. They could feel an exponential easing of H's nerves;[72] everything would be stellar if she continued to maintain her wit. Thank God for the almighty distillery.

"That could be," said Speed with a low chuckle. "Or it could be a master ale maker."

"Now that's a classic martini deck answer!" cheered H, sipping her freshly shaken gin and tonic after a quick clink with Wendi's glass.

"We could use an ale maker on this vessel after all the all-hands-on-deck situations we've been through," said Speed.

[72] There definitely was an inverse relationship in H between the volume of gin consumed to the intensity of nerves exhibited, if one could quantify stress vs. alcohol consumed numerically.

"You know, on our first voyage the shaft broke? And then the damn anchor ripped a hole in the bough like a wolf's canines through a rabbit carcass!"

"Yes, honey. We've heard all the mishaps. You skipped the part when you went aground and had to jettison a thousand pounds of iron ore overboard," said Wendi. "Your back hurt for weeks!"

"Better ore than cows," added H. "Poor ol' Cumby."

"One time you even lost your rudder!" Penny exclaimed. "Meow. We're doomed!"

"Even the cat knows all my stories," said Speed, shaking his head.

H grabbed a wildflower out of the glass mason jar on the table and gave it a sniff. She used her finger to trace around the doily under the jar, thinking to herself. "I wish we had a way to ask Chester what really happened."

"I'll tell you what," said Speed, harnessing his full captain energy, "I will send a couple of crewmen off in their little wooden lifeboats to make sure our friend Chester is faring eternity peacefully without intruders. They could use a task, and you've spiked my curiosity."

"I'm probably overreacting," said H. "I'd appreciate the investigation, though. I've never seen so much death. Thank you, Speed." Speed relinquished his carving throne, tossed the gleaming tool back to H, and exited the room in search of his reliable crew. Penny followed him out the door.

"Now that it's just us girls, we can discuss the subject in further detail," said Wendi. "Human women go through changes throughout their life, with varying hormonal levels that create moods, untimely feelings, and symptoms of discomfort! Your body could be working through changes." Wendi slowly swirled her drink in her hands.

"I don't lay eggs, and I don't ovulate them either," answered H. "It's pretty hard to do when you don't even have a *beaver*." Wendi smiled. "Pretty sure I'm a sterile hybrid, much like a tiger muskie! But I'll consider the theory if it happens again."

"Is it a full moon? My best friend back on earth used to do the craziest things during the full moon," exclaimed Wendi.

H held back giggles. "Last I checked, we are still on earth."

Wendi chuckled. "Oh, you know what I mean, love. Solid ground earth, not the third planet from the sun."

"If the moon can control the ocean tides, it can definitely influence weak-minded humans! Maybe *weak-minded* is the wrong term, but I digress. The wolves love the moon, and singing to her brings them such joy, and the moon loves their symphony in return." H slurred her words, buzzed and bull-mooseing like she took the master class. "What if the moon wants to control all bodies of water but can't due to negotiations with the Gods? She's bitter and creates occasional frenzies to remind those who deny her what she wants of her powers."

"The moon is a puppet master, and we her humble marionettes!" Wendi joined H in laughing.

"Another shipwreck? Blame the moon! Snowstorm in April? Blame the moon! Pollution in our waters? *Still* the moon! Barnacle Bob clad in just an apron? *Moon!*" H could hardly blurt the banter through her giggle fit.

"Grumpy old husband? All the moon's fault!" Wendi bent over in laughter. "I'm not even going to ask about good old Bob."

H adopted her best moon voice, emphasizing each word with her hands. "How dare you talk shit about me! I'm up here glowing in the sky, working hard and shit, orchestrating fiascos! The audacity of you feeble women to consider my job anything less than necessary." The moon somehow sounded like an Italian chef who had burned their marinara and was now furiously stirring for an impossible resolution.

Wendi snorted. "In this light, your tail looks like the glimmer of our friend the moon on the water," she said.

H looked around the room and soaked up the ambiance. Wendi collected vintage glass bottles, using them to house candles or tiny strings of Christmas lights. It looked as though twinkling stars lined the room. It probably helped her creative display that Speed was a trained and respected electrician back in his day, skills which helped him greatly in the navy. Some well-known brand names were etched into the glassware, and a few bottles still sported faded labels.

A glass bottle caught H's eye, and she popped out of her seat. "Good Nite Cough Syrup," she read aloud. "Alcohol, cannabis, chloroform, and morphine—now that's an all-star lineup! No placebo effect there. Sounds like something that could knock a storybook princess out for years! Is this the secret behind Sleeping Beauty? Or the evil apple that dropped Snow White? It's probably the only thing that could make a Red Delicious taste good." H crinkled her nose in disgust.

"I agree with you fully. I much prefer an apple with a tart zing. It sounds like you're wanting a new series of fables. *Fairytales of Pharmacology*—that has a nice ring to it!" Wendi sighed. "Aah, the good old days. Back when the soda pop actually contained cocaine! No wonder the industry flourished."

Speed returned to the hysterical ladies and shook his head. "I knew I shouldn't leave you two unsupervised. I'm surprised you haven't burned the lake down." Penny wound around his heels, her beautiful blue eyes watching and waiting for his lap to open.

"Oh, honey. We are only just getting started," Wendi answered. Speed nestled back into his carving cocoon.

"I'll be right here where you left me when you need me to bail you out of sea jail," answered Speed without looking up. He placed a hand on his beard and peered thoughtfully at his carving.

"I'd wholeheartedly welcome a little mishap with the law," teased Wendi. "As queen of this vessel, I'd challenge them to try and stop me!" Speed smiled but didn't avert his gaze from this work above his sleeping lap cat. Wendi turned back to H. "You'd best eat a bit, dear. I don't want you to have a headache tomorrow." Wendi pushed the platter of beautifully assembled charcuterie toward H.

H picked up a green olive and a piece of white cheddar cheese and started snacking. She made her way around the tray, sampling each and every tasty morsel. She quickly felt satiated and hopped over to the sofa, where she dozed off for quite a few hours.

Chapter Eight

"GOOD MORNING, DEAR MERMAID!" SPEED sat in his chair with a cup of coffee and a cinnamon roll, Penny nestled on his lap. He held a newspaper, but H wasn't sure if it was old or current. Ghosts had their ways of acquiring things. "Are you well rested and ready for breakfast? My three best men, Twiggs, Crockett, and Weasel, report no suspicious activity near Chester. It was quiet and still, with no Reefers to be found. The bodies were gone. They did mention a couple of squiggly lines in the sand, but that was likely just the current making her art."

"That's good to hear," said H, sitting upright and rubbing her eyes. As if on cue, Wendi flitted in from the kitchenette and placed a cinnamon roll and a cup of tea on the end table next to H, whose stomach growled.

"I best feed my mermaid," said Wendi. "We don't want to find out what she's like when she's hungry. She might turn into a vampire or a piranha!" She sat down at the table with her own roll and cup of tea. "Perhaps a good breakfast will make for a good day for all of us. Breakfast food fixes all ills."

H ripped off a piece of roll and dipped it in a small dollop of whipped butter. "I think you might be onto something, Wendi!" exclaimed H. "Your cinnamon rolls are perfection, and I love what you did to this butter."

"Only the best for you, dear mermaid," gushed Wendi. "We have high standards on the big, wild martini deck!"

Speed finished his roll and looked toward H. "What's going on under the frigid sea today? Do you have plans for adventure, or does the current take you where she pleases?"

H looked up from her meal. "I have yet to visit the *Monarch* on this go-round, and I want to find a fox named Chaos on the main island. I'm not entirely sure where she lives, though."

"I thought you knew all the animals up there," said Wendi.

"Quite a few of them, yes," replied H. "But it's a big island."

"I'm sure they've all heard of you," said Speed matter-of-factly. "Birds talk a lot. Now that I think of it, maybe my sweet Wendi is part bird."

"You know birds came from dinosaurs." H didn't miss a beat. "I wouldn't mess with the great-to-the-umpteenth descendant of the Tyrannosaurus rex."

"Finally! A logical explanation as to why I'm all ass," said Wendi with a wink. "Hourglass figure by T. rex." She bent her arms at her elbows and bared her teeth in a smile. "I bet I look much better in a dress, though." Speed and H giggled.

"The *Monarch* was but a fine wooden vessel," Speed commented. "You'll have to send Jack our best regards. Lord knows he probably gets lonely over there all by himself. He's welcome to visit us anytime."

"I'll relay your sentiment," said H. "If he knew there

were cinnamon rolls and mixed drinks, I'm sure he'd be here in an instant."

"Before you go," said Speed, "I have a little something for you." He held up a single black bear claw at the end of a brown leather cord. H swam over, and Speed tied it around her neck to join her chains of agate pendants. "This is for luck and for the strength of the mighty black bear to protect you."

H left the *Emperor* in a much better mood than when she'd arrived. She headed toward the SS *Monarch*, which was just a short swim away off Blake Point. H playfully swished her tail as she neared the wreck. The real vessel was scattered in disintegrating pieces on the floor of the lake, cargo strewn like a seasick sailor's lunch. The water-logged oak scraps, weathered with time, no longer formed a masterpiece. But the ship's ghost glimmered in the depths of the lake, as Jack spent his afterlife making sure the ship looked as good as she did the day she was born.

A sudden low rumble interrupted H's frolicking. A shadow engulfed her, and she spun around to locate the source. A chill traveled down her backbone, and her heart galloped. She froze in a panic, waiting for the Red Delicious apple of underwater encounters.

H called out into the darkness. "Hello?" Her voice quivered. Water echoed in her ears.

"Mooooo," said the low rumble.

"Betsy?!" exclaimed H. "Is that you?"

A large brown cow descended from above and swam face-to-face with H. Her kind, large brown eyes peered curiously at the mermaid, eyelashes fluttering, as she let out a low grunt. H reached out and pet the sweet cow right on the head.

"Yes, you're a good girl, Betsy," H cooed. "You really scared me, though! Don't be so sneaky next time, or I'll tip you over while you're sleeping." Betsy smiled, perhaps remembering the pranks of farm life past.

"Can you talk?" H asked the rogue sea cow. "This might be the first time we've truly crossed paths, but I'm pleased to make your acquaintance. My name is H."

"I don't trust humans," replied Betsy sweetly, and she shyly hung her head.

"Well, shooting skunk stink, who could blame you?" responded H, giving Betsy another pat on the head. "Lucky for you, I'm only half human! Do you ever visit other ghosts? It must get lonely wandering the depths of the lake for all eternity."

Betsy made a face that tried to hide her pain, but H saw right through it. She was treading water in a sea of anxiety and man-made fears. "I don't much talk to anyone."

H asked, "What about your fellow livestock? Surely you have some friends from your past life."

"I've never come across the herd," said Betsy. "I think they either swam to shore or made peace with death and went to the big red barn in the sky."

"I've never seen them either," said H. "I do enjoy the ghost ships, though. Do you ever visit Cumby?"

"No," said Betsy. "It feels like betrayal. I know it's not her fault, but still . . ."

"That's fair."

"I've always loved the fair. Only the best were chosen to go. We'd see cows from all over! The food was the tastiest. That's the only social event I'd care to attend."

H laughed. "Did they put your food on a stick?"

"What?" Betsy's nostrils flared in confusion. "Most of the humans put their food in glass jars."

"I've heard stories of the Minnesota State Fair," H explained. "They put all the food humans eat on a stick!"

"That must have been after my time. Leftover fruit and vegetables went to the livestock," said Betsy. "It was a treat."

"I'm on my way to the *Monarch*, Betsy. Have you ever visited her?"

"Nooooo," Betsy mooed. "I keep my distance from most vessels."

"Well, come along for a swim! I'll tell you all about her," H said with excitement. "She was a wooden vessel, just like the Cumby, but iron reinforcements made her more durable. Her job was to haul humans as well as freight."[73]

"I bet they never threw humans overboard to lighten the load," said Betsy.

H chuckled. "The *Monarch* has a history of tragedies her very own. She survived her bow running aground and a very rough Thanksgiving in 1896. The weather hissed sleet and snow at the Thanksgiving crew. Waves crashed over the deck, like sinister gravy on a mountain of mash!"

"I love potatoes," said Betsy.

"As do I," said H. "Anyways, the *Monarch* battled the nasty weather and made it into Two Harbors, where the grasp of the waves hurled the ship full speed into the docks. The captain used wicked evasive maneuvers to spare both ship and pier. Damage to the hull was minimal, considering all she was up against!"

"They had something to be thankful for," said Betsy.

"Yes, they did. On her final voyage she was carrying oats, flour, and salmon. Snow and fog blanketed the water with a cloak of fleeting visibility. They couldn't even see Passage Island Light Station."

"Oh, dear," said Betsy.

"They lost track of their location. Her path intersected a wall of rock so hard that it cracked open the hull like a chipmunk with a peanut!"

Betsy gasped.

"Bitter December winds swept across the lake. All the crew made it to shore except one.[74] They clung to each other for warmth, surviving on meager rations. Much of their time was spent trying to keep fires going to alert the lighthouse keeper of their distress."

"Fire is dangerous," said Betsy.

"Both dangerous and lifesaving," clarified H. "A few years later,

[73] The SS *Monarch*, built in the late 1800s, had sixty-five luxury cabins and electricity. Her oaken hull was originally white and later repainted black, which made her look like a tribute to the common loon.

[74] Cause of death is unknown. Some say Jack had fallen asleep in his bunk, while others said he had gone blind and couldn't make it to shore. Another report said he grabbed the wrong rope and fell into the lake.

they upgraded the lighthouse. Her beacons were important—passage between islands was only about three miles wide, and ships needed to stay on course to survive."[75]

"If only one could go back and change the past," Betsy lowed.

"That's a sentiment we all feel from time to time," said H. "Alright, my dear. We're here. No more running from your past; it's time to meet some more ghosts." H led Betsy to the ghost of the *Monarch*. "You need to meet my friend Jack. He'll adore you."

"Moo." H couldn't tell if it was in agreement or protest. Regardless, the dashing brown cow followed her closely .

"Jack," H called out, "you've got visitors. We come in peace!"

Jack promptly materialized on the main deck. Jack was quite the dapper fellow, with clean-cut hair and a pair of dark-gray wool trousers with a knit fisherman sweater. Gaze drifting to Betsy, his eyes enlarged like a marshmallow in a microwave. "Heavens to—well, to Betsy! She is real!"

"Indeed," said H. "She's not just another mythical Lake Superior creature of the deep."

"I've been wandering the waters since 1874," contributed Betsy. "A lot has happened since then."

"I've only been here since 1906," said Jack. "Do you remember when the *Monarch* joined Superior's ghost fleet?"

"Yes," nodded Betsy. "I've seen many shipwrecks over the years but never ventured too close."

"Can you imagine a drowning sailor whose last dying thought was, 'Is that a cow?'" H laughed at her own joke.

Betsy smiled. "I'd haunt the man who threw me overboard if I knew where to find him. I'm a blue ribbon winner, you know." Jack and H chuckled. The thought of a vengeful cow delighted them both.

"Oh, he's rotting in hell with the Devil for sure." Jack reaffirmed what Betsy had always suspected—which surely meant more, coming from a devout Catholic.

Betsy looked forward very seriously. "You know, I've always

[75] Passage Lighthouse was upgraded to a 50,000 candle-power light. A few years after that, she was given electricity, which makes a much brighter light than an oil-burning wick.

thought I was clairvoyant," she murmured. "Back in my young farm days near Moose Lake, I always knew the world would burn. I had vivid dreams and even visions while awake."

"Did it come true?" Jack asked.

"Not during my lifetime. I warned the calves to tell their future offspring of the horrors a wildfire would cause. It was all I could do."

H looked pensively toward her newfound cow friend. "Did you see the Cloquet Fire of 1918 in your visions? The one caused by railroad sparks?"

"Neither of us were alive for that," said Jack with a tinge of sadness, locking eyes with Betsy.

"I heard people drove their cars into Moosehead Lake to escape the flames," said H.

"That could be the one," whispered Betsy. "I don't know anything about the actual tragedy, but it still stings. The visions looked so real."

H explained, "Hundreds of people died, hundreds of trees died, and many animals lost their lives. It was the biggest fire the region had ever seen."

"Aah, the trees. A robust logging industry sets the groundwork for an extreme bonfire," said Jack. "Sounds like there's not much anybody could have done to stop it beyond the rains from Mother Nature."

"I had the gift to see and warn the others," explained Betsy. "Most of them thought I was just a nutball full of sour milk." Her head drooped, large eyes cast downward. "I never got my chance to lead the stampede to safety."

"Your warning came far too early, Betsy," said Jack. "Perhaps the flames you saw were a different fire altogether, or perhaps history took a different course. You were just born before your time."

"The afterlife is your greener pasture, dear Betsy," said H. "The burden of that vision was too large for just one bovine to bear. I'm sure your message made it through the generations, because the livestock that survived had the right instincts."

Betsy looked upward toward Jack and H with a small smile. "I also had visions every day about what color shirt the farmer would be wearing. Every day, I was correct; the other cows thought I was sneaking peeks at the laundry!"

Jack chuckled. "Now that's a skill that has potential in a betting world!"

"I even dreamt about the day I died," said Betsy. "Looking back, I didn't get the metaphor. I would have taken off!"

H changed the subject, hoping for Jack's insight. "How is life on the *Monarch*? Has anything exciting happened since we last visited?"

"Oh, you know," started Jack. "Retirement is peaceful. I do a lot of reading and crossword puzzles. Sometimes I go fishing. Once in a blue moon, I get out my sketchbook and make a greeting card or two."

Jack had drifted closer to Betsy and was petting her head and scratching her behind the ears. She leaned into him, thoroughly enjoying the attention.

"Your life is a lot like that of a lighthouse keeper," said H. "I think you may have missed your calling."

"Life on the water always brought me joy," said Jack. "Death in the water is just as nice, especially with a luxury ship."

"I don't want to dampen the mood," said H. "But when I visited Chester, I found hundreds of dead whitefish, all with circular wounds. The smell was horrible."

"That's awful!" exclaimed Jack. "How did it happen?"

"I was hoping you would have some ideas for me." H looked to Jack and then to Betsy. "There's a bit more to the story." H regaled everything, starting at her visit with Glenny. She finished with, "Speed's crewmen assessed the situation and the bodies were all gone! I'm wondering if it was the work of Reefers. What kind of creature do we have on our hands?"

"I don't like this. I don't like this one bit," said Betsy.

"Neither do I," said Jack. "You know I love a good mystery, but I hate to hear the lake is in danger."

"I had a dream the lake was full of snakes," said Betsy.

"That's not a dream; it's a nightmare," said H.

"It was awful," remembered Betsy. "The water turned red with blood. What if it is another vision?"

"Let's hope it wasn't, dear Betsy," Jack comforted.

"I don't want to go back out there until you sort it out," murmured Betsy. "I've been through enough."

"I am hoping to find some answers soon," H empathized. "I don't want to face it alone, either. I'm scared too."

"I'll say a prayer for your safety and for the Lord to give you strength," said Jack. "We must trust He has a plan."

"Maybe Betsy could stay here with you until I figure it out, Jack," H suggested. She looked back and forth at both of them.

"I had another dream that I was sleeping in a ship's cabin!" exclaimed Betsy. "That made no sense to me."

"I've never hosted a cow," said Jack. "But I'd be willing to accommodate your needs." He'd been petting her throughout the entire conversation.

"Do you run up and down the halls for fun?" Betsy asked through ear scritches.

Jack let out a chuckle. "Why don't you hang around and find out? I'd enjoy the company."

"Are you sure he won't turn me into cheeseburger?" Betsy whispered to H. Jack smiled. "I don't want to be cow-napped, either. Dottie got beamed up by a ray of light into a metal bird one night. Never heard from that cow again. Can't say I didn't warn her, either."

"I assure you this ship is entirely safe. Any shenanigans reminiscent of uncomfortable farm times do not exist in this place. Although I would like to hear more about this metal bird," said H.

"I don't think ghosts have to worry about either of those things," added Jack. "It would be my honor to house you as a guest of the *Monarch*. Let me show you to your quarters, where you will have your very own king-size feather bed to curl up and rest in."

"Alright," Betsy mooed. "As long as we agree to no tipping and no tossing. If you try anything, I'll kick you! And I'd be delighted if you read me a story. I love stories, especially fantasy tales."

"We have lots of stories to exchange, dear cow." Jack appreciated how Betsy knew exactly what she wanted.

"Oh, you don't know the half of it. These eyes have seen many strange things." Betsy followed Jack to the door leading belowdeck.

Their budding friendship made H grin ear to ear. "I'd love to stay," she said, "but I've had the tour before, and I need to see a fox about some land business that might help our underwater situation."

"Leaving so soon? You just got here," said Jack.

"I'm on a mission to solve all the unknowns of the universe," explained H, "and by *universe*, I mean the island we all know and love. We have to get to the bottom of the whitefish massacre!"

"In that case, carry on, my wayward mermaid! I will say a prayer for your safe return." Jack waved goodbye.

As H flitted up to the surface, she could hear the conversation continue.

"On the top deck, I've got my very own garden," Jack exclaimed. "It's growing beets, carrots, potatoes, and lots of tomatoes. I would love to hear more about your visions too!"

"You had me at beets," said Betsy.

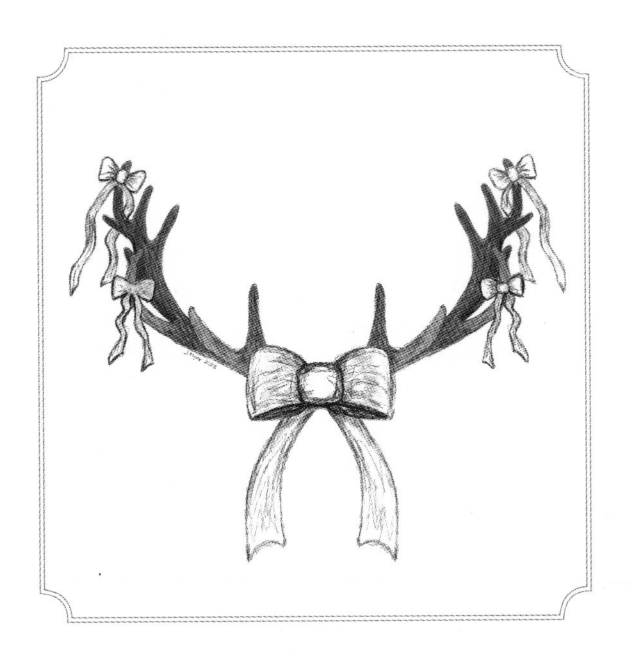

Chapter Nine

CHAOS, UNSUNG INTROVERT OF THE red fox realm, would be difficult to find. More sightings of Bigfoot have been reported, according to the many riveting tales Revna had told her. H just could feel it in her bones. Isle Royale was big for an island; all she could do was scour the Siskiwit Bay shoreline for a flash of sneaky orange of the swift, petite mammal with dainty steps and a haunting song.

H's curiosity wandered back to Chaos. She wondered if that shy little fox ever lived up to her name but was sure her mother would be proud of her gifted kit regardless. Did Chaos come from a family with a history of paranormal powers? H had a feeling Chaos had a mother stronger than one of Fourball's neat whiskeys. H knew it would be impossible to know every furred, scaled, or winged being around the lake, but she would try her best, damn it. Somehow the wildlife always knew about H, and she felt like she had a reputation almost as big as Fury's mom.[76] Obviously one of her winged friends would be glad to help with eyes beyond the perimeter, but self-sufficiency was a virtue H held near to her heart. If that shy fox enjoyed a frolic in the sunshine here and there, luck could be a vibrant four-leaf clover in the hands of a mermaid. H suspected Chaos much preferred the dead to the living, making her gift of communication a true blessing. She probably didn't like people, either. If H made it to Siskiwit Lake, Howard, with an inner circle akin to a private detective, could use his resources to stir up a search party. Everyone loves a good, strong beaver on their team.

H had turned the corner on Blake Point now and was taking the waters outside the tiny islands lining the shore. She planned on swimming toward the rocky shoreline as soon as she passed Park Headquarters. Her body moved gracefully, silver tail shimmering in the filtered light that penetrated the depths, while she hummed Teyla Sjoberg songs.[77] Her braids flowed behind her with the forward momentum, as every so often she would spin her body 360 degrees while swimming because it was fun and also helped her keep up her speed.

H surfaced from the depths and poked her head out of the water. Beads of water trickled down her forehead, reflecting bits of liquid crystal sunlight. Her wet hair clung to her body as she scanned the area for human presence and proceeded shoreward. Her silver tail glimmered like an oil slick, flashing purples, pinks, and teals with every delicate propelling movement.

The island appeared calm and still, a garden of serenity. Wildflowers dabbled the shoreline leading up to the trees. The thick forest and ground foliage hindered visibility into the woods. H continued west, the sound of splashing waves overtaking the song in her head.

H had soon traveled farther than the site of the *Algoma* wreck. She longed to stop and visit Lou over a blueberry tart, maybe even cheesecake, but there would be time for desserts later. H was seri-

[76] Fury's mom is a cougar who wanders a wide geographical range. The birds nicknamed her Thunder Puss for her mighty roar—nobody knows her name, but everyone knows her stories.

[77] H heard the songs while spying on a party cruise at midnight in the Duluth Harbor. If the fearless sirens of modern folklore could sing like Teyla, we'd have many a sailor drawn to their death in tales so chilling you'd need to don a cardigan.

ously curious about the human ghosts on the island and wanted to know more. She needed help deciphering their cryptic message and wondered if it related to the whitefish massacre. She felt like they knew something important, maybe even relating to survival of those in the waters.

H spotted a fishing vessel on the horizon and slunk back into the natural blanket of invisibility provided by deeper water. She moved slowly, her braids suspended in the water as though snakes arising to a challenge, continuing west, in hopes of surfacing to an empty sea. She hoped to find the company of her favorite posse of lake trout, as they often fed on unfortunate souls in this very same region.

Deepwater darkness enveloped H as she continued to swim gracefully toward Siskiwit Bay. Surely the lack of fish in this area meant the vessel would move on, and they'd know that if they had the latest electronic fish-finding tools. Cool water caressed her scales and massaged her skin as she fluttered on the lake floor. The black shadow moved closer to H as she swam onward, and she wished that the boat creating the shadow would hurry away already. Suddenly the shadow expanded and slithered alongside, above, and below her. H thrust forward as fast as she could, neck hairs standing straight up. It wasn't a boat—it was a creature, maybe even multiple creatures. Her body collided solidly with a slender wriggling being; at the same time, she felt a stabbing pain in her back shoulder.

H spun around, trying to free herself from the tangled darkness. Pain shot through her shoulder and down her back as her human heart pounded in panic. Adrenaline rushing, she reached an arm behind herself, trying to free her shoulder of the weight. Her shoulder throbbed in agonizing fear as six snakelike creatures wrapped themselves around her thrashing body, baring sharp teeth from their round mouths. She cried out in pain, hoping someone would hear and come to her aid. The largest was as long as she was; it circled the struggle, slowly approaching the seemingly well-set mermaid trap.

Whatever was stuck to her shoulder shot bullets of electricity down her body, silencing any rational inner monologue she still possessed. The creatures were long and moved like snakes, but they had mouths more like a lamprey. They were slender but also strong, with fins near their faces and one dorsal fin along the long body. H felt as though she was being drained of life, and something really started to stink. The fire that burned in her soul flickered as she lost the substance she needed to continue her fight. Her thrashing grew weaker as the internal voice in her head told her to keep fighting.

She thrust her arms backwards, trying to reach the seemingly inherent dagger that had been stuck in her back. The black creatures wrapped themselves around her arms, holding her back. It was like being attacked by Medusa's hair. H fought harder, throwing a punch in the direction of the larger monster that was watching the smaller ones take her down like a three-legged zebra in the Serengeti. Her gills flared open and shut as screams of resistance escaped her quivering lips, laden with the worst burning and stabbing pain she had ever experienced. She couldn't see much through all the thrashing, and the water looked foggy.

"Son of a bitch!" H yelled desperately. She was confused and scared—but mostly really pissed. She thought of Betsy's dream where the lake was full of snakes. "Damn it, Betsy!"

"Not today, mermaid." The voice was deep and scathing. A chorus of snickers echoed in the darkness. Something swirled through her braids, and she struggled as her hair tangled and became untamed. Yellow eyes glowed back at her through the mayhem of slithering bodies.

H gasped. "Motherfuckers!" Her scream made the water tremble. She threw a strong right hook, startling one of the creatures and loosening its grip.

A vortex of mayhem ensued as a tornado of slithering beings surrounded her. H's momentum increased with a free arm as she smacked them. Every time she hit one creature away, another replaced it. Her anger felt electric. They yelped in pain at the impact of her fist. Her shoulder throbbed as she struggled to stay upright. Tears welled up in her eyes at the pain, and they fell off her face as icicles.

A sleek black tentacle wrapped around H's neck. Somehow the water grew darker, consuming her existence in layers like a cake with buttercream frosting. She bellowed with all her strength, but her tail ceased its swishing. *Reefers,* she thought, blinking slowly. Her arms relaxed and fell to her sides. She was paralyzed and numb.

What did I do to deserve such torture? H asked herself, eyes fluttering. She heard an earsplitting roar and was sure her life was over.

Amidst the thrashing, H saw a glimpse of opalescent antlers.

They must have drugged me, she thought. *That was the awful smell.*

Eyelid flutter—copper fur breaking through the evil. Eyelid flutter—gleaming, snapping, snow-white teeth.

It's not real.

Claws slashing, pouncing. Blood. Antlers covered in ribbons. Bows or snakes?

I'm hallucinating. Her arms were free, but she couldn't find the power to lift them. Eyes closed, she could feel the struggle in the water surrounding her—then, suddenly, she was falling.

Oh, shit. Her eyelids weighed a hundred pounds. She poured all of her energy into hoisting them upward. One weary peep showed an opaque world.

"Wake up, mermaid. Balance has been disrupted, and we must fight. Nature as we know it needs restoration. We need our water back." The creature spoke with the most beautiful voice.

H felt antlers lift her body through the water. "I'm dreaming?" H slurred. "Who the heck are you?"

"My friends call me Trippehjay for short, but . . ."

Her will was strong but her body weak. Before losing all consciousness, she wondered what ship she would choose to haunt if given the option in the afterlife.

Chapter Ten

"WAKE UP, YOU SKANKY SIREN! You passed out for a while there!" Nigig's little nose twitched furiously. "What flaming atomic beaver butt did this to you, H? How did you get here? Can you even swim with that fancy tail all shredded?"

"I . . . don't quite remember. I was attacked in the darkness by swimming snake creatures. I think a deer saved me? I was scooped up by antlers . . ." Her voice trailed off as she tried to make sense of it all. The sequence of events clouded her foggy brain. "Everything hurts and I'm dying."

"A deer? Under the water?" inquired Nigig. "Oh, honey, you are one friggin' mess—drama queen comments justified. Were you out smoking the devil's lettuce with Speed?"

"Something stabbed my shoulder, and I fought to free myself

until I passed out. I was outnumbered at least six to one, and no to the lettuce. I think it was the Reefers the trout warned me about."

"Well, that's a scalding dumpster fire of a story if I ever did hear one."

"Honestly, the only thing that saved me was the angry lynx. They hissed like a thunderstorm, clawed quick as lightning, and definitely saved my ass-fin."

"Wait, you were scooped up by antlers *and* saved by a lynx?" Nigig's eyes grew as big and pensive as the harvest moon yet again.

"I think that's what I saw. My memory is baked like a hotdish." H shrugged and leaned over to put a hand on her little friend. Her blue eyes closed in agony. "Speaking of food, some zebra mussels would hit the spot right now."

Nigig waved his tiny paws up and down in feigned hyperventilation. "A lynx and antlers!" His voice was even higher than normal. He looked at H as though she would put the pieces together and get it. "You were saved by Mishipeshu!" He paced back and forth. "Oh. My. God."

"It said its name was Trippehjay. That's all I remember. Why didn't they slaughter me?"

Nigig smiled. "Perhaps you placated the beast."

"Well, now, that just sounds naughty," answered H with a half-grin. She hurt too much to enjoy Nigig's witty banter right now. "Isn't protecting copper more of its standard operating procedure?"

He thought for a moment. "I suppose Mishipeshu would have their own names. Trippehjay . . . I like it! And, yes, they do protect copper, but not all tales of Mishipeshu result in death and misfortune, silly. Sometimes the beasts serve as protectors and guides. I'd definitely want them on my side in a bar fight."

"What do you know about bar fights?" H struggled to hold her head upright. A whiskey or, better yet, Wendi's signature cocktail would sure hit the spot right now.

"Sandbar fights? Where my brothers and I used to wrestle over treats from Mom? It's smooth and luxurious on the paws, but you know what they say—beaches be crazy. Sand gets in your everywhere."

H collapsed on the rocks, her undone braids a dark wet mess that draped over her pale skin and hid the oozing sore on her back. Teardrops grazed her skin like daggers. She cringed in pain, hoping Nigig didn't see her agony. Waves lapped in her reeling mind trying to place her memories.

"It's getting dark soon, honey. We need to get you some serious help. Even your sharp blue eyes look dull. What's mermaid for 9-1-1? How do I get you a hot fireman? Have you ever dreamed of riding a moose? Do you know any sled dogs?" Nigig rattled off questions like semiautomatic rounds. He rubbed his best friend's back with a tiny paw. "It'll be OK, H. We'll figure it out."

"Of course I know sled dogs. Bler and Q live in Wisconsin, though, and it's springtime!" H looked westward to see the hot-pink sunset dissipate into nighttime. On a normal day, they'd be relaxing on the rocks, watching the colors for entertainment. "I'm not sure we can fix this alone, but I don't want to expose myself to a human."

"Well, yeah. You'll go to jail for that!" Nigig laughed at his own joke. "Listen, girl. I know a guy, but we need to find a way to get you there. My friend Blue has a crush on this saucy black cat who lives with a medicine woman in the woods. Not terribly far from here, but it would be a trek."

"So if I sell my voice to a sea witch, I can get a potion to grow legs and walk there, right?" meekly asked H trying to remain herself through all the pain. "I've read the book; I know how it works! Hans Christian Anderson books were on the . . . oh, great. I can't remember which wreck!"

"Oh, my Little Mermaid! You've told me the story before. The fairytale mermaid did it for a man, but you'd do it for a walk through the woods with your best gay otter, looking for trouble. And I'm pretty sure it's sea *bitch*, not witch—let's be honest."

"She may be the most famous mermaid, but I have the most fabulous entourage," whimpered H. "I'm sure her sidekick was a whiny little bitch who floundered about."

Nigig giggled. "Wait till they write our story and Hollywood finds us. I will not rest until my name is on a star." He pumped his tiny otter fist.

"I'd rather have my name on a star in the sky than on the sidewalk," said H. She looked toward the sky lovingly and saw her favorite constellation, Ursa Major, watching over her like an old friend. Stars were reliable, stars were consistent with their lack of drama, and they didn't trash the planet to get rich. H loved and cared for the stars as though they were living friends.

She played with the cord around her neck, fingers trailing down to the bear claw. If there was ever a time she needed the great black bear to watch over her, it sure as hell was now. *The* makwa *will save me,* she thought, rubbing the claw.

"Great Mama Bear, give me your strength and courage to get through this." H prayed skyward, rubbing the smooth claw with her fingers. H would have sworn the stars twinkled slightly brighter like fairies, as though they had heard her plea.

A large teardrop dripped slowly down her cheek and fell into the lake, where it burst into twinkling stardust. H looked toward the sky as the stars shed their dust into a sparkling spiral that materialized into a moving shape. H reached her hand over and closed Nigig's open mouth, his dark pupils illuminated by the shimmering spectacle above.

The stardust floated to form a three-dimensional animal originating from the stars of Ursa Major. The four-legged beast leapt across the galaxies above, and with but a few hops the shimmering stardust creature was standing on shore in front of H and Nigig. The glow of the stardust evaporated into thin air as the animal shook like a wet dog, and a beautiful black bear materialized in front of them. Her fur had a glowing purple sheen in the moonlight.

"Wow," uttered Nigig. "What in the unsalted shore nuts . . ."

"Hello, inhabitants of Earth. I come in peace," said the bear in a very official tone. She chuckled at her own joke, then continued in a more relaxed tongue. "I've always wanted to say that. My friends nicknamed me Ursala since I never left the Big Dip, and I've been sent to be your protector and get you to safety."

"Did you just . . . crawl out of the sky?" Nigig asked.

"Pretty much. It feels good to stretch the ol' legs."

"Are you the spirit of Ursa Major?" H struggled to get the words out.

"You could say I'm one of them," said Ursala with a gleaming white grin. "Ursa Major was named by the Greeks. I've been chillin' for centuries with the OG[78] sky bear and my fellow Indigenous animal spirits."

"The Anishinaabe men said *makwa* would save me," recited H.

"It's me! Rarr. I'm the *makwa*, it's me," Ursala sang. "I share the constellation, you know. The Ojibwe call it Ojiig, which is a fisher, not a bear.[79] Different cultures have different names for the constellations. I am here because you rubbed the bear claw and prayed to the Great Mama Bear. That's me! Mama makwa."

"Who else is up there?" prodded Nigig. "Any famous otters?"

Ursala avoided the question and continued, "Obviously I represent the bear clan. We watch over our earth family. I'm basically an *Ursus americanus*[80] guardian angel and healer for Turtle Island."

"It's beautiful that we can all see the same stars but read a different message," H marveled.

"These multiple Gods and spirits are so confusing," groaned Nigig.

"Not really, when you get right down to it," chuckled Ursala. "Most of us focus our efforts to certain regions or earthly resources. Anyway, the fisher in the sky pushed me out of the stars before I could even stretch. Strong little bugger! Said something to the effect that mermaids can indeed survive on land. Gosh darn

[78] OG is slang for original gangster, now used as a term denoting admiration and greatness. I just realized Ursala means Original Greek as a play on that. LOL.

[79] The fisher saves birds from spirit monsters that shoot arrows at him in revenge. They hit him in the tail and pinned him to the sky forever like a bingo flyer on a bulletin board.

[80] That's the scientific name for black bear. Sounds fancy.

it, you're hurt, mermaid. I can't *bear* to see you in pain. Let's get you healed."

"Are you going to lick her wounds with mystic saliva?" asked Nigig excitedly. "Healer clan win!"

Ursala shook her head. "No, Sir Nigig. The makwa clan may be known for their healers, but I'm here to escort you to one instead. I may be a mystical bear, but I can't practice earthly medicine."

"You heard my wish." Her voice quavered with gratitude—and more than a little anxiety. "I trust dead humans, but I'm not sure I trust the living," she admitted.

"Well, have a little faith, my darling," assured Ursala. "The world brings us together for many reasons, and we must trust our Mother's judgement. When the stars align, we get shit done, don'tcha know."

Nigig composed himself enough to ask, "Can you get her to the healer in the woods?"

"You betcha," said Ursala with a confident wink. She smiled at H and lowered herself to the ground. "Climb aboard and hold on, mermaid! You're going to be out of the water for a bit, but I've been told by the powers that be it will be just fine."

H reached toward Ursala, grabbing the rich black fur of her neck and hoisting herself upward. Her arm ached as she struggled to pull herself and swing her tail over. She was about to ride a bear side-saddle, like a rugged lady in an old western; she wished she weren't injured so she could fully enjoy her first trip on land. She wrapped her arms around the bear's neck and embraced her as though she simply needed a hug to survive. The warmth of Ursala soothed her injured soul.

"Ope—I'm just gonna sneak past ya," said Ursala as she jumped over Nigig and a rock to get H on dry land instead of the rocky shore-line. Ursala again looked toward Nigig. "Show us the way, little otter."

Nigig lead Ursala off the rocky shore, toward the forest. He knew the way all too well. As they frolicked through the woods, dancing stardust illuminated their way. They passed a river with bubbling waterfalls, and H soaked up the scenery from Ursala's back. Old trees lined the trails, with exposed roots telling the tales of their age. Through the canopy of the forest, H could see the night sky watching over them. A cloud of bright-green fireflies followed, chasing the stardust as if it were a fun game.

Nigig was much faster than H had expected for a critter with short legs. She held on as long as she could, but the bear's comforting presence combined with the pain in her shoulder had her sleeping again despite her mental protest.

Ursala followed with ease while Nigig ran as though his life depended on it. After about an hour, they hit a small clearing with a little white house. A single light near the front door lit up the grassy yard.

A dog barked inside. Something clattered near the back door. H blinked slowly, half-awake and wondering if the whole day had just been a dream. Seeing she was still on land riding a black bear, it seemed the unrealistic events had unfolded just as she remembered.

"I can't stay," said Ursala. "You're on your own from here, H. I'll keep my Merak and Dubhe eyes[81] on you."

"Thank you, magical bear lady," said Nigig. "If you have any bear cub friends, send them my way!"

Ursala smiled. "Your journey has just begun, young adventurers."

"You will always be my favorite constellation." H whispered the words softly, secretly, into her velvet ear.

"I know," smiled Ursala. She walked her precious cargo to the front door and knelt down, letting H roll off gently into the grass. "I'll miss you, dear."

H looked up at the bear. "You're just a wish away, right? That's what fairy bear-mothers are supposed to say."

"You betcha. Do the clan proud." Ursala leaned over and kissed H's forehead, turned, and walked away into the darkness, her body turning to stardust that climbed back into the sky. H would swear Ursa Major twinkled with extra vigor for the rest of the evening.

[81] Merak and Dubhe are two of the seven stars comprising the Ursa Major constellation; they point towards the North Star (Polaris).

"I suppose we pound on the door like civilized humans do when they want to get someone's attention?" Nigig looked at H, who melted into the ground like a puddle, for guidance.

A voice in the darkness answered. "I recommend that over knocking over trash cans. She swears in Spanish every time I do that!"

"Blue!" Nigig bounced up and down.

"The one and only, still kicking, and not sure how I feel about it," answered the blindfolded eyes emerging from the darkness. Blue the raccoon had a slight chonk build. He scampered over to H to assess the situation and placed a tiny black paw on her injured shoulder while looking her up and down. His bushy striped tail swished behind him as he waddled.

"You definitely need the medicine lady, and you're in luck. I saw her get home from work. She's probably inside watching TV with the lovely Nebula," said Blue dreamily. He sniffed the air. "Perhaps you could get her to spare me some fresh eats while you're here. I think it's Taco Tuesday. Watch out for the dog. She might try to eat you!"

H had butterflies in her stomach. Big, orange, flapping Monarch butterflies.

Nigig sensed her nerves. "Let's get this over with." He took a step forward and pounded his slender body against the door three times. Someone inside barked. H waited to meet her first living human.

Chapter Eleven

SAMANTHA HAD CHANGED INTO HER favorite sweatpants and Fall Out Boy concert tee and was nestling into her cocoon on the plush gray couch under her softest fleece blanket. A long-haired black goddess of a feline, Nebula, curled up on her lap. Gabby, a chocolate Lab mix, jumped up on the couch and curled into a little ball next to her.

She sipped a glass of blue-raspberry vodka mixed with lemonade as she flipped through the channels. She was in the clear to watch whatever trash she wanted, as her fiancé, Dan, was out of town visiting his large Italian family in Chicago for the week. She had fallen in love with a Cubs fan, and that was probably the strangest thing she would experience in her life.

Samantha reached toward her wooden coffee table for a plate of food that had a half-eaten softshell taco on it with a side of pinto beans. She relished in the fresh flour tortilla her mom had made and sent home with her. God, it was good. Tacos were proof God loves us and wants us to be happy, she was sure of it. With her dinner finally finished, Sam could focus on finding something good to watch. There was baseball on standby, but it just didn't feel the same since her favorite player, Joe Mauer, had retired.

She settled on *Ghost Hunters* because she'd always had this looming feeling that her house was haunted. While she watched the show, she grabbed her phone and took a moment to doom scroll through Twitter. Her pharmacist friends online helped her get through the day with their similar frustrations about the profession and funny stories. She relished the updates from Dr. Waffles and The Really Cranky Pharmacist. She also loved Larry the Potato dog.

Thoroughly entertained by her phone and down the rabbit hole of social media, it's no surprise Sam was startled when Gabby leapt off the couch and started barking out of nowhere. "Quiet down!" exclaimed Sam. "It's probably just that pesky raccoon again."

Nebula opened her eyes for a moment before closing them and nestling back in. Gabby settled back into her spot but seemed a bit restless and distrusting of whatever she heard outside. Sam patted her head.

A couple of minutes later, someone was pounding on the door. Who the heck was out and about this time of night? Sam hopped up, and Gabby let out a quiet woof.

"What is it, Gabby Girl?"

Gabby danced to the door because that's what dogs do when they get to see other humans. Sam opened the main door and looked out through the screen of the second door. Sam, stunned, just stared into the night at the three sets of eyes looking up at her. This sounded like a scenario that was about to be followed be one heck of a punch line: *An otter, a raccoon, and a mermaid walk into a bar . . .* Gabby snapped her out of her head by letting out a woof. "Quiet, girl," said Sam, unsure of how to proceed.

"Hello?" said Sam shyly, a little unsure if communication would even work. Introverts really hated the bullshit that goes along with introductions.

"Hi," answered Nigig. "We are in need of a healer."

Sam wasn't sure if she was more surprised by the silver-finned mermaid or the talking otter.

"Are we in danger, Mom?" asked Gabby. "Do I need to do one good heckin' protect?"

Sam blinked again, because her sweet chocolate lab that she'd had for years just talked to her for the first time. "I think we're OK," answered Sam cautiously, the words stuck in her throat.

"The mermaid has a nasty sore," groaned Blue. "And I have a bone to pick about how you pack your trash."

"That second part can wait," snapped Nigig. "Our mermaid, the fabulous H, has traveled through dark of night on back of bear for your assistance. Yes, she was riding bear back, no pun intended. My name is Nigig, and this fluffy bandit here is Blue."

"Is 'H' short for something?" Sam formed words that didn't feel real.

"No, it's just H," said Nigig.

Gabby looked at Sam confused, like she wanted to eat Blue's tiny masked face. Sam, too, wanted revenge on the fat raccoon that made a mess of her trash. However, the current circumstances warranted further investigation. The thought crossed Sam's mind that she was the chosen token Hispanic fairytale princess, who could talk to animals much like the other princesses. Her winged eyeliner was on point for that line of duty, but she was far too punk rock to wear a gown while singing niceties during house chores with her cat and dog, let alone around the pharmacy.

H leaned over in the grass, black hair dried and draping over her pale body. Her movement exposed the volatile sore on her back, catching Sam's dark brown eyes.

"Oh, shit," said Sam. "Let's get you inside and clean that wound.

Let me start that over," she quickly added. "My name is Samantha, and I'm a pharmacist, which means I deal with human medicines. I have never treated a mermaid before, obviously. When I wake up from this very weird dream, we can all have tacos."

"I love tacos!" Blue enthusiastically clapped his tiny black paws together in a swoon.

"Her skin half is mostly human," shrugged Nigig. "She even has a tattoo like you do!" He pointed at the tiny music notes decorating Sam's wrist.

"Where does a mermaid go to get tattooed?" asked Sam curiously.

"It's actually a birthmark," answered H. "I've always had it. I just pretend it's ink to fit in with the sailors."

"It's au naturel, baby," tittered Blue, giving the fluff of his tail a shake.

"Do you have a way to get her inside?" asked Nigig. "We feel kind of out in the open here. Privacy would be nice."

"Hang on," said Sam. "I'll be right back!" She returned a moment later with a rolling computer chair. "Let's prop her up on this and roll her inside. Does she need to be in water?"

"I have lungs and gills," said H. "I don't think I'll dry out. My tail's not covered in slime like regular fish scales; it's just shiny and impermeable. The outer layer seems to be protective."

"The bear just said—" Nigig stopped abruptly before completing the thought. "Never mind. Do you have a spray bottle? We can mist her just to be safe."

A comedic ensemble ensued: Sam squatting in a deadlift with two furry woodland creatures trying to help, their tiny paws pushing fruitlessly against the almost seven-foot-long mermaid. Blue stood like he was holding H up all by himself, while Nigig's slender body shook with muscle failure. Sam had been regularly biking, so she had lower body strength like a kangaroo. It was just really awkward trying to lift a half-fish, half-human up to a chair without hitting her wound in the process. Nebula watched the escapades from the window, very much amused.

Sam rolled H into the house, around a corner, and into a black-and-white tiled kitchen with bright-white cabinets. She turned to the sink and grabbed an orange towel with a black cat on it that said "Trick or Treat."[82] A white ceramic skull covered in glitter sat on the counter next to some bananas and a white box.

"First we need to clean the wound," said Sam, grabbing a bottle of antibacterial hand soap and a washcloth. "What type of creature did this to you?"

"I'm not entirely sure," answered H. "We've been calling them Reefers. They're long and slender but not as skinny as a snake. They slithered as they swam and had glowing eyes. It's probably some sort of hybrid sea lamprey."

"That's not at all disturbing," responded Sam sarcastically. "The bite mark checks out. Sea lamprey have almost perfectly round mouths that attach to their prey with sharp little teeth." Sam ran some warm water on the washcloth, added soap, and made some suds. "They've been trying to eradicate them for years."

"That could explain your stabbing feeling," warbled Nigig.

"They were not regular invasive sea lamprey," continued H. "I've seen plenty of them in my day and lost a friend or two by their sick mouths. They've been here since the 1930s and can be a formidable opponent, but not supervillains who hunt in packs. And the four species of lamprey that are native to the Great Lakes actually help the ecosystem—as a food source and with habitat modifications."

"What made them different?" asked Sam. "Humans are invested in decimating invasive lamprey. Geez, they even set traps near the rivers where they breed and use chemicals to kill their larvae!"

It hurt to remember. "They were black instead of a grayish brown. Their eyes glowed yellow. They had small fins near the head. I think they emitted a substance that made it hard to see," said H. "Oh! They had the ability to wrap around my arms and neck like a

[82] Decorating for Halloween is Sam's specialty, and she always starts a few months early—or is it that she ends a few months late? Either way, I've grown to enjoy it.

strong tentacle. That makes them much longer, size wise."

"They're actually parasites from the Atlantic Ocean," added Sam and she pushed H's mess of hair aside to reveal her injury and started to pat it down with soap. H nodded in agreement, well aware of where the assholes came from. "I suppose they'd have to be pretty nasty to survive out there."

"Those invasive stinking skunk butts." Nigig did not miss a beat, wagging a furious finger.

"Toxic chemicals make me nervous," admitted H. "What if they caused the lamprey to turn into mutants?"

"It's possible," confirmed Sam. "OG lamprey suck your blood like a vampire and even ooze an enzyme that prevents the blood from clotting. They literally suck fish dry while feeding."

"Their teeth looked like Rolf's canines!" exclaimed H.

"Rolf?" Sam hesitated.

"A wolf from Isle Royale," said Nigig.

"I suppose we can thank the Welland Canal." H winced at the soap scrub down on her back. She could do the math and recognized that was a clear path to the Great Lakes from the Atlantic Ocean. "It's not like the evil bastards were dropped by planes. I can't see them coming from another Great Lake, either. Someone would have warned us!"

Sam was surprised that the mermaid knew her geography, but then again, she was giving a goddamn mermaid a sponge bath in her kitchen. "Yeah, the bad lamprey have spread farther west as of late and have wreaked havoc on fish populations. Most fish don't survive an attack." Sam grabbed her phone, did a quick internet search, and held up a photograph of the sea lamprey for all to see. She zoomed in on a photo of the round, pointy teeth in their mouth.

"At least they eventually spawn and die," muttered H.

"That's why I'm never having kids," Sam quipped.

"Well, how do we kill the fuckers?!" Nigig bounced up and down, equally furious and excited.

"They have no known predators in Lake Superior," answered Sam. "Perhaps that's why they saw you as a threat."

"How would they taste deep-fried with a little ketchup?" asked Blue while licking his lips.

"Eww, even I wouldn't put those nasty underwater snakes in my mouth," huffed Nigig. "Instead of blood, sweat from Satan's ball-sack runs through their veins!"

"Gross!" Gabby barked.

"Maybe the indigenous lamprey can oust the colonizers?" wondered H. "Teach 'em some respect! I don't talk to the little friendly 'reys much, but the invasives are giving them a bad name! They've gotta be mad."

"At least when the little ones feed, they rarely take the life of the host," Sam added.

"Would the enzyme that makes blood flow freely feel like electricity?" H asked, deep in thought.

"Maybe," said Sam. "Hard to say for sure, and those who would know are probably dead. It honestly sounds like more of a trait of an electric eel." Sam had finished gently cleansing the wound, inspecting it closely as she worked. She walked over to the shiny silver refrigerator and pulled an ice pack out of the freezer drawer. "I'm going to ice your sore for a few minutes to bring down the swelling," she explained, placing a thin cloth towel over the wound. "Hold this cold pack in place. I'm going to go grab my first aid kit." Sam disappeared down the hallway.

Gabby walked over from the doorway and placed her head in H's lap. "You need a snug. I can help."

"Thank you, sweet Gabby," said H. She pet the dog and gave her ear scritches.

"How d'you know how to do that?" Gabby asked. "Have you met a dog before?"

"I've got a friend under the sea, the best good boy poodle named George," explained H. "He guards the Miss America."

"Oh, that's heckin' cool," said Gabby.

"I feel like absolute garbage," said H, looking up through her mess of tangled dark hair. The color was drained out of her somehow-even-paler-than-normal skin.

"Well, lucky for you, this guy loves garbage!" Nigig joked, pointing to his chonk of a raccoon friend.

"It's OK," said Blue. "I'm not fat; I'm fluffy. More to love. Nebula, you pretty kitty! Do you want to cuddle?"

The silky black cat poked her head through the doorway. "Don't touch me. I bite you." With a sassy wave of her tail floof, she strutted back to the couch like a couture model on a New York runway.

"What's your supervillain origin story, Nebs?" prodded Blue.

Sam yelled from down the hallway, "Retail pharmacy!"

"The ladies always crush my dreams," Blue sighed, "and then I eat my feelings. Vicious cycle."

"And that's exactly why I don't pursue anything with ovaries," sneered Nigig.

An old woman in a chunky knit red shawl emerged from the darkness of the living room and poked her head through the doorway. Her eyes widened as she looked at H for a moment, then wandered back to the living room.

"You have a ghost," whispered H.

"That's just Shirley," said Gabby. "She's harmless and doesn't say much. Sam doesn't know."

Samantha returned with a bright-purple plastic Caboodle and a small white case bearing a red cross. She opened both cases and rifled through her selection of drugs and Band-Aids. The purple case held over a dozen translucent orange pill bottles, while the white case had all sorts of sterile bandages and tubes of topicals.

"I don't know anything about medicating fish," Sam admitted. She thoughtfully added, "However, your top half is your human half, and I'd assume your torso contains human organs that will metabolize medication much like they would in a 100 percent human. Then again, you live underwater so perhaps your organs function a bit differently. You might have extra parts. This might be a weird question, but are you allergic to anything?" Sam needed to cover all her bases.

H nodded and adjusted her ice pack. "I've never had an allergic reaction to anything, but I've never dabbled in pharmaceuticals before—unless you count alcohol."

"It appears to me that you are fighting off an infection and it is spreading throughout your body, not just the wound. I can't judge your immune system by taking your temperature because nobody knows the healthy temperature of a mermaid . . . but your symptoms are pretty telling. You need assistance from our lord and savior, the antibiotic." She set aside two pills and poured a glass of water, then froze. "Do mermaids eat and drink like people?"

"You know it," answered Nigig. "All this girl talks about is dead sailor chow."

"Wait, what?" Sam asked, looking surprised with her large brown eyes.

"Don't mind him," H responded. "I can consume food and beverages the same as a human would. I do it all the time."

"She eats zebra mussels too," squealed Nigig.

"OK." Sam hoped the feisty otter would explain more later. "When is the last time you ate?"

H examined the whirlwind of events in her mind. "Earlier this morning, I had breakfast with my friend Wendi, and I haven't had a snack since."

"What about second breakfast?" asked Blue, his eyes large and full of concern, paws clasped in a plea.

H shook her head no. She had been too distracted by Betsy and Chaos to stop for a meal. *I did find chaos,* she mused, *just not the one I was looking for.*

"Alright. We need to feed the mermaid," said Sam. Afraid her tacos might be too spicy, she opened her freezer and pulled out a sausage pizza, Chicago-style, from Dan's favorite restaurant.

"Do you like pizza? Are you vegetarian, or will you eat sausage?" Nigig giggled.

"Pizza is good," H answered weakly. "They have it on the *Edmund Fitzgerald*." Her stomach growled at the mention, which was a good sign. "The only thing I don't eat is fish, for obvious reasons."

"Great!" Relieved, Sam turned the oven on and waited for the beep. She wished she had something fancier, but she hadn't exactly anticipated a mermaid at the dinner table. She wasn't much of a cook anyway. Remembering a white box on the counter, Sam turned to the mermaid. "Do you like pie?"

H's eyes lit up like a Roman candle on the Fourth of July.

"It's not homemade, but that's for the best," said Sam somewhat jokingly. "My friend Lyn over at Betty's Pies made it, and it's my favorite—blueberry."

"Yes!" H clasped her hands together in joy and smiled through the pain.

"You know what my friend Mama Sue says," quipped Sam. "Life is uncertain; eat your dessert first!"

H recognized that phrase. Mama Sue, whoever she was, would get along well with Frosty.

Sam looked around and read the room. Every furry creature except Nebula was intense-eyed and drooling. "I suppose we can all enjoy a slice together." Blue danced as Sam plated the pies, hesitated when she went to grab forks because only she and the mermaid needed one, and placed a plate in front of everyone.

"This is the best day of my life," Blue said from his plate, whiskers stained purple and tiny paws covered in goo. "Do you need help with dishes?" Blue licked his plate clean. He couldn't help himself.

"I agree." Gabby's body shook with wags. "You should share the pie with me more often. I mean, I love you, Mom!" She sat down politely and did an epic doggy head tilt.

"I think we are officially friends," declared Nigig. "I'll be visiting you more often for sure."

H felt soothed by the familiar taste of blueberries. The comfort of food was second to none. "Your friend Lyn makes a darn good pie! She's as talented as my friend Lou."

Sam smiled. "I'll let her know she has fans, or we can write her a review online later to pass the time." Betty's restaurant was famous for her pies, and people from all over the Midwest came north to seek her sweet creations. Sam was fortunate enough to be just a short drive away.

Nigig looked at his friend. "Blue, were you named after the way you eat fruit pie? Your face, dude!" Everyone giggled.

The stove timer dinged a pleasant sound[83] and Sam popped up from her seat. She sliced the delicious-smelling pizza and looked around again. "We need to let it cool a bit; I don't want you guys to get burned tongues because you can't control yourselves." She was looking specifically at Nigig and Blue. "In the meantime, I think it's safe to medicate our mermaid." Sam sorted her meds, handed two pills to H, and gave her a glass of water. "These are antibiotics—Bactrim and Keflex—used to treat nasty skin infections. They complement one another to provide full coverage for possible bacterial assailants. The downside is they can mess with your digestive tract and cause stomach upset. That's why I fed you first."

H nodded. She popped the pills and chugged her water like a sailor with a beer stein. They left a nasty aftertaste in her mouth, which assured her they were going to work.

Sam didn't bother getting out new plates for her friends. They were woodland creatures, after all, and probably didn't have high standards. Blue liked to eat off a trash can for fun. Everyone got a piece of pizza, and everyone devoured it much like the pie.

"Anything round and sliced is delicious," observed Nigig. "True story."

Blue began to sing in a thick Italian accent: "When the moon hits your eyes like a big pizza pie, that's pie for Blue." Nigig bobbed his head along, and Gabby smiled.

[83] The ding of the stove timer has brought more joy in the history of mankind than anything, even kittens.

"Why is the sauce on top of the cheese?" inquired H between bites.

"That's how they do it in Chicago," answered Sam. "It keeps the crust crispy."

"Is this heaven?" purred Blue.

"No, it's pizza. Same thing," said Gabby, tail wagging.

When the consensus of the room was a content full belly, Sam cleaned up and turned to H. "I'm going to treat your wound with a numbing antibacterial spray, and then I want to cover it with a bandage for the night."

H nodded, feeling a smidgen stronger now that she had food in her belly. Her blue eyes had regained some color.

Nigig took a moment to play with the water spritzer and misted H like she was in a salon chair.

"Should we do something about your hair?" Sam asked. "I could help brush it for you."

H smiled. "That would be one step in the direction of looking normal once again."

Sam looked to the living room in preparation of making a comfortable spot for H to rest. What she saw was a translucent woman sitting in the leather armchair with short gray hair, large plastic glasses, and a red knit shawl. She immediately reached for a large plastic container of salt, as if her favorite ghost hunting show was a documentary and their tactics for protection would work effectively in real life.

Noticing her gaze, Shirley looked up and said, "Hi, Samantha! My name is Shirley. I used to live here. I'm your resident spirit, I suppose."

Despite the fact her face drained of all life fluids, she managed a meager smile at the old woman. Sam was experiencing supernatural overload; at this point, nothing surprised her. A flying saucer could land in her backyard any minute and she would just roll with it.

"Pleased to meet you, Shirley. I still get your mail sometimes!

Gosh, that Medicare sure kills a lot of trees!" It felt like the most awkward thing she had ever said.

"Mail!" said Shirley. "I love getting mail. Has anyone accidentally sent me a postcard? I suppose not . . . most of my friends are in the ground by now as well. I just love travel and looking at photos on postcards, especially ones that note historical places."

"No postcards," stammered Sam. "Only junk mail."

"Say there, merlady," whispered Shirley, "I can't wait to hear about the depths of the lake. All this lamprey talk reminds me of a 90s sci-fi show with aquatic symbiotes called Goa'uld. Maybe we can watch it later; it's got one of my favorite local actors—he also played MacGyver! Rest up. I'll be keeping an eye on you."

With her hair brushed, belly full, and wound bandaged, H got rolled to the couch where she nestled in under a blanket cocoon. She fell asleep as a movie played about a girl pretending to be a boy to play soccer, which was hilarious and entertaining. Nigig and Blue snuggled in on top of her blanket and kept watch over her as she rested.

Chapter Twelve

"H," COOED SAM. "H!"

H rolled over beneath a wildflower-covered prairie of warmth and cracked open an eye. *So this wasn't a dream after all.* She was in a house with a living human.

"It's been twelve hours, and you need another dose of medicine," said Sam, her large dark eyes full of concern and looking hot with her perfect winged eyeliner. "Eat this first." She placed a plate of hot buttered toast with blueberry jam in front of H, which she quickly ate. Shirley was nestled in a large leather armchair, intently staring at her.

H longed to stay awake but soon succumbed to rejuvenating rest . . .

Sleep coma. Sam at her side with more pills. Drinking a fruity elec-

trolyte beverage. Misting the tail. Dreaming again. Sitting up, weary. Sam cleaning the wound and replacing a bandage.

Eyelid flutter. Cat butt in face. More pills. Nigig and Blue curled up on her. Tacos. Back to sleep. Half awake. Pitter-patter—Nigig and Blue sneaking off for snacks.

Eyelid flutter. Raccoon nose. Gabby curled up by her tail fin. Another round of meds. Nebula looking out the window. Comfort. Warmth.

Eyelid flutter. Mist. Television playing movies about vampires. Nigig cheering for a 'Team Jacob.' Swallowing tablets. Eating a cheese sandwich. Snooze.

Woken up by a loud car engine and men hunting demons on TV. Experiencing FOMO about television shows. Lights out again. Deep rest. Nigig arguing about misting. Sam left for work. Nebula was in charge. Shirley scolding the boys for crumbs. Awake. Sam burning a needle to pop and drain a blister.

Wound cleaning. Pills. Sleep. Repeat.

Her eyes fluttered like hummingbird wings. She could feel warm sunlight filtering through the window.

For the first time in days, H woke up on her own and looked around the room. She was still being cuddled by furry creatures, the show on the television was about a high school singing group with cheerleaders, and she could hear Sam milling about the kitchen. H propped herself upright with a pillow and sighed. Her shoulder was no longer bandaged; it felt smooth and healed over. Clarity returned to her once foggy mind as she settled back into normal consciousness.

"Good morning, sunshine!" Nigig popped his head up like he'd been waiting his whole life for this one moment. Then he turned to Blue and grumbled, "You snore, buddy."

Blue shrugged. "Samalama!" he hollered. Apparently, they'd become comfortable enough to dish out nicknames. "What's for lunch? H is awake!"

"Broiled sasquatch steaks and lutefisk," teased Sam, poking

her head through the doorway. H wrinkled her nose in disgust and opened her mouth to speak.

"She's kidding," explained Gabby. "I smell wild rice soup and grilled cheese sandwiches."

"Spot on, girl," praised Sam, who had become accustomed to feeding her entourage of furry friends. They were total foodies and utterly grateful at every meal. She honestly enjoyed their company more than that of most people.

"While you all were asleep, I took it upon myself to visit my friend Lyn and get us a few more pies. I also picked up some pasties for dinner."

Blue and Nigig's eyes lit up in unison, and they clasped their tiny paws together in joy.

Blue's nose twitched. "I smell blueberries and strawberries and raspberries!"

Sam giggled. "Good nose, Fluffy! I can't get anything past you."

"The sooner you learn that, the better!" exclaimed Blue triumphantly. He smiled at the use of his nickname.

"Thank you so much. For everything," said H, feeling very grateful to have found the right human to help her heal and regain her strength. Most importantly, Sam appreciated good food as much as she did. *I may have found my soulmate.* At the very least, if she were ever to grow legs, Sam would surely be her best friend.

"It's been my pleasure, friends," assured Sam. "You've got a couple more days of antibiotics left, H, just to be safe. Everything has healed up quite nicely."

Nigig looked up. "And we are going to have a movie marathon and adventures to pass the time?"

"Whatever your heart desires, little otter," said Sam.

"Oh, honey. Don't tempt me," he challenged.

"Movies and popcorn, that's what he desires," Blue yawned, picking his teeth.

"Well, that's easy," said Sam. "What shall we watch? I was going to suggest Dan's favorite movies—*Lord of the Rings*. It's got action, a wizard, and little people with hairy toes called hobbits!"

H squealed in delight. "I've read the book! Well, the one about the original hobbit, at least. It's the only book I've found on more than one shipwreck."

"I love those movies," added Shirley, surprising everyone with her sudden interest. "That Aragorn is so handsome."

"Let the movie marathon begin!" Blue pumped his little fist in happiness. He liked being a house raccoon. It suited him.

Sam served H a mug of soup and her buttery grilled-to-perfection cheese sandwich as they all sat and ate, eyes glued to the television. The movie sucked all of them in as they became thoroughly invested in the outcome of the tiny heroes. By the last movie in the series, they were all eating piping-hot pasties and munching on popcorn. They ate two pies in one day, and Blue claimed he was bulking up for winter. They all slept that night with content bellies and spirits high on the storytelling masterpiece encompassed by the movies.

The next morning, H awoke to Shirley's spectacled gaze. "H! I've been thinking a lot about your life underwater. There are over 350 shipwrecks in Lake Superior. Humans don't know where over half of them are! Inquiring minds want to know more."

"I've visited most if not all of them," answered H. Before she could tell Shirley tales of her deceased friends, Blue distracted them.

"Sam! Do you have any cookies?" he yelled. "Not the store-bought kind; I've seen the wrappers in the trash. The homemade kind that smell good."

"Oh, good heavens," said Shirley. "I used to make oatmeal chocolate chip cookies for the county fair. I got the blue ribbon seven years in a row until Gayle Johnson showed me up. I think she staged a coup to peek in my recipe card box. She had very loud and distracting sisters." Shirley talked matter-of-factly, as though everyone knew the alleged Johnson sisters.

"Maybe you should give your secret family recipe to our friend Sam," snapped Blue, eyes ablaze.

"I'd prefer the aroma of delicious cookies than the stench of feral heathen peasants," meowed Nebula. "I'll help!" She jumped to the coffee table and knocked a pencil onto the floor, then watched intently as it rolled toward Shirley.

"Good morning, lovelies!" Sam sang as she entered the living room with H's medicine and a slice of pie for everyone (except the furry boys, who had to eat in the kitchen).

"Pie has fruit, and fruit is part of a healthy breakfast. The logic is solid as bedrock," crowed Shirley.

"I have so many questions about the world you grew up in," said H solemnly. Sam nodded in agreement as she licked pie filling off her finger.

"Me?" Shirley sounded shocked. "I'm watching a cryptid eat pie. Back when I lived in small-town Barnum, before I moved up the North Shore, we'd joke at the municipal liquor store about deer hunters finding Bigfoot. Do you know Bigfoot? When the trappers came to town, well, that's when the stories flowed like Gooseberry Falls. Back in the glory days, the railroad folks always thought they saw things in the woods out the window. They have logbooks of their sightings."

"It's entirely possible that Bigfoot is real, but he's not one of my current woodland friends," confirmed H. "I doubt he'd walk the shoreline or live on an island because he needs cover to hide, so there's no way I would ever find him."

"My college roommate used to read me Bigfoot sighting stories. They were hilarious," Sam grinned. "I'd want him on my zombie apocalypse response team."

"Your what?" asked Shirley, adjusting her glasses as though it would make her hear better. "Are we talking about the end times, when zombies take over? I know how to shoot a gun!"

"Actually, a machete is a better weapon," Sam clarified. "You don't have to waste time reloading." She thought for a moment. "How come we are so sure Bigfoot is male? Every single time I've heard a story or account, they use he/him pronouns."

"Well, Sam, it's the goddamned patriarchy," snapped Shirley as she sipped, pinky up, from a ghostly floral teacup. H and Sam locked eyes, surprised at the modern-day revolution leaving her lips.

Even from the kitchen, Blue's slurping was loud enough to capture everyone's attention. His nose scrunched against a clear pint glass decorated with Iditarod sled dogs. As he drank, tiny teeth bared, his pink tongue hopped up and down and water splashed over his whiskers. He popped up, sufficiently hydrated, and looked toward Sam. "I'm ready for my pie. Raspberry this time, please."

"Pie again? You just had a slice. Oh, I know. You want second breakfast." Sam dished up a small second helping.

"Tricksy hobbit, manipulating our sweet Sam-wise," yelled Nigig from the kitchen, still nursing his first piece.

Shirley commented, "Besides my cookies, I always made a raspberry pie for the county fair; but that Sue Smith always beat me. There was just something about her crust. She even had her own raspberry patch—it attracted bears across their lake." Shirley looked down and whispered as though revealing a secret: "Maybe scared raspberries make better pies."

"You know Mama Sue from Barnum?" stuttered Sam in shock, putting together the pieces from the previous story. "I went to college with her daughter. She's like family to me."

"Of course," laughed Shirley. "I don't think there are any other famous Sues with raspberry pies. I grew up knowing her grandma. This whole state is just one small town, don'tcha know."

"Oh my Gods, they know the same person," announced Blue to everyone, already done eating. His face was purple and red, while Nigig continued to eat in small, precise bites. Gabby licked her bowl clean, tail wagging violently the entire time.

"How come your ghost friends can eat and I can't?" Shirley looked a bit grumpy and pensive as she asked the question. "Tea is good, but I want more!"

"Life's a bitch, Shirley," groaned H. "My theory would be you *can* eat, but it has to be food from your human days. Maybe if you went in the kitchen and poked around, you could figure out how to do it. I can ask my friend Lou and get back to you."

"What's on the itinerary for today, Captain?" Nigig prodded. "Besides your nomination to make cookies . . ."

"I was thinking we could roll H outside and get some sunshine," Sam answered. "It's going to be a beautiful day, and you guys have been cooped up in my living room for far too long."

Gabby jumped up and did her happy dance. The pooch had no poker face. "Can we go for a car ride?"

"I'm not sure that's a good idea," Sam quickly answered.

Nigig thought a moment. "We could roll H to the car, and you could drive her down the highway and show her what a human town looks like. Maybe we could visit Betty's since we are now out of pie yet again?"

H grew excited at the thought. "I could put a blanket on my lap and nobody would know I have a tail! I don't need to get out of the car."

"She's always wanted to see Split Rock Lighthouse," revealed Nigig. "She talks about it all the time." It was true. H thought it was the most beautiful of all the lighthouses on the lake, especially because it sat high on a cliff overlooking everything.

"There will be a lot of human activity there," dithered Sam. "We wouldn't be able to get close, but we could drive through the parking lot."

Blue and Nigig scampered about in excitement.

"It's not exactly looked upon with favor to keep wild animals as pets," sighed Sam. "You two will have to hide in the back with Gabby and keep your whiskers out of human sight." The rowdy boys nodded in agreement. Sam turned to H. "You look human from the waist up, but let me disguise you a little more."

Sam disappeared and returned with a black Panic! at the Disco T-shirt, which H threw on over her knit top. She pulled her hair back behind her ears to hide her gills and felt like she could pass as 100 percent human.

Sam grabbed her *F* the Patriarchy* keychain from a hook by the door, ventured outside, and moved her bright-purple Wrangler as close to the door as she could. The ensemble rolled H's computer chair all the way to the car door, using the lever to change the height to help roll her into the car. All the furry creatures—except Nebula, who preferred to reign over her palace—piled into the back seat and got comfy. H pulled a blanket over her tail. She felt like she was in some sort of spy movie.

Shirley looked sad, watching them from the living room window. H turned to Sam. "Do you think we could bring her along?"

"Can she leave the house?" Sam asked.

"Ghosts leave their ships all the time," explained H. "They can travel the whole lake if they want."

"Yo, Shirley!" Blue hollered. "Get your buns in here, old lady!"

Shirley appeared by the car door. Sam leaned to open it as Shirley went right through it and sat in the back with the animals. "I've never been in one of these newfangled automobiles," said Shirley. "My last car was made in 1972 and didn't even play cassettes! Thank God for NPR."

Sam slid into the driver's seat. "Safety first," she said as she buckled her seatbelt. H followed suit. "Put these on." Sam handed H a pair of hot-pink mirrored aviator shades. She instantly felt like a movie star. Sam was definitely one of the cool humans.

They took to the road, emo music booming from the Jeep's speakers. Sam turned to H and asked, "What would you like to listen to?"

"Do you have any Teyla Sjoberg?" H asked shyly. "She's my very favorite."

"Of course!" Sam answered as though the question was silly. "I have her entire catalog on standby." They enjoyed the masterful crooning of the beautiful blonde songstress as they cruised down the highway.

H watched silently as the world passed them by. She soaked in every quaint little shop, restaurant, and house along the way. Land was very much like she'd pictured it from books and old newspapers but even better, because she could see humans milling about and living their everyday lives on land.

The time passed quickly, and H relished every moment. Road signs indicating they were nearing the lighthouse lined the highway, and Sam slowed the vehicle and turned at a marked sign. A tan brick building met them at the parking lot.

Shirley lit up. "The lighthouse is maintained by the historical society. The mighty storm of 1905 claimed nearly thirty ships and inspired her construction. There are over a hundred steps to get to the top! I've climbed them quite a few times. Sure did make my gams tired."

H had looked up at the large 130-foot-tall cliff holding the glorious lighthouse hundreds of times. They couldn't see a whole lot from the parking lot, but it was still amazing in her eyes. "The *Madeira* and her first mate went down in that storm! They're right up the shore," H added.

"On the grounds, they have restored the lighthouse keeper's brick houses too. It's just like the house I grew up in and honestly doesn't look like it was a bad gig." Shirley added, "They retired the lighthouse in 1969. I remember the day the light went out as if it were yesterday."

Sam schemed, "If we had a shred of creativity, we'd have brought a wheelchair and a sleeping bag to get you closer. This is a high-traffic area, though. We probably shouldn't linger here too long."

H nodded. Everything looked so different from land. People were walking the trails, reading informational signs, and taking pictures. Her heart warmed at their appreciation of history.

"The light burns once a year in honor of the *Edmund Fitzgerald* on November 10," said Shirley, finishing her train of thought. "She's the most famous wreck in these waters, and her death still captivates most everyone. There's even a song about her."

"The *Edmund Fitzgerald* went down all the way on the other side of the lake," murmured H.

"A testament to her legacy," confirmed Shirley.

"The view from the water is actually better than what you see here," said Sam. "I don't get out much, but when I do, I love a good scenic boat ride."

Nigig and Blue had poked their heads up and were peering out the back window. Luckily it was tinted, so they were fairly well concealed. Gabby had her head hanging out the slightly open window and smiled with her tongue out.

"I've been here once before," mentioned Blue. "In my young and fit days, I could make some time and cover a good area. I was chased around by a man with a big camera and decided I didn't want to come back. Too many people."

"Pictures! I love pictures," Nigig enthusiastically squealed. "Well, I love the concept of pictures. I never get to actually see them, but I know I'm a model citizen, with a body like this."

"It's a trap!" exclaimed Blue. "A tourist trap. Everyone wants to see the water and the lighthouse. Nobody wants to feed the raccoon. Rule followers are so boring."

Sam smiled. "Are you the reason behind the 'Please do not feed the fat raccoon' sign?"

"Pretty sure they don't use the F word," sneered Blue, "and I'll never tell."

"Should we go get more pie?" Sam surveyed the crowd.

"You're kidding, right?" guffawed Nigig.

Sam turned the Jeep around and returned to the highway. They resumed their mini road trip, music blaring. Everyone was content to travel in silence and enjoy the scenery. After a while, Sam slowed the vehicle again and turned into the parking lot of a brown-and-white restaurant with lots of windows. A bright-blue sign invited people in for pie, and Sam parked the car and pulled out her phone. She scrolled and did a quick search. "These are the flavors of pie on the menu today," said Sam, handing the phone to H. "Which one would you like to try?"

H grabbed the device and followed Sam's guidance on scrolling. She looked at pictures of delicious pies. Not all of them had fruit filling, and some had cream or chocolate filling. Her stomach growled in anticipation until she read the name of one glorious looking dessert. "Turtle pie?" gasped H disgusted. "I can't imagine putting a turtle in a pie let alone eating one!"

"Turtle eggs are delicious!" Blue squealed, smacking his lips. "Sign me up for that!"

Sam laughed. "*Turtle* is a term in the sweets world for a chocolate caramel treat with pecans that resembles the shape of a turtle. No turtles were harmed in the making of that pie. Do you not have chocolate turtles under the sea?"

"Oh, thank Gods," giggled H. "In that case, I will try the turtle coconut cream pie! Strawberry-rhubarb sounds good too." H thought of Wendi and the magic she could do with rhubarb. She continued to play on Sam's phone, mystified by the technology, scrolling up and back down again.

"We'll get both! What would the rest of you scoundrels like?" Sam turned toward the back seat and realized she would probably be buying pie for these filthy animals for the rest of her life.

"Blueberry!" responded Gabby, Blue, and Nigig in unison. Everyone laughed.

"You can keep playing on my phone. I'll go in and place our order. There's usually a line—it might be a bit," said Sam.

Sam walked into the restaurant. The cheery blue-and-white floor tiles welcomed her like an old friend. She soaked up the retro vibes of the diner. Speaking of friends, she wondered if Lyn was baking today. She peered behind the counter and didn't see her, so she joined the line behind a few other folks.

"Samantha, darling!" said a voice from behind. Sam spun around to see Lyn in a ruffled apron dusted with flour.

"Hey! I was hoping I'd run into you," Sam grinned. "Last time we spoke, you were experimenting with recipes. Didja ever figure out a good way to incorporate crispy bacon into a pie?"

"It works well on a breakfast pie," said Lyn. "We sort of knew that already, though."

"That's just another name for quiche," Shirley gurgled.

Sam turned beet red. Shirley had followed her in. She looked around. Nobody was looking at them, so she concluded they were safe and carried on as though nothing were wrong.

"What about the one with chocolate?" Sam nodded toward the French silk on display.

"I'm still perfecting the chocolate-to-peanut-butter ratio," Lyn confided. "It will have a delightful layer of bacon sprinkled on top with a chocolate drizzle."

"I want to be the first to try it!" exclaimed Sam. "You might see more of me than usual. It turns out Gabby loves blueberry pie as a treat. I can't say no to her pleading eyes and tilted head."

"Aww, she's such a good girl," Lyn gushed. "Give her some pets for me. I best get back to work! We've got a busy kitchen today." Something dinged behind the counter, and Lyn scooted off.

"See you next time," said Sam. She placed her order with Shirley by her side and returned to the Jeep. Once they were inside, she complained to Shirley. "Oh my God, next time you follow me into a crowded place, please warn me first! I can't talk to you or I'll look like a crazy person."

"I know," Shirley wailed. "I just wanted to see if there were any other ghosts in the diner. It would be nice to meet some of my kind."

"Were there any ghosts?" H asked.

"No," sighed Shirley. "It was nice to see the old diner again, though."

"You guys are not going to eat in my car," insisted Sam, turning to the critters in her back seat. "I love you, but I don't want to clean up that kind of mess."

"If you drove like a normal human being and not a race car driver, we wouldn't have a problem," pleaded Blue.

"Exactly how many car rides have you been on, Fluffy?" questioned Sam. Nigig laughed.

H was glued to the phone, silently scrolling through the news. She found the interface quite intuitive and was mystified at the mass amounts of information at her fingertips. She had looked up Teyla Sjoberg and read more about the lighthouse. "I love your phone," said H. "This is fantastic."

"They make waterproof cases," Sam explained. "We could get you one, although I don't think you'd have signal in the middle of nowhere. And charging the battery would be a pain, but if you left it off most of the time, you'd probably get a couple weeks off one charge. Then you could call me to meet up for pie and a recharge."

H waved her hands up and down, unable to find words that adequately conveyed her excitement.

"I think that's a yes," cheered Nigig. "You better let me borrow that to look up otter stats."

"Stats, you say?" Blue snorted. "Dude, no way she's letting you watch otter porn on her phone."

"No, I want it for the articles!" replied Nigig, paws balled into little passionate fists.

Sam snorted. "Alright, kids. Buckle up. We're going downtown to get H a phone." She backed the Jeep out of her parking spot and exited the lot, returning to the ribbon of highway connecting blissful morsels of goodness on the land realm.

Nigig snidely continued, "You're just jealous of my significant baculum, Fluffy boy!"

Blue was excitedly gesturing with his hands. "I have one too, and it's *Procyon lotor* perfection, thank you very much. Don't be so *Lontra cana-dense, sis.*"[84]

H broke her pensive silence: "According to the internet, most mammals have a baculum. Yours is not a unique penis bone, friend—tis but an average dick." She had learned how to use Google.

"Oh no," squealed Nigig, "we've armed H with unlimited information. With great power comes great responsibility!"

"The mammal with the largest baculum is the walrus," answered H.

Blue snorted. "Remind me never to mess with one of those bad boys."

"They can reach thirty inches long!" exclaimed H. "That's over one fish length!"

Nigig wrinkled his nose, and his whiskers quivered. "I'll believe it when I see it."

Sam giggled. "I have a friend in Alaska. We could all go visit."

"Don't tempt him," groused Blue. "We'll never get the mermaid safely across the Canadian border."

"She looks enough like my niece Chelsea that we could just borrow her ID. Wouldn't even need to make a fake one," answered Sam.

"Oh, now we've resorted to breaking the law?" H feigned disgust. "Alaska Natives call the walrus baculum the *oosik*. The late Congressman Don Young brought one to a hearing once and brandished it like a sword!" The phone screen glow reflected off the pink sunglasses on her face. "His successor is much classier. She's *pro-fish*!"

"As we all should be," Shirley agreed. "A woman's place *is* in the House."

Blue added, "Where she can bake pies for raccoons!"

[84] Today I learned that *Procyon lotor* is the scientific name for raccoon. *Lontra canadensis* is the name for river otter. Sometimes I can't get a word in around these critters!

"Missed the point entirely, Fluffy," chuckled Nigig.

"This is huge," H exclaimed. "The Council of Fins has a human ally!"

Sam wondered what her search history would be like after getting her phone back from the information-hungry mermaid. "You're drunk on information, my dear! Initiate self-control!"

"Information hangovers are the worst." Blue spoke like he had experience in the subject.

"Tell me more!" Shirley was soaking it up.

H enjoyed the scenery as Sam drove. The reflection of the sun hit the leaves as they shimmered in the wind. A full palette of spring greens tickled the landscape, worthy of a leading role in one of Vera's paintings. The winding highway continued relentlessly onward, trees breaking occasionally to offer a brief glance at the mighty blue lake.

They returned to town, where cute shops lined a quaintly bustling main drag. Sam nestled her trusty steed outside a shop named Skyrizen. She turned to her passengers and said, "I'll be right back. No funny business, kids!"

H watched Sam through the large shop windows. White counters lined the room, displaying the latest smartphones on glowing pedestals. Candy-colored cases and cables littered a sidewall.

Sam was chatting with a salesman, looking at two different phones. She quickly glanced at the Jeep as though to make sure everything was OK. Gabby stuck her head out the window, smiling broadly. Sam pointed to a metallic pink phone, and the salesman grabbed a case from the wall of goodies. They proceeded to the register, and Sam exited the shop with a brown paper bag.

Sam hopped back into the car. Smiling, she pulled a rectangular white box out of the bag and smoothly slid the top off, revealing a shiny new phone. "Check out this beautiful piece of human technology." She revealed a clear plastic box that, upon closer inspection, held a phone case.

Nigig squealed with excitement, "Hey, that case is named after me! Well, the Middle English version of me." He scrunched his nose and flared his whiskers.

"Indeed it is," said Sam. "You're agile, rugged, and waterproof. That's what everyone wants in a phone case!"

"I'd normally describe myself as sleek and sexy, but that works too." Nigig strutted in the back seat, paw to the air, praising himself like a God.

"Nigig, can you read?" gasped Shirley.

"I recognize combinations of letters like they're a picture. I know the word *otter*," shrugged Nigig.

H hugged her smartphone close, eyes welling with tears. It was as precious as the One Ring. "Thank you, Sam. For everything. Was it expensive? I can repay you with treasures from the sea."

"No need to repay me. My student loans are all paid off! It is a gift, and, yes, they are expensive. Take good care of it," said Sam. "Now we can stay connected and you will have a world of information at your fingertips. Be sure to dim the screen, and shut it off when you're not using it. It's easy to burn through battery when you get enchanted by the internet."

"I'm going to install your waterproof case, plug you in to charge, and then you should be all set! There will be a tutorial on how to use it too. They make them so boomers don't struggle so much."

"Hey now!" screeched Shirley, pretending to be offended.

"Almost all set," answered H. "I hate to ask another favor, but I could use a skein of yarn and some knitting needles to make another pocket inside my top."

"Another pocket?" asked Sam. "Whatcha got hiding in there?"

"Oh, just a multi-tool," replied H nonchalantly. "I got it from my favorite beaver."

Sam stifled a laugh. "The more I learn about you, the more I love you. You're in luck. There's a cute little yarn shop that Mama Sue showed me just down the street."

Sam pulled up to a quaint lilac building with white trim. A warm glow illuminated oaken shelves stocked with yarns of every color, neatly organized in rainbow order. A woman sat in an armchair in the back, peacefully knitting what appeared to be a sweater.

Vera would absolutely fucking love this place . . . H felt an idea travel through her with such tenacity that she jumped. She pulled out her phone and snapped a picture out the window. A movement caught her eye, and she noticed a gray tabby peering out at them through the glass.

The bright-yellow door of the shop jingled as Sam entered. The woman in the back met her with a smile and what seemed like midwestern niceties, as H tried to lip-read the conversation. She wasted no time in grabbing a skein of gray yarn from the wonderfully organized display and a pair of wooden knitting needles as she proceeded to the register. Sam was a very efficient shopper—or maybe it was that her introverted side didn't mess around with chitter-chatter. When Sam returned to the vehicle, she handed a brown paper bag to H.

H peered inside, delighted at what she saw. Up close, the yarn was a dark gray with subtle splashes of color, mostly teals and dark blue with a tiny pop of purple and fuchsia. It felt like nothing she had ever handled before, soft yet sturdy. The texture was calm and smooth like chocolate pudding. The glorious skein was locally made and dyed, and of course named after the lake H called home.

"This is perfect," said H. "Thank you again." She picked up a knitting needle and examined it closely.

"Are you going to make me a sweater?" Blue popped his head out from the back seat. The whites of his eyes twinkled against his furry black mask.

"A sweater? Don't conform to human ways. Nudity is so hot right now," said Nigig with his snide fashion guru voice. "You're just asking to catch rabies: *'Bite the clothed one! He's clearly a little bitch!'*" Nigig waved his paws around like a frenzied beast.

"Your mom has rabies," Blue retorted with a slight baring of his bright-white teeth. He clasped his paws together and continued, speaking dreamily, "Animals in tiny human clothes look cute. Cute animals get food. Food includes blueberry pie, my favorite."

"I take it back," Nigig snorted. "Not even the rabies would want you."

Gabby chimed in, ignoring the teasing. "I twelve-out-of-ten would wear a heckin' sweater if it meant I could have some pie, yes, indeed! Pie and Frisbee, my two favorite things." Her tail bonked noisily against the side of the Jeep. "Just make the shirt short enough for butt scritches and good pets!"

Sam giggled. "Oh, Fluffy boy. Now that we're friends, you're going to be spoiled. You might have to make friends with Dan, though, if you're going to hang around like our own personal trash bandit. Sweet Gabby, you probably need a Christmas sweater, because we all know that giant T-shirts from drug companies with blue pills were not your favorite."

"Oh, sweet biscuits, I remember. That free T-shirt was too big for you, so you made me wear it! Good thing you gave me treats after I modeled it for you and your friend. I only did it with a wag because it made you laugh." With that, a huge smile erupted over the chocolate Lab's face. "I'm so glad I could amuse you with my cuteness, but next time ask the drug reps for a shirt in a normal human size. Dogs don't take Viagra, but I wore the darn thing anyway. I would say their free stuff is a bamboozle—free pie would be much better."

H had once again become engrossed in her phone. She looked up as Sam asked, "Is there anything else you want to see or do before we head home?"

"Nope. I've enjoyed seeing the world and being spoiled by you. I am so grateful; I owe you big time."

"Thank you for visiting dry land. Please keep your hands and feet inside the vehicle at all times," Blue announced. "If you look to your right, you will see trees. If you look to your left, more trees. *Leaf* it to them to keep you breathing clean air with no hidden agenda or corporate profits." He waved his stocky arms from side to side as he spoke, inflection dipping and climbing like a pro tour guide.

"Well, since you only have a couple more days at my house, what would you like for dinner? Besides the pie, of course." Sam glanced at H and then back to the winding pavement.

H sat thoughtfully for a second. "Honestly, I'd just like some tacos. My seamen friends don't make much Mexican food! I'd like to eat them again now that I'm more conscious."

"Well *that*, I can do," answered Sam, relieved. She wasn't much of a cook but knew her mama's family recipes by heart.

"*Tacos!*" Blue and Nigig squealed in unison. Furry woodland creatures really did love human food, and H was sure it had ruined them forever. Being friends with a mermaid has unforeseen side effects.

"You guys are basically domesticated now," said H. "You're gonna end up vaccinated with collars and a whole list of tricks."

"There's nothing wrong with doing a good trick now and then," barked Gabby.

"Oh, of course not," said H. "I just realized these wild boys are very tame."

"We're wild and crazy, and you know it," Nigig boasted, twirling in a circle.

"You're downright feral," agreed Blue looking at Nigig. "I'll act tame for food. I'd even let them pet me. But if they dare touch my fluffy tail, they're dead." Blue tried to act solemn and serious but had clearly failed in the delivery as Nigig cracked up and even Gabby was chortling.

Sam turned down the narrowing road that led home. H recognized the patterns of the trees. The pavement soon ended and narrowed even more as they proceeded down a gravel road leading to the small clearing in which Sam resided. She parked snugly beside the front door, where the rolling chair awaited their return. She herded

Blue, Nigig, and Gabby out of the Jeep while Nebula watched from the window, unamused.

"Missing me, are we?" asked a voice from above. H looked up from the open car door as Revna swooped down from the sky.

Her eyes lit up at the sound of feathers beating against the air. "Revna! Where the hell have you been? I could have sworn I heard your voice during the Isle Royale aurora show! I've had questions galore—and even more strange adventures."

"Oh, I've heard about your so-called adventures. And, yes, that was me talking." Revna glanced toward the house where Shirley was now peering out the window next to Nebula, whose large eyes followed every move of the large black bird. "Getting a little help from the spirit realm, I see. Next time you summon a sky bruin, I'd love to be around for the ride." She perched on H's outstretched hand.

Sam returned to the vehicle with her trusty rolling chair and blinked slowly at the sight of the bird.

"Sam, this is Revna. She's kind of a big deal," said H. "This is my human friend, Sam."

"Oh, I know," answered Revna quickly. "I've been watching. A bit risky to go out in public, don't you think?"

"I'm in my rebellious teenage years," H joked. "Try to ground me; I dare you!"

Sam had always thought birds were a little bit creepy, but she mustered a "Nice to meet you, Revna." At least ravens were gothy and liked shiny objects, which was a relatable and respectable trait.

"Likewise," answered Revna politely, bowing her head. Her eyes glistened as she spun her head around. "We have important information to discuss, as I must hasten elsewhere. The realms keep me occupied and burdened."

"Are we talking about my ability to converse with spirits? The ghosts I saw on Isle Royale? The Reefer monsters who attacked me? The mysterious creature, Trippehjay, that saved me? The bear who crawled out of the sky?" Revna hopped off H's hand as she crossed her arms. "Is it something else completely? Is the fate of humanity on the line?"

Revna's eyes danced in what H assumed was a smile. "You are special, young finned one, as you are well aware that you are one of a kind," cawed Revna. "For once in your life, you have a definitive purpose."

"This is gonna be good," said Nigig, sprawling his long brown body in the grass.

"Ooh, should we make popcorn?" Blue excitedly plopped his fluffy bulk next to Nigig in anticipation.

H braced herself for something cryptic. "I'm the only known mermaid on this planet," she stammered. "What does my existence have to do with anything remotely life-changing?"

"In the beginning . . ." began Revna.

Blue jumped to his feet. "Spare us the mother-fluffing drama! Get to the good part." He huffed his fluff back down to his seat in the bright-green grass.

Revna happily bounced in the grass to entertain her anxious audience. Sam had nestled herself onto the rolling chair, Gabby at her side.

"The answers you seek, with as much detail and historical accuracy as possible, lie only in the mind of the wise old one who still lives today, as she has lived through it all. As darkness spreads throughout our lake, you are the light that may hinder the black flame." Revna switched directions in the grass and paused to look at her captivated crowd. "Elusive, she lives in the depths of her hidden underwater cave. To search for her without direction would be cumbersome, but solace lies in the classification of records. Humans would refer to it as a library of sorts or even a tree of life."

H had a solemn, pensive look. "*The wise old one* . . . The oldest known resident of the lake is Nancy Sturgeon. Nobody knows her actual age, but she's rumored to be at least two hundred years old."

"Never ask a woman her age," warned Blue.

"Ew. I bet she's got that deathbed swamp smell about her," Nigig groaned.

"So, this Nancy—a friend of yours?" Blue spoke the words with much anticipation.

"No," answered H. "I've never met her. Sturgeon tend to love the deepest, darkest parts of the lake because they are bottom-feeders. I spend most of my time adjacent to land and near my shipwreck friends. Our paths have yet to cross. Sometimes I've wondered if she was but a myth."

"Bottom-feeders!" Nigig grabbed his sides and rolled around, giggling. "Now, that's a club. How much for lifetime membership?"

"Your mom is a bottom-feeder!" Blue joined in the shenanigans.

"You know I spend more time underwater with the dead than the living, Revna," said H.

"So, to find Nancy, H needs to slide her public library card and visit the historical record keepers of the underwater realm. The only hope is that they will know her approximate location. Wouldn't they also have historical records? Verbal, magic, or otherwise?" Sam summed it up quite efficiently.

"They're not necessarily a physical entity," said H. "Underwater, we rely much on verbal history. It's often skewed, and we tend to sugarcoat things for those in the afterlife."

Revna hopped forward with a fiery glint in her eye. "As you return home, time nears expiration for life as you know it. Make the best of it. Trees grow black, and darkness consumes life. Zeus sends his regards and enjoyed your adventure with Ursala." She nodded toward H, waved a wing goodbye to the crew, and hopped into a gliding takeoff.

"What should I do about the Reefers?" H called after her.

"*Ca-caw! Ca-caw!*" The boys flapped their arms and made raven noises from their grassy seats.

"Well, that was definitely not the Minnesotan long goodbye I'm familiar with," said Sam.

"She always does that," said H. "She says something cryptic[85] and flies away before you can drill her with questions."

"She's a master of mystery and an absolute queen," gushed Nigig, clasping his paws under his chin.

"*I* thought she was kind of a frigid bitch," Blue fumed. "Tell us exactly how to fix it. Don't leave us a riddle and hope we can solve it in time to avert a catastrophic event!"

Sam had never seen Blue so worked up. She leaned over to pet his head and scratch his chin. "It's OK, Fluffy boy. We'll dissolve the chaos. I think you're getting hangry."

"It's true," nodded Nigig. "If the Fluffy boy gets angry, you best get food in his little belly."

The gang moved inside to settle in for a night of contemplation. Nebula met them at the door and growled, "Which one of you pooped in my litter box? It smells like something dead. I bite you."

"Not it!" Nigig hastily answered and put a paw on his nose.

Blue threw his paws up. "I'm not toilet-trained, so the box of sand felt more like home! Geez, woman, would you rather I do it on the floor?"

"Don't mind him. He's just hungry," explained Sam. "How's my pretty kitty?" She leaned over and scratched Nebula's chin just how she liked it.

"I require fresh ice water and sardine cutlets. Thanks for asking," Nebula mewed her polite yet snide demands. She wrapped her long, silky body around Sam's leg and flicked her tail sassily for her human.

"No need to snark at your mother," said Shirley. "She took allergy shots for you, for heaven's sake!"

"I bet your cat ate your beady eyeballs when you died," purred Nebula as if the words were sugar.

Shirley looked a little frightened by the thought but gave her a kind smile. "There, there, my pretty little morbid one. No felines violated my body, thank you very much."

H resumed her place on the couch, making herself comfort-

[85] Revna never simply says what she means. The Gods warned her not to meddle in human affairs, as changing the course of history could be catastrophic. She routinely provides guidance, although humans would never know the voice they heard while sleeping was actually a diva bird and not a dream. Revna was merely the gardener who planted the seed, and it was up to the individual to let it bloom into its full potential. Reminds me of the prime directive.

able with her knitting needles and yarn. She worked carefully as Vera taught her. Blue and Nigig nestled on her lap while Nebula perched on the back of the couch and looked out the window.

"If we were superheroes," said Blue, breaking the silence, "and this were our secret lair, the world would laugh to find us cuddling around a knitting mermaid."

Nigig perked up, and his whiskers danced. "Superheroes! Take off your mask, Fluffy boy! Show us your real identity!"

"Leave it all on," mewed Nebula. "Nobody wants to see that."

"She's the token antihero, that one," said Blue. "A beautiful, silky, black vixen breaking hearts and legs. A straight-up ruthless assassin in a gorgeous body."

Shirley walked in wearing a pink floral blouse with poofy sleeves, a large gold rhinestone brooch, and a flowing skirt. "Mind if I join you whippersnappers on the davenport?" Seeing H knitting, she added, "I used to wield a mean cross-stitch. I could even out-doily Alvera Lanari."

"Sam would be like our Squad Mom," said Blue. "She'd be the one making us cookies and putting on our Band-Aids."

H had already completed knitting the phone pocket and had slipped off her knit crop top. She wore Sam's T-shirt while sewing the pocket into the top, opposite from the multi-tool pouch.

Sam poked her head into the living room. "Tacos are almost ready! Furry boys gotta eat in the kitchen, and we will not judge the mess you make."

H's stomach growled at the word *tacos*. Gabby followed Sam across the kitchen, waiting for her to drop something. Clean-up duty was a very important job.

"Why would anyone ever want to leave Mexico?" Blue asked as he hopped off the couch to scamper into the kitchen at the sound of clinking dishes.

"Where are you going with that, Fluffy?" Nigig poked his head up curiously.

"They have authentic tacos!" Blue passionately said, clasping his paws lovingly at the side of his head.

"If I ever head south, I'll be sure to take you with me," promised Sam to her hungry raccoon friend, who was ravaging a plate of tacos on the floor. Nigig ate more cleanly, with precise bites using his bright-white teeth. His teeth could snap open a mollusk and adequately crunch a taco.

Sam made sure H could reach the coffee table and scooted it closer to the couch, placing a plate of tacos in front of her.

"Sorry you can't partake in the fiesta," said Sam to Shirley from the armchair she had parked in to eat. "I hope you were at least able to enjoy tacos in your lifetime."

"Oh heavens, yes," answered Shirley. "At the church potluck, there was always a delightful taco salad, which I would annihilate if I didn't fill up on Lutheran sushi first. You know, pickles wrapped in cream cheese and ham. It always tasted so good after spending all day in the hot summer sun for the Lutheran Women's gun club skeet shoot. You should have seen the selection of dessert bars. I always wore my stretchy pants." Shirley lifted her hand perpendicular to her mouth as though she were telling a dirty little secret.

When dessert was served, the usual events transpired with the furry duo. Blue wanted second helpings and ended up covered in fruit. Nigig ate cleanly.

H had two slices of pie. "The turtle pie is better than I dreamed it would be," said H. "Thank Gods no turtles were harmed in the making of this delicacy. The rhubarb pie is tart yet sweet. My friend Wendi would love it!"

"I'm so full I could burst," Blue bellowed.

"Same," groaned Sam. "I need to get out and exercise."

"Merely existing is exercise," said Blue.

Everyone had settled into the living room. It was time to get down to business. "What did Revna mean by all her chatter?" Sam asked. "You need to find Nancy . . . and to find her cave, you need to visit the library? What the heck is an underwater library?"

"I've heard you can store facts and stories for future generations below the depths of the lake, but I never dove into it," said H, smiling at her own pun.

"Such a party girl," said Nigig. "What about the cold hard facts and data, ma'am?"

"A life I envy," said Blue dreamily, then turning and pointing to Nigig. "And I think *you* are the party girl!" Blue and Nigig giggled.

"Revna mentioned a tree of life and trees going black," Sam mused. "Is that a metaphor, or is there a literal tree of life? What about an intact submerged tree?"

"Well, I can assure you there is no physical library under the water, despite changing water levels and erosion over the centuries," answered H. "There is no Atlantis—at least not in Lake Superior—and no trees grow down there."

"What about your ships and sea-dwelling ghosts?" Shirley inquired wistfully. "Did they convert an old vessel into a record keeper?"

"The ghosts I know live their afterlives in the depths apart from what transpires on land amongst the living," said H. "They are rich in history, yes. Some even try to keep up with current events. But there is no soul or group that keeps track of everything. If anyone were in charge of history, it would be Wadeen on the Loops."

"What about the lighthouses?" Samantha asked like a lightbulb went off in her head. "They guide vessels and watch over the waters."

"They're also made by the hands of man," said Nigig. "How old is the oldest lighthouse on the lake?"

"Whitefish Point Light Station was built in 1861," Shirley rattled off.

"Nancy Sturgeon would be older than that structure," said Sam. "We have got to be in search of a natural landmark."

"It's got to be a literal living tree," said Shirley. "We do have a coniferous celebrity nearby. In fact, you can only visit it with an Ojibwe guide."

"*Manido Gizhigans!* It's also known as the Witch Tree or Little Cedar Spirit Tree!" H exclaimed as her eyes burned with excitement resembling the morning star.

"The Witch Tree is over three hundred years old," said Shirley. "It makes me look like a spring chicken. I suspect it is much older than we think."

"She is beautiful indeed," said H. "I've admired her from the water and in Vera's art."

"I've honestly never been to see the tree," said Sam. "I know she grows out of a rock up the shore, but I've done most of my exploring seeing local waterfalls. I love waterfalls, and Dan loves lighthouses." She shrugged.

"The first written account of the Witch Tree was penned in the early 1700s by a French-Canadian fur trader, a man with explorative pursuits. However, the local tribes have known of her for much, much longer. A couple of theories were made as to describe her appearance." Shirley sat herself more upright from a slouched position and leaned in to the group as though she were going to tell a fireside horror story. "At one point, it was believed a hawk spirit lived inside the tree; the hawk could bring rough waters to paddlers who didn't bring a gift before a journey across the waters."

"What are the other theories?" H was captivated and confused. She had never heard these legends before. "Spill, Shirley!"

"What kind of gifts?" Nigig asked with a twitch of his nose, eyes intent on the storyteller.

"Generally, they'd bring tobacco," answered Shirley. "Sometimes they'd avoid paddling near it altogether unless they were in large groups. They'd play drums and sing to appease the spirit."

"Perhaps that explains the lack of Indigenous vessels and ghosts underwater," said H. "The exploring European immigrants had no idea they had to barter for safe passage."

"So if we find a smoking hawk, we are on the right path!" Blue jumped up and down excitedly—then froze, softening with concern.

"Similarly, the tree was thought to be home to an evil spirit. The rowdy European settlers' gunshots startled the spirit, scaring it away for all eternity. It is not known where the spirit may have relocated." Shirley shrugged.

"Do we really want to find an evil spirit?" asked Nigig.

Nebula yawned. "I could take it, you know."

"Yes, you are the glorious Queen Bitch," said Blue. "Winner, winner. Bend a knee!" He bowed down to her excellence, sprawling prostrate on the floor.

All eyes twinkled in the falling darkness and stared intently at Shirley, consumed by the tales emerging from the old woman.

"The final theory," Shirley continued, "was that a woman was sent to the point to stand guard over the lake. She had a vision, which told her to look for a change in the water." Shirley relaxed back into her armchair. "Regardless of the lore, the tree is believed by many historians to be the oldest living landmark in the entire state."

"That's gotta be the place," yelled Nigig. "But which theory is true? What are we dealing with?"

Shirley wasn't done, now that she had the spotlight. "The tree has only been nicknamed the Witch Tree for about a hundred years. The legend also specifies that the underwater lynx lives nearby. Oh! There is another unofficial rumor that we don't even count as a theory. It states that the spirit in the tree is the reason the Vikings can't win a Super Bowl."

"Trippehjay," whispered H, ignoring the silly rumor. "They saved my life, but I don't think they'd come out of hiding for just any reason. The sacred tree on Hat Point has got to be where I need to search for answers," said H. "I'm betting everything on it."

"When I release you tomorrow, you won't have too far to swim," said Sam. "We best get some rest, as we need to be up bright and early to avoid prying eyes and traffic."

"We ride at dawn," said H as she snuggled in on the couch

under a blanket with a raccoon and otter curled up on her and a brown dog at her tail fin. Nebula lounged upon her pillow and rested her head on H's neck. She was really going to miss her human, Sam. She felt overwhelmed by the thought of returning to the water and needing to save the world. Shirley's knowledge was a blessing, but for the underwater portions of the puzzle, she'd be on her own.

Chapter Thirteen

"I SMELL SIZZLING BACON!" BLUE jumped up and bounced right on H's belly like a tennis ball made of fluff.

"Breakfast is the most important meal of the day," remarked Shirley from her armchair as she sipped her tea in a vintage floral china cup.

H reached up an arm and petted Nebula as the whole lot on the couch untangled and stretched. Nigig and Blue headed straight for the kitchen, where Sam was scrambling some eggs.

Sam smiled. "Hang on, boys. It'll be ready in a few minutes." Nigig and Blue looked up at her like two excited children on Christmas morning. They were her furry little shadows, scampering around behind her, eyes wide with anticipation.

H blinked slowly. The week had gone by so fast. She had shown up on the doorstep of a living human who graciously gave her medicine and tacos when she was at her lowest point. She could have died without knowing modern movies, the dumpster fire of social media on the internet, or turtle pie. The misery of saying goodbye to a friend tickled her emotional cortex, as she wiped a single teardrop from her eyelid. Everything was going to be fine. She had a plan, she had a phone, and, most importantly, she had her squad. She stretched, somehow determined not to let the weight of the world weigh heavy on her shoulders. Gabby, sensing her turmoil, placed her head on H's tail affectionately for comfort.

"I wish I could visit the tree with you," sighed Shirley.

"You could join me. I'd love the company," said H. "The ghosts on Isle Royale went from water to land. I'm sure it goes both ways."

"I don't think I entirely understand the rules of my realm," Shirley hesitated. "I've never pushed the envelope."

"The ghosts I know basically do whatever they want," H explained. "They live their lives to the fullest, even in death."

Sam's voice echoed from the kitchen. "You want *pie* for breakfast? On top of the bacon and eggs I've already prepared?"

H giggled as Blue tried to sweet-talk his way into a little morning dessert. "I'm not an addict," he insisted. "I just like good food. That's not a crime, you know. Blueberries—that's fruit. Humans and their furry companions alike need to eat their fruits and veggies."

"Winter is coming, and he needs an extra layer. It gets cold up north, don'tcha know." Nigig tried to help his friend's argument. "The fluff only gets him so far."

"It's almost summer, don'tcha know," responded Sam, nevertheless loading their plates with both breakfast and dessert.

H ate her breakfast quietly, wondering what she would find later. Sam had already agreed to house (and feed) Nigig and Blue for as long as they wanted. She would just have to convince Dan that she learned how to talk to animals and that neither of the boys had rabies. They wanted to have the squad assembled in case H phoned for help.

Sam looked at H and asked, "Are you ready to go?"

"Yes. I'm fully charged and ready for battle."

Sam pulled her purple Jeep up to the door. H hopped her butt onto the rolling chair while Sam and two furry woodland creatures helped navigate her down the hall and out the door where the open passenger door welcomed her. Sam queued up the Teyla Sjoberg music and they were ready to ride in the dim light of dawn. Everyone piled in the Jeep except Nebula, who watched the circus wide-eyed from the front window.

Sam drove quietly for the majority of the trip. She and H listened to music contentedly with no need to small-talk or further discuss current events. This was the sign of a true friendship, H was certain. Sam slowed the vehicle and veered right, continuing onto a dirt road. It curved and dropped steeply, navigating with ease like she was born for off-roading. The road sloped downward to a flat area where she drove through a small stream and proceeded onward. Lined by trees, the road narrowed and was riddled with large sprawling tree roots. Large rocks created an obstacle course—H suddenly realized why the vehicle had such large tires—and the road forked multiple times. Sam took the corner and suddenly the lake in all her glory appeared. Waves gently lapped against the rocky shoreline as the sun poked her head out over the clouds. The light pink sky glowed with the aftermath of a reliable sunrise.

With a final maneuver, Sam pulled the Jeep as close to the water as possible and parked. "This will be our secret meeting spot. If you ever need anything, I will meet you here."

H nodded. It was easy to see why Sam chose this location, as it was hard to reach with most vehicles and the privacy was superb. Sam opened the passenger side and helped H plop down onto a rock. From there, she used her arm strength to inch her way toward the water and hop her body from rock to rock as her iridescent silver tail reflected the colors of the morning sky. She plunged into the cold lake with a splash, the cool, blue-gray water welcoming her home by embracing her body. H's long, dark braids soaked up the water and dripped down her pale skin.

H leaned against the large rock, tail gently slapping and massaging the water. "I don't have words adequate to thank you, Sam," she said. "I know I will see you again, so this isn't goodbye. It's a later, buddy! Next pie is on me." It all came out sounding like a comical sitcom.

Sam smiled. The mermaid understood her more than she realized. "Until next pie, friend." She leaned down and gave her mermaid friend a hug.

The four-legged creature brigade hopped over to say their goodbyes. Gabby couldn't stop wagging even though she was going to miss her mer-human. H nestled a wet hand on Gabby's head. "Goodbye, sweet girl. We will swim together when this is over!" Gabby's paws did a little tapping happy dance and she kissed the mermaid's face.

"Bye, friend!" grunted Gabby as she wagged her way back up to Sam.

"I can't do it," sobbed Blue. "I don't want to say goodbye. The week of pie shall not end, nor shall our mermaid swim into danger. Be careful out there, love. We're cheering for you."

"Blue! I almost forgot." H reached into her tank top and pulled out something that was hidden in one of the pockets. She unfolded a knit object to reveal a tiny, raccoon-sized fisherman sweater. "I made you this to keep you warm on those cold, lonely nights." H held it up for all to see. She had used the leftover yarn from her secret pocket. "Now you can lay off the pie," she whispered with a wink.

"Now *that* is the cutest thing I have ever seen," commented Sam. "I can't wait to see Fluffy boy model it for us!"

Blue tiptoed over, grabbed the sweater, and hugged it to his chest. "Thank you, H. I will wear it with pride like I'm your little bitch." He was holding back tears, but everyone laughed to ease the sadness.

"Well, jeez, honey. You went all in with that one. Where's mine?" Nigig joked with a paw on his hip. He scurried his slender brown body over to his best friend. "Be safe out there, OK?" His eyes solemnly looked into hers and he wrapped his short arms around her for a hug. "And when you make *my* sweater, I want it in rainbow!"

H chuckled. "Deal."

Shirley stood quietly, watching the goodbyes. "I don't want this adventure to end," she said. "Back in my day, it was rare for a woman to take to the sea."

"Come with me, then! At least to the Witch Tree, and then you can go back home," requested H.

Shirley dove into the water. "I'm going to see the lake from the inside and return home with the full story," Shirley vowed.

H looked back at the rest of her friends. "Behave yourselves. I'll be in touch. Onward, Shirley!" She waved and took to the water like a hot moose on a summer day. Her silver tail glinted in the sunlight, and with a splash, she was gone.

H twirled underwater, spinning her body as her tail propelled her onward. "I missed you, old friend," she murmured to the lake. She stayed close to the surface, but just enough below it to maintain her stealthy cover. H thrusted herself onward and glided smoothly with the grace of a ballerina. Swimming was fantastic; she had missed it dearly. Shirley floated next to her without doing a trick or saying a word.

H poked her head out of the water, dark hair glued to her soaking wet noggin. She could see Hat Point in the distance. She felt lightning bugs in her stomach as she drew nearer, eyes fixed on the sacred timber. She pulled out her phone and snapped a quick photograph of the tree, texting it to Sam with a note that said she made it. H pictured her friends surrounding Sam's phone, waiting anxiously for updates.

"There she is," said Shirley, awestruck. "I've never been this close before."

The roar of the waves splashing consumed H's auditory senses as she focused on the tree. H swam all the way up to the wave-beaten gray rocks and placed her hand flat against them. She looked straight up toward the gnarled tree and admired the wind-battered rocks covered in colored mosses.

"She was carved by the hands of nature," said H. She had almost forgotten about their plan and reached into her pockets for a small leather pouch that Sam had filled with tobacco. She gently tossed the bag up to the tree. "For safe passage."

"And the Vikings," whispered Shirley. "Skol!"

H took her hands and walked them down the rock wall toward the water. Her hands followed the rock straight down as her whole body was consumed once again by the lake. She was upside down, nose-diving, slowly following the rock line toward the bottom of the lake, moving her body forward only with her hands. Another twenty feet had passed, and she put down her right hand to find a gaping hole. She pulled her head down to look inside. It was roughly five feet in diameter and appeared to form a dark rock tunnel. "Hey, Shirley! Stay with me. Your glowing helps me see," called H. Shirley was gazing at the rock formations. "We go in together."

"To the fires of Mordor!" Shirley cheered.

H smiled. She swam inside, following a few bends and turns, shimmying around a couple of large rocks, and found herself in a large cavern. A couple of smaller holes were in the rock wall as though leading to more rooms. H looked upward and gasped. Shirley placed her hands on her heart.

Tree roots poked through the roof of the rock cavern. In the darkness, H could make out that some of them came out of the rock and re-entered, while others hung down like wooden stalactites. It was beautiful and furled and even more gnarled than the tree above ground. H reached up to touch the roots, and out of the darkness a voice spoke, stopping her finger at the tip of a wooden icicle.

"We've been waiting for you, mermaid," spoke a soft yet expressive woman's voice.

H, startled, turned away from the roots, her hair suspended messily in the water as though to speak her feelings for her.

Illuminating the darkness from one of the holes in the wall swam a walleye, approaching H with her glowing scales. Although she was a fish, she also appeared to be made of copper. H watched in awe as the most beautiful fish she had ever seen spoke.

"My name is Elizabeth," she said. "I am keeper of the sacred texts and histories of life in Gitchi-Gami. The young fry joke and call me Liz in the Library."

"Pleased to meet you. I am H, the mermaid of the lake. I've never actually heard of you." H looked around the cave, a bit embarrassed.

"Me neither," Shirley chimed in.

"We all know who you are," Liz proclaimed. "Unfortunately, we don't have any hydro-memories as to where you came from." Her dorsal fin appeared to be made of pure copper while maintaining the sheer quality of an actual fish. H couldn't keep her eyes off the beauty. "You, my dear, are a bit of a mystery."

"That's not why I'm here, although my curiosity would be quenched and delighted by that information," answered H. "Where are your books?"

"Yes, the books!" Shirley exclaimed. "If you've got history books, I need to read them."

Liz chuckled. "We don't have actual books." Her large eyes glistened and reflected H's body back to her like a looking glass. She swam around H in a circle. "The water sees all; the water knows all. The molecules exist with nature, and we cannot survive without her. We are water."

H tried to understand but needed more. "Do we read the water?"

"Not quite, but close. The water feeds the grass, the flowers, the trees. The Little Cedar Spirit Tree soaks up the water with her roots. She does not grow upward—she grows inward."

"The water feeds the histories to the tree . . . so we must read the histories from the tree," H speculated, "like a deconstructed book." Somehow, she understood. Her silver tail reflected Liz's glowing metallic scales.

"Precisely," Liz confirmed. "Gnarled is our tree by the centuries of loss, but her scars make her beautiful, as there is much love in these waters. She has watched over this lake and will continue to watch over this lake for all eternity. She feels what we feel, collectively, from the depths to the shores."

H locked eyes with Shirley and knew they were both thinking about the woman standing watch over the water. "I'm looking for information on Nancy Sturgeon. She's the oldest known resident of the lake and might have information that can help me defeat my attackers."

"Grab ahold of the root," Liz instructed. "Tell her what you need, and open your mind." Liz flicked her tail and it glinted in the darkness, a candle in a dark room.

H closed her eyes and clasped onto the exposed root protruding from the rock ceiling. She opened her mind for nature's wooden chandelier. "I need to find Nancy Sturgeon," she implored. "Please help me find where she lives."

Shirley grabbed a root next to H and listened in.

Whispers surrounded H as her mind's eye saw a vision of rushing waters and bubbles. It felt as though she were moving down a twisting, turning waterslide. Clarity broke through the television static, and she saw a sturgeon with a noticeable nick in its tail, swimming peacefully across the bottom of the lake. The vision gained momentum, taking her from the depths of the sea to the recognizable rock structures of the Apostle Islands. The sturgeon swam onward to a waterway and turned down what appeared to be a river. The water wasn't as deep as before. The sturgeon looked up and saw a white-and-blue metal lift bridge. She continued past large brick buildings, then stopped at a rock hole—similar to the one H was in now—marked by a large gray boulder. The sturgeon entered the rock hole and kept swimming onward, downward, deep below until she was surrounded by darkness.

H opened her eyes, startled by the vision that now encompassed her brain. She expected Nancy to be in deep open waters, but instead she chose a shallow waterway to a secret hideout only accessible through a tunnel of sorts.

"The first time is always such a rush," said Liz. "The water has a way of showing us exactly what we need to quench our thirst for knowledge."

"I'm dizzy," Shirley yelped. "That was a trip through class five rapids!"

"Enough with the water puns already!" a voice said from the cavern entrance. "Did that mermaid ever show up?" The words slowed as his giant, radiant eyes fixed on H in the middle of the cavern.

H turned to see another glorious copper walleye illuminating the dark cavern, followed by two much smaller fry.

"This is my mating partner and life companion, Keetaq," said Liz. "He and I are the sole keepers of the Cavern of Liquid Truth, as he calls it."

"It needed a cool fortress name," Keetaq remarked. "I keep an eye on structural integrity, while Liz handles the library functionalities." The glowing fry began to swim around them, weaving in and out of the overhead roots like it was their own personal playground. "Covalent bonds of water do more than hold the molecules together. These are *spicy* polar covalent bonds, and within the atoms lie the knowledge."

"Our fry love living here, and they are growing into little history lovers," Liz said proudly. "Someday this will all be theirs, as it was passed down from Keetaq's family."

"How did you learn so much about water chemistry and its ability to hold history?" H asked curiously. "There is magic involved, right? There's more to the science?"

"We learned it in school, is the running joke," answered Keetaq cheekily. "I come from a long line of hydro-engineers. The magic within is placed by the Creator and works synergistically with the chemistry. Also, we suspect valence electrons feed off drama. They've got a thing for being negatively charged."

"I yearn for that knowledge as well," longed H. "Today I'm on a time crunch, as there is evil afoot. I must make like a mackerel and hit the road toward the Keweenaw."

"Yeah, we saw what happened," admitted Keetaq. "The waters brought us no memories of you for over a week. We thought you were dead."

"You've been watching H?" Shirley inquired. "What a grand show that must be!"

"Her water memories are some of the most exciting!" Keetaq declared. "We've been waiting for new contributions to the memory bank since the attack. The lake brings us a lot of content every day, and we have to sort through it to find the important matters. We have millions of historic reels of fish pooping." The small fry giggled.

"Revna landed in the tree and said you were coming," revealed Liz. "We heard the whisper of her feathers filter down through the roots."

"Of course she did," remarked H, completely unsurprised by her debonair feathered friend.

"We wish you the best in your travels, and may the sea fates be kind," invoked Liz, blessing their journey.

"Thank you for everything. I hope to return someday when I have more time!" H swam through the tunnel leading to the cavern as she said her goodbye.

"I want to revisit this place again someday," yearned Shirley. "I know the land history quite well and would love to explore the memories of the water." Liz smiled and bobbed her head. Shirley, realizing H had gone, scooted out to catch up.

"H," Shirley yelled. "Where are we going?"

"East toward Houghton," H commanded.

"Ahh, Yoopers!" Shirley squealed with glee.

H couldn't move her mermaid body fast enough. Part of her feared another lamprey attack—fewer stops meant fewer opportunities for the creatures to latch on. She didn't want to stop in fear that it could give the predatory bastards a chance to catch hold. Her anxious mind found comfort in following the shoreline, much like in the vision. She was going to trace the journey of Nancy Sturgeon like her life depended on it . . . because, indeed, it probably did.

H journeyed across the open water, with loyal sidekick Shirley by her side, toward the Apostle Islands, from which she could follow the shoreline all the way to the Keweenaw. Her body and mind raced in tandem. As she left Minnesota waters, she said, "Hello, Wisconsin. Same water, different jurisdiction. Silly humans and their invisible borders."

"Greetings, Cheeseheads," bellowed Shirley so the whole state could hear her. "The government has a fetish for fine print and absolute control. We know the water has a spirit and will all her own, human laws be damned."

Time passed reliably as they swam on, with H poking her head up for a peek here and there. She could see the Apostle Islands in the distance. Aware that humans frequently occupied the beautiful area, she kept her journey deep enough to hide from prying eyes.

From the rocks below, she could tell she was passing Bear Island, Otter Island, and Cat Island. The rock formations here were the most exquisite on the whole lake, but their proximity to shore made it easy for humans to lurk in the fickle waters. Coniferous trees grew out of the rocks, reflecting in shallow pools of blue-green water, capturing the hearts of photographers galore.

Breaking the silence, H spoke to Shirley. "Black bears live on the Apostle Islands," she said. "It seems odd because they are much smaller than Isle Royale, but bears have never made it to Isle Royale."

"Really?" Shirley asked with surprise. "I've never given a thought to bears residing on islands."

"Stockton Island is a black bear playground," explained H. "I like to watch the cubs play in spring but can't get close because the humans are all over the place."

"I can see why! This part of the lake is so beautiful. It looks like it was carved by the hands of God himself."

"Nesting birds love it here, but some of them gossip like gulls. They'd be fun to talk to if we weren't in a hurry."

"Indigenous Nations called this area home for hundreds of years," relayed Shirley. "A French explorer named the islands after the twelve Apostles, but they already had proper designations from the locals."

"Humans have big egos," H agreed. "Somehow, history feels like a contest of the big bitchy egos all trying to out-bitch one another. Why is it always the men?"

Shirley smiled. "Have you heard the history of Madeline Island?"

"Not in depth," H admitted. "I do know it's the biggest and most populated."

"Madeline Island was a spiritual ground for the Ojibwe," Shirley murmured. "The Great Spirit had led the people to an area rich in natural resources, especially the wild rice growing on the waters of the bay. Chief White Crane's daughter Madeline, namesake of the island, married a French fur trader. She helped her tribe thrive and her husband become successful in the fur trade."

"I love a strong female lead." H wished she could have befriended Madeline.

"When the government tried to remove the Chippewa from the area, Chief Buffalo fought the United States for the right to their lands. They signed the treaty of La Pointe in 1842, establishing reservations. You might be interested to know the Isle Royale agreements happened two years later, after a holdup on British territory clarifications."

"Now Madeline Island's sacred lands are a hot spot for tourism and rich people," H sighed. "I've even seen cars drive on the ice from Bayfield to reach them in the winter."

"America is but a melting pot of hot wild rice soup," quipped Shirley. "She has scalded many along the way."

"The story does seem vaguely familiar." H shrugged. "I wish I could visit La Pointe Indian Cemetery on Madeline Island and talk to the ghosts. The humans seem to think a lot of haunting happens there."

"Here's a thought," schemed Shirley. "When this is all over, you can head back to the Witch Tree and see early island life unfold before your eyes."

"Even more motivation for me to find Nancy and beat these skeevy, miscreant Reefers!" H cheered.

They reached Michigan Island, and H knew they had passed all twenty-two islands, and made a beeline toward the Porcupine Mountains, from which she could follow the shoreline north. She refocused her thoughts, which had scattered like driftwood on the rocky shore. Motivation ignited her soul as she realized all the amazing things she could discover through the recordings made by the water.

"We're headed toward the Porkies!" exclaimed Shirley. "The forest there is billions of years old and considered an old-growth forest! The rolling mountains are a sight to behold."

"They're beautiful," agreed H. "My favorite time to visit is in the fall, when the leaves turn yellow, orange, and red."

"I also enjoy winter, when the snow sprinkles them like sugar on a delicious donut," replied Shirley. "If you could travel inland, you would see some breathtaking waterfalls and basalt rock formations."

"My friend Fury the cougar lives here," said H. "She always has the best stories."

"Large predatory cats are glorious beasts—the epitome of power and grace."

"I dunno . . . Nebula may actually be more vicious."

Shirley chuckled.

In the realm of Michigan waters, H popped up to see her beloved Porkies, then followed the rocky shoreline north. Old, wise trees grew out of the earth for miles. This was one of H's favorite spots to watch the sun rise and set. The loquacious waters splashed rhythmically as night encroached on the sky's perimeter. She was just in time for one of those candy-coated sunset treats, which did not disappoint with an exquisite excess of pink and a splash of orange.

As the scratchy woolen cloak of night descended upon the lake, H continued north, tracing the outline of the Upper Peninsula. In the dark, she felt safer near the surface, where she could poke out and peek at the earth whenever she pleased. Shirley danced across the water. Once they had passed Ontonagon, human activity near the shoreline decreased substantially.

"The Upper Peninsula is proudly known as the Copper Country," said Shirley in her tour guide voice. "At one point in time, she was the world's largest source of copper."

"Humans sure do love shiny minerals," H observed. "How do you think dull minerals feel about that bias?"

"Well, humans had a particularly ferocious appetite for copper, especially for uses in technology like electricity. It began with a man named Douglass Houghton, the prestigious geologist for whom the city was named," explained Shirley. "People from all over Europe immigrated to one of the snowiest places in North America to work in the mines."

"That sounds like a hard life," replied H. "Manual labor and blizzards? No thanks."

"It is rumored that this area of the country has some of the highest populations of ghosts," whispered Shirley.

"I suppose they've never considered the waters of the Great Lakes as a contender," chuckled H.

"Ghosts can be friendly or harbor vengeance and resentment," said Shirley. "I saw it on that television program Sam watches. Anyway, when the mines closed, most of the people moved elsewhere."[86]

They had reached the Keweenaw Waterway, and H knew they had to use stealth moves. Spying eyes in Houghton or Hancock might spot a large fin in the water.

H approached the Portage Lake Lift Bridge, connecting the cities of Houghton and Hancock, and realized her squad was probably wondering about her whereabouts. She poked her head out of the water and snapped a delightful night photo of the bridge all lit up. The hillside covered with old houses graced the background like a time machine to the past. H sent Sam the picture with a note saying she was doing alright and looking for Nancy with Shirley.

"I love swimming under the bridge," grinned H as she and Shirley passed below the cheerful white-and-blue metal construction. "It lifts up and down like the bridge in Duluth!"

"It was originally a wooden swing bridge when they made it in the 1800s. The current structure is the result of multiple upgrades," added Shirley.

"How do you know all this?" marveled H.

"I'm familiar with a lot of Lake Superior history," answered Shirley. "I'm a bit of a fan."

H hadn't been near Houghton in quite some time, and although she was in a hurry, she filled her eyes with the bliss in front of her. Aged brick buildings with faded painted signs lined the downtown area. People drank and ate out on a large wooden deck overlooking

[86] Let's be transparent (ghost joke, LOL), a lot of work is required to move eight feet of snow with just a Yooper scoop shovel. Life was hard up north; it took moxie to simply survive. Also, when the mining industry died, the shipping activity dwindled along with it.

the water as music and muffled conversation raced through the night. Women laughed and made "woo" noises. The air faintly smelled of delicious artisan pizza. Warm streetlights illuminated the once busy mining town that was now flush with college students.

H continued onward, pausing for a moment to admire a turreted yellow mansion close to downtown. It was her absolute favorite antique house, and she couldn't help but imagine what it would be like to live there. It had large clear windows overlooking the water and ski hill across, but also intricate and colorful decorative stained glass windows. The windows were so large they were probably a hazard to the poor birds, especially the grouse.

Faint voices snapped H out of her daydream and nighttime sightseeing, and she tuned in to aggressively eavesdrop. Shirley joined in on the spying.

The first voice pierced the night like a dagger trying to make a noise that resembled singing. "I can see paradise by the lift bridge lights."

"That's not how it goes!" squealed another. Giggling followed.

It was dark and quiet, not a human to be seen as H moved closer. Chipmunks. Three chipmunks were bebopping near the water. One of them staggered as they opened their mouth to make more off-key singing noises. H didn't know many of the creatures in these parts, so she figured it was worth making their acquaintance before continuing onward.

"Hello," said H. "It sounds like you guys are having one heck of an evening."

"Oh my God, it's a water woman! How much fruit did we have?" The trio scurried in frantic circles, trying to hide behind one another. "And an old lady ghost!" they shrieked. They grabbed at each other and at their own faces, little paws all in a tizzy.

"I'm not a woman, really. I'm a mermaid. The name is H, and I live in Lake Superior. Perhaps you've heard of me?" H splashed her silvery tail, a quick glimmer in the dark water.

"We have heard legends of a mermaid but thought it was just another tall mining tale," slurred the chipmunk in front. "My name is Carol, and this here is Toni and Elithe." They appeared less frazzled now and came forward toward the water all in a line. Their noses twitched as though trying to legitimize her claim via smell.

Shirley introduced herself. "My name is Shirley, and I am indeed an elderly woman."

Toni had a stumpy front leg. She crouched in the grass while looking H up and down. "Well, Mermaid of Lake Superior," she prodded, "what are you doing in our backyard?"

"Today I swam all the way from the North Shore of Minnesota." H stopped her thought for a moment as she realized she was justified in taking a moment to catch her human breath. "I'm looking for Nancy Sturgeon, who allegedly lives in a secret underwater cave around these parts."

"We don't know any fish," revealed Carol. "Just a few birds and the man in the yellow house. Seagulls talk a lot, and sometimes we listen, but they're mostly full of sloppy white excrement."

"Gulls like to gossip, right, H?" Shirley chuckled.

H's curiosity was piqued. "The man in the yellow house? The beautiful yellow house?" She pointed up the hill at the gorgeous abode.

"Beautiful indeed," gawked Shirley.

Elithe shrugged and hopped forward. "Yep, that house up the treacherous hill. The man who built the house still lives there, along with a bunch of rowdy young women."

"Except he's dead now. Jeez!" Carol whispered it loudly as though it were a secret. Her tiny nostrils flared passionately.

"Oh, so he's a *ghost*, not a pimp!" exclaimed Shirley. "Whew! I thought it was a brothel."

Toni started talking with her one paw and stumpy arm. "You see, this house was built of the best lumber. Every corner of the house was built with affection and lots of money. It's been kept up better than all the others too."

"James was filthy rich," Elithe confided. "They didn't skimp on exquisite decor. You should see the elaborate brass light fixtures and the floral wall paintings!" She swooned.

"James?" H tilted her head, dark hair dripping.

"James Pryor," Carol babbled. "He worked in mining but not as a grunt. Business fella, made a lot of money running the mines. He had a lumberyard too."

"That sounds familiar," muttered Shirley.

"How do I know that name?" H thought out loud. "I've heard it before."

"He grew up in England and moved here with his parents, then moved back again," added Toni. "He even at one point worked for the company that helped build the canal you're swimming in right now."

"He's very protective of his former house," warned Carol. "She was his pride and joy. It's almost creepy."

"He doesn't much talk to us," sniffled Toni. "We're 'vile rodent filth bags.'"

"Oh, honey," comforted Shirley.

"Maybe he'd talk to you if you hadn't plucked his knob-and-tube wiring like a bloody guitar string," barked Elithe. "You brought that on yourself." And that's when the chipmunks giggled so violently that they rolled on the ground in the green grass.

"I'm not the one who chewed a hole in the wall!" exclaimed Toni. "Blame Nat for that one."

"Um, Nat? Where *is* Nat?" Carol's mortified eyes searched in all directions as she scampered in a circle.

"Nat ate too much fruit and passed out behind the back porch," squeaked Elithe.

"I thought she went to see a squirrel about a nut," answered Toni quickly.

"We should probably get going," said H. "It's getting late, and I need to find a sturgeon."

"What kind of fruit intoxicates a chipmunk?" inquired Shirley, with both curiosity and concern.

"The kind the rowdy women soak in vodka," proclaimed Carol seriously. "So, our sister Nat thought the fruit in the trash was just normal discarded fruit. Nope, it was a liquor trap."

"By the time she figured it out, she was one strawberry too late. We had just started snacking, so we're still standing," sloshed Toni, wrapping her stumpy arm around the shoulders of Elithe and Carol.

"We'll be OK," assured Carol. "This is just like the blue gelatin incident of 2019." She looked up wistfully, basking in the reminiscence. Toni and Elithe snapped their paws and waved their arms in agreement.

"It will wear off," promised H. "My squirrel friend Angie has gotten into her share of sun-fermented berries, although I think it was intentional."

Shirley's curiosity got the best of her and she had to ask. "What happened to your paw, Toni?"

"Those rowdy women set traps and tried to kill us," Toni sputtered forcefully. "There I was, just trying to get in from all the snow and warm up. I saw a piece of cheese and thought they had graciously left me a snack. Nope—not a buffet. My reflexes were fast enough that the trap only got my paw, so I chewed my way out and warned the others. Goddamn women put my paw in the dumpster! The audacity!"

"Paw-dacity," corrected H.

"One of the women chased Toni out of the house with a railing spindle," Carol stammered.

"We spend most of our time outdoors nowadays," confessed Elithe. "Except in the winter, we can sometimes sneak in the basement through the commotion. The ladies of the house like to build snow sculptures, and it is choreographed mayhem."

"They also boil water just to freeze it," yipped Carol. "Humans are seagull-level odd sometimes."

"Speaking of water," H interjected, "we should really hit the seas, Shirley."

"The gals, a bunch of total nerds, are weirdly obsessed with anchors. Nautical chic is always in, I suppose," Elithe mentioned astutely, lifting her arms in the air as if to question it all.

H, ready to leave, glanced out at the house and saw a man in a suit looking out the window. He had graying beard and wavy hair flat against the top of his head. Despite her familiarity with ghosts, she felt a chill go up her spine. "Is that James?" she asked.

"Yeppers indeed, eh," said Carol.

"His portrait is in the hallway of the *Algoma*, but he looks much younger." H felt victorious in placing the memory. "Why do successful businessmen always look so stern?"

"It's because they're hiding something and are grumpy about how much their suits cost," Shirley snarked.

"His stare feels cold," shuddered H. "Which reminds me, there is darkness lurking in the lake, and we should probably move on before we, too, fall victim to toxic fruit."

"I suppose so," agreed Shirley.

H snapped a quick photo of her favorite house before leaving—and did a double-take at the unexpected guest in the image. As she peered intently at the house, James touched his finger to the windowpane, and it started to freeze just like the frame on the Algoma.

You did this, he mouthed. He proceeded to take his finger and write the word *FROSTBITE* across the glass.

"Now, why didn't I think of communicating like that?" Shirley tutted.

"I don't know what to make of James freezing the window up there, but I find your company absolutely delightful. We're on a mission and need to skedaddle," said H to her three new chipmunk friends.

"Likewise," said Elithe, trying to stand up straight. "It has been our pleasure to meet you, real living mermaid legend of the greatest lake of all! God bless the cryptids."

"Be careful out there," jabbered Toni. "I wouldn't want you to lose a paw too!" Carol and Elithe chuckled from the ground.

Shirley said, "Please excuse us. Goodbye, ladies. Make smart choices, or at least mediocre ones!"

"Bye, new friends," H said. "Be safe. And watch for eagles!"

The waterside karaoke continued as they bobbed away, and the high-pitched chipmunk songs echoed across the portage. H was already by the university the next time she poked her head out of the water. She remembered the tall brick building resembling male genitalia, a building with large windows overlooking the portage, and a very long building that looked like a ship with dozens of small windows. There was the small open area where humans parked their snowmobiles in winter, which is all H remembered from a choppy, icy day a few years back.

H imagined what it would be like to be human and have the gift of science at your fingertips, with microscopes and machines at your disposal to study the world. Imagine the glorious books in that remodeled college library, and the extensive local archives full of black-and-white photographs! This place could be heaven. Nearing the performing arts center meant she was near the end of campus and needed to find the rock with the hidden portal, shifting the focus of her excitement toward the task at hand.

H dove to the sandy, mucky bottom of the canal, where there wasn't a whole lot for the eyes to observe. Not a soul, besides Shirley, was out for a midnight swim. A lack of vegetation made the ground completely visible, which had gentle ripple marks in the sand from the flow of the current. A large gray boulder sat alone along a steep shore side, resembling the one from the Witch Tree vision.

"That's the rock," said Shirley.

From a distance, there was no visible opening; but as H neared, she could see the hole had filled up with sand. She cupped her hands to scoop away enough sediment to enter, working sloppily and briskly. It didn't need to be pretty. She tried to make her hands and arms as large as possible, like a half-human Yooper scoop. Shirley floated by her side, cheering her on. It took a good fifteen minutes, but finally a tunnel entrance emerged and ominously gaped before them.

Chapter Fourteen

DARKNESS ENGULFED H AND SHIRLEY like a raccoon eating a piece of blueberry pie (except much cleaner). The dark, winding pathway beneath Portage Lake was cavernless and varied little in size.

"We've entered the intestines of a giant beast," murmured H. "We'll be swimming for an eternity."

"The trail has spiraled so much. I thought we were headed toward Torch Lake, but now, I'm not certain," Shirley wavered. "Maybe the tunnel isn't even directed toward a body of water."

"I keep telling myself there's a pot of gold at the end of this twisted rainbow." They continued to swim in silence.

As H descended into icy-cold darkness, her mind wandered like a spotted baby deer in a fairytale forest illuminated by rainbow moonbeams. Glaciers had once covered this entire area, long before the Great Lakes even existed. She longed to see a real glacier, but not if it meant remodeling the entire planet. H overheard a conversation among humans near Duluth about how the final remaining fragment of the glacier that formed the Great Lakes, the Laurentide Ice Sheet, will completely melt, much like her heart the first time she met George the poodle. Warming of the arctic was an unfortunate yet undeniable truth. H could point fingers all day, but blame never got shit done. To her dismay, the humans of the world in power didn't seem to love the planet as much as she did. She wanted to meet a polar bear before she died. She wanted to breach with orcas during the summer solstice and worship the sun. H didn't even know if she could survive in salt water; still, she wished for the gift of teleportation or at least flight. Maybe she could send Sam on adventures so she could get some pictures, as wanderlust could be very contagious. Perhaps she could sneak into a zoo . . .

Shirley was just happy to be out of the house.

H dropped her hustle as she heard voices rich with the sanctimonious glow of elder beings. She rounded a dark corner, Shirley right on her tail, and the two found themselves in a large, sparsely populated cavern. White crayfish scampered across the floor, orange eyes flashing. Pearlescent fish swam in perfect synchronized schools.

"Oh, for cute," gushed Shirley, peering down at the luminous crustaceans.

H gasped. It was rumored that the floor of Lake Superior, at least in some parts, was indeed the roof of a cave that housed freshwater species never seen before.

Shirley and H proceeded to the center of the cavern in awe. Schools of fish stopped swimming and stared. A few sturgeons rested near the bottom. H twirled around and found herself face-to-face with the largest-finned being she had ever seen. Its large gray caudal fin was distinctively sharklike, and its body was long and smooth—a textbook specimen, minus a nick in the tail. Wanting to ask a million questions without looking like a blubbering fangirl, H was left tongue-tied like an anchor rope.

"You've gotta be Nancy," concluded Shirley, unphased by the underwater celebrity. "Your ancestors were alive when dinosaurs walked the earth! Your species has undergone millions of years of evolution—oh, heavens. I got a bit off topic. My name is Shirley, and I'm pleased to make your acquaintance."

"Likewise," said Nancy. "I have waited for years to meet you, Mermaid H. I hope your journey to the lair was fulfilling." She rotated to look H right in the eye. "I do not believe you truly know who you are, or you wouldn't feel quite so flabbergasted." She circled H, inspecting her shoulder. "Your injuries have healed nicely, although we carry our scars for all eternity."

H met Nancy's gaze. "Emotional or physical scars?"

"It's impossible to exist without both, my dear."

H didn't know what to ask or if she was going to get real answers or Revna answers. She started with, "Why was I attacked?"

"Invasive species succeed by disrupting the circle of life and altering the food chain. They take more than the earth can give," offered Nancy.

"They're here to make the lake their personal Glensheen Mansion and screw the current residents in the process?" H asked the question with fire in her eyes. She wanted revenge and didn't care if that made her come off a bit ugly.

Nancy chuckled politely. "That's one way of putting it. They'll outcompete native organisms for resources, leaving just enough to reproduce and feed themselves thoroughly. You pose the largest threat of any being in this entire lake. Eliminate the threat, dominate the terrain. Death feeds new life."

"How awful," sputtered Shirley.

H finally asked awkwardly, "Why am I perceived as a threat? Do I have a secret destiny, or is this my hero origin story?"

Nancy looked up, a bit startled at her directness. "You, my dear, are Hanging Cloud Astrid, daughter of the Norse Gods and the Anishinaabe Spirit Elders known as Moon Keepers. Your sole purpose was to protect these waters. Without water, life ceases to exist."

"What?" H blinked slowly. A chill traveled from the back of her neck all the way down to her tail.

"Come again?" said Shirley. "I think our girl is in shock."

"As explorers visited the region, they found their travels exhaustingly dangerous. The Norse Gods watched over their sons on these journeys. Odin had a vision from his beloved raven about the death and destruction of the water. He reached out to the spirits already present around the lake and watching over the living. Odin needed to return home but did not want to leave the Great Lakes without hope, as fresh water—especially flush with fish—was a gift from the Old Gods. He'd never seen anything quite like Lake Superior."

"What in the world are you talking about, Nancy Sturgeon?" H stuttered.

"It's ironic how water gives us life, but the waters of Lake Superior also harbor death," Shirley thought out loud.

"You were forged from the ice of the North Shore, a bolt of lightning, and a piece of my tail." Nancy motioned toward her damaged tail fin.

Shirley gently rubbed H's back with love.

"Infused with the powers of the Norse Gods, Thor himself placed lightning in your veins. Freya gifted you knowledge from her personal library and love of animals; the Moon Keepers gave you the gift of communication encompassing all creatures, alive and dead. The Moon Keepers' Woman of Solstice plucked a star from the sky and encased it in your heart for you to be a beacon in the darkness and guide those who may be lost."

H lifted her hands to her heart.

"You're made of sky glitter," Shirley whispered, peering through her spectacles at H's star-dusted tail.

"The Moon Keepers offered Mishipeshu a copper sacrifice to ensure your safety. Odin's wolves howled to provide you nourishment and a warrior's blessing. You were born in the water inspired by the Nibiinaabe mermaids and encapsulated with a celestial timer to release you into the waters when times grew rough. After your creation, the Norse Gods returned home. The Moon Keepers continue to spiritually guide this area, but those who believe in their Earth Mother have dwindled. Much has happened between then and now."

"Nibiinaabe mermaids?" asked Shirley, butchering the double vowels.

"The half-fish, half-woman is not a new concept to the Anishinaabe," replied Nancy. "Aquatic fairies have graced the waters of the lake in times past."

"Why am I made out of your tail?" H questioned, somewhat horrified.

"Oh, heavens! It was not a burden that brought me any pain. I was chosen as one of the leaders of the lake fish—or Council of Fins, as it is now called—to gift you my ability to swim and have a capacity to enjoy history and learn from it. My ancestry is notable."

"I won't ask how old you are if you don't ask how old I am," responded Shirley with a wink.

Nancy nudged H to lighten the mood a bit. "You should have seen Thor and the Thunderbird debating who had the best powers. The storm was so bad that it sunk a couple of ships."

H stared forward at Nancy, sea-blue eyes revealing turbulent rumination.

Nancy's tail bobbed. "Your silence is deafening, mermaid," started Nancy. "To which we shall begin, your life has a definite purpose. You are the mer-woman water defender of the greatest freshwater lake in the world."

"I always felt that deep down I was Indigenous at heart. I could feel it in my bones," H confessed. "How did I never know my full name?"

"I suspect it was lost in translation during your hibernation period."

"I hibernated . . . like a bear?" wondered H.

"It was a magically induced sleep," answered Nancy. "You were alive for over a hundred years before your cocoon, so to speak, released you into the wild. Your creators could sense the lake would eventually be in some sort of danger. They wanted to save you for battle. The Moon Keepers have other spirits guarding the lake, and you've met at least one of them."

"The antlered lynx," Shirley blurted.

"Yeah," agreed H. "I see the compromise and marriage of two cultures. I represent the best of both worlds."

"The Gods and Moon Keepers worked together to make you powerful. After all, the protector of the lake must be more powerful than the lake itself," explained Nancy.

"Why didn't you go find H and tell her where she came from?" Shirley sputtered. "Poor girl. Had no family, no purpose, no sense of being!"

"She made her own family," observed Nancy. "We never expected her to gain so much love in friendship. Love makes one even more powerful."

Shirley prodded, "How'd the name come about?"

"You were named for Hanging Cloud, the only Ojibwe woman ever granted the honor of full warrior. She even had permission to carry weapons and hunt. She was of the bear clan, which specializes in defense and healing. Modern historical records tell very little of her story, besides the men she married. People today may never know her true greatness. We chose to honor her with you. Astrid means 'beautiful god,' so they weren't straining themselves too much with that one." Nancy explained it all with such precision and tact. "It's basic Norse."

"So that explains why Ursala told me to do the clan proud," confirmed H. "I didn't realize I was a claw-holding member." She clutched the bear claw from Speed.

"Indeed," replied Nancy. "You should have seen the ceremony. We were under the old-growth trees in what is now Hiawatha National Forest, gathered around a fire under the moonlight. I was a lot smaller back then. The elders filled a birch canoe with water, put me in it, and carried me onto land! I've never had such an adventure. You'll have to ask Revna about it sometime."

Exasperated, H exclaimed, "Revna was there?"

"Shut the front door!" squealed Shirley.

Nancy chuckled. "She's a lot older than she looks. At the time, she was just a child, accompanied by her parents, Huginn and Muninn. Keeps a secret like a body in a locked tomb, that one. Her parents were much more talkative. Revna serves multiple Gods in different realms and always gets the job done without meddling in the affairs of mortals."

"She never even called me by my name," sang H.

"I know that song!" said Shirley.

"You would have had so many questions," said Nancy. "Revna never would have answered them. It was a risk to let the events unfold, but I think this is what the universe intended."

"I was injured very badly. I thought I was dying. Am I . . . a mortal?" H asked meekly.

"Yes and no. You have powers, you know, more than just talking to animals," Nancy relayed brightly. "You've made us all so proud thus far, H. Making the creatures of the world important and bringing together those on land and sea has accomplished much for species everywhere. You eat invasive zebra mussels with delight, and you clean up plastic and trash out of the water for fun. The time you cleaned up the small oil leak had us cheering for days. We never thought you'd have a human friend, for that matter."

"So . . . ?" H waited for a real answer.

Nancy offered up, "I didn't think you could die considering the powers used by the Norse Gods to create you. Your near-death experience was confounding. You do have godlike powers, which you must learn to harness, so you're more like a demigod in all technicality. Honestly, I think if your powers would have been engaged for protection, you would have never become so ill."

H realized Nancy didn't really have all the answers. H summarized tactlessly, "I am a threat to the invasive sea lamprey-like creatures who attacked me because I am a demigod created to spill the brains of any asshole who tries to flub up these pristine waters. I am a predatory student loan coming to collect interest until the day they die."

Nancy smiled at her crudeness and excess of passion. "Yes, my dear. Exactly that. We need you to fully harness the gifts you have been bestowed. And, for the record, I'm not sure those assholes you're up against have brains!"

Nancy Sturgeon was feisty. H loved that. "What do we know about the current threat—the Reefers?"

"Well, I don't get out as much anymore, but I do have my ears and eyes on the lake," said Nancy. "It's rumored they are headed toward the Soo Locks to show the rest of them to their new boastful residence. Strength in numbers appears to be their attack strategy."

"Alert the papers," yelped Shirley. "Or even the gulls!"

Nancy swished her long body back and forth.

"Loss of fish due to invasives overfeeding would be catastrophic,"[87] huffed H.

Nancy nodded. "Many factors come into play when you consider the entire ecosystem saga. Lake Superior's temperature has been increasing at a faster rate than many other bodies of water. We postulate that within twenty years, the lake may cease to freeze over in winter ever again."

"If the lake gets too warm, she'll start giving up her dead," exclaimed H, wide-eyed. Bodies surfacing from the depths would be a living nightmare. Would a ghost whose body was recovered continue to haunt their beloved ships? She shuddered.

Shirley cringed.

[87] In the early 1900s, the lake was flush with fish. In the past century, fisheries have decreased tenfold. Fish populations have never rebounded, much like the animal populations of those victim to the fur trade.

"The humans could have done us all a solid and stopped driving their cars so much," said Nancy. "The culture of freedom and exploration has deep roots, and I'm afraid the owl in the ore mine has been a skeleton for at least a decade."

"I was hoping the millennials would kill the bottled-water industry and then come for the giant gas-guzzling RVs as well as demanding higher automobile mileage standards. A girl can dream, I suppose. If they weren't working so hard to simply exist, I'm sure this would all be history." H sighed.

"I always saw so much potential in renewable energy," added Shirley. "Politicians don't care about the planet anymore. They all sold their souls to the oil companies."

"Just like the humans, Reefers are going to harvest the resources until nothing is left. Then what?" H demanded, voice cracking.

"Those who lack foresight make up for it with ignorance," declared Nancy.

"Much like many men in history, unfortunately," Shirley agreed.

"Well, I'm not the crusty old patriarchy, and I won't fail the most innocent, vulnerable creatures of this planet," promised H. "Without water, we are nothing—every last one of us."

Nancy nodded sincerely. "That's the spirit, my dear Hanging Cloud Astrid. You must be on your way, though. Evil waits for no merwoman. No pressure."

"Wait, what about powers?" H was confused, overwhelmed, and distracted. "What will protect me in a fin fight?"

"Lighting and ice." Nancy nudged H's arm. "Look at your birthmark. You are bestowed with the powers of that from which you were made."

H always forgot about her tattoo—er, birthmark. She traced the line with her fingertips as it all suddenly came together. It *was* a lightning bolt forming a snowflake, not tree roots. Lightning and ice. Electric and cold. Shocking and frigid. "But how . . . ?"

"That, my dear, you'll have to figure out on your own. Empty your thoughts, and channel the essence of the molecules that form you," said Nancy. "Thor tends to be a bit theatrical at times." She smiled and nudged her mermaid. "To exit the cavern easily, follow the tunnel in front of us. You will pop out of Lake Superior near Copper Harbor."

H had a lot of information to process. She wanted to explore the underwater cavern, study her ancestors, and give Revna a hard time for making her dance like a puppet. Starting toward the dark tunnel, she turned to Nancy and said, "Thank you, Nancy Sturgeon. You'll be hearing from me again, I'm sure."

"I don't doubt that for one second. You know where I'll be! Be brave, be strong, and, most importantly, be electrically charming yet frigid."

"Goodbye, old fish!" yelled Shirley.

"Goodbye, old lady!" replied Nancy.

The exit tunnel spanned much less distance than the entrance cave. "Why do I feel like we're being flushed down a toilet?" asked Shirley.

H wondered how vast the caverns were and if multiple caves were connected by passageways. It was rumored that hundreds of years ago, an explorer discovered underwater caves and died trying to go deeper than his suit could allow. Perhaps she would someday find him haunting these depths. Then again, it could just be another Lake Superior myth.

Chapter Fifteen

NIGHT HAD NOT YET LIFTED when H and Shirley neared Copper Harbor. H popped out of the water, did a 360-degree check for humans, and punched out a frantic text to Samantha: "OMG. Found Nancy. I was forged by the Norse Gods and Moon Keepers to protect the lake. Superpowers TBD. *Lightning bolt emoji. Snowflake emoji.* The Reefers are coming! We must cut them off at the east side of the lake. I've got a plan. Shirley says hi. Tell the furballs I miss them. *Heart emoji.*"

Sam responded with a simple "OMG WTF." Another text came back: "Nigig says he's not a furball, but Fluffy fits the bill." Next came a selfie of Nigig with Blue poking his head up, crazy-eyed, in the background. She smiled with her mouth and her heart.

With a swift tail surge, H propelled herself toward Isle Royale, where she would spread word of the attackers and warn the others. Her lake trout family had initially reported strange encounters around the reef, so she would relay the full description of the creatures there. Shirley stayed on her six, at the ready. Information would travel fast if H found the correct cascade. Bird-to-bird news traveled faster than viral Twitter memes, especially with Revna involved. No doubt the lake's inhabitants—furred, finned, and ectoplasmic alike—had already heard their mermaid was in danger.

H approached Isle Royale in record time. The air was still, the waves were calm, and not a human was in sight. The crisp smell of the impending morning danced in her nostrils as she surfaced in Siskiwit Bay. "This better work," she said, propping herself on a rock near shore. H cupped her hands around her mouth and let out a high-pitched bark, almost a scream. Hopefully it was just the noise she needed. H repeated the screeching yelp one more time.

Shirley popped up beside her. "Chaos!" she yelled. "Chaaaos! It's your new friend, Shirley!"

There was a quiet rustle in the tall grass near shore, followed by an eye peering through and blinking slowly. First a little black nose appeared, cautiously followed by the bewhiskered snout of a red fox. The creature was so cute that H immediately wanted to boop that snoot.

"Chaos?" desperation carried through her vocal cords.

"Yes, that's me. Hanging Cloud Astrid . . . you have finally arrived," answered Chaos shyly. "I was looking for you just west of Wright Island a little over a week ago. I've been waiting for you because they said you would come."

H looked puzzled. "Who said what?"

"The Anishinaabe men. They'd seen you before and knew you'd be back for information," replied Chaos. She sat on the damp sand and flicked her bushy tail. "They bring their birch bark canoes ashore every night and walk the island."

"I can't believe I never saw them until just recently. Are they the Moon Keepers who helped make me?"

"No," responded Chaos. "They know the story, though. You are a bit of a legend. They are swift and quiet; you'd need perfect timing to see them."

Foxes were shy and generally needed a little prodding. "Do they have insight to help me battle this evil?"

"Perhaps," she barked quietly. "The men said you have to find some hidden pictographs near the Pictured Rocks to learn how to use your powers. There's a small cave near the turret rock that you can't find unless you're underwater, which used to be accessible for humans hundreds of years ago." Chaos tilted her head sideways, much like a puppy trying to be cute for a treat.

"Oh, great, a hidden quest," muttered H, unenthused. "Well, I trust them. Everything else from their message has come true."

"Yes," Chaos confirmed. "You were saved by a bear, and Revna finally told you something useful."

"We're just missing the Thunderbird," mused H. "Maybe it's waiting for the perfect moment. I'll need strength in battle."

"Perhaps," Chaos replied, timidly breaking into a smile. "We're all here to help you."

"You've got that right, Chaos," cheered Shirley.

Chaos nodded her head and flicked her tail.

"I appreciate that very much," acknowledged H. "What I really need right now is a songbird. Has anyone seen Athena?" Daylight had begun to creep above the tree line to the east. The island was still quiet except for a few chirps and rustling noises in the distance.

"She's a friend of mine," Chaos divulged. She gave a screechy yelp, breaking the silence like a chainsaw. "Sometimes I even sing with her."

H tried to hide her surprise as she peered skyward. Shades of orange and pink painted the horizon, signaling the sun's dramatic entrance.

"Good morning," sang a beautiful voice from above.

"Athena! I'm in dire need of your help," said H, brushing her wet hair out of her face.

Athena gracefully swooped down and landed on the rock in front of H. "Anything," answered Athena quickly, sensing desperation. "We've been looking for you! I was worried."

"Alert the birds, all of them—divers especially. Today, fly for the glory of our dear Lake Superior. The Reefers are coming in even greater numbers, and we must stand our ground, water, and air. Meet me in Whitefish Bay," explained H. "Send a voice or two toward Thunder Bay and a couple more to Duluth, where they can hit the Apostle Islands and Wisconsin shoreline on the way back. Invite any birds you encounter along the way. Arne and his brethren are particularly crucial."

"We're forming a flying bird gang to intimidate the bad guys? Cool!" Athena took to the air. "I'm already on it, sista," she chirped as she flew away.

"More like a diving kill squad." H pivoted to the silently inquisitive fox. "Thank you for the assistance, Chaos. I have so much more to talk about, but I must gather my underwater army."

"I can help recruit," interjected Shirley. "I can head back home and tell every creature I pass to head east. Even if they can't see me, sometimes a ghost whisper can spark an idea. I can at least warn the birds at Sam's house."

"Great idea, Shirley. Get on it, and we'll meet again," said H.

Shirley sank into the lake.

"Goodbye," whispered Chaos. She disappeared into the brush with a flash of her orange tail.

H dove gracefully into the clear water of Siskiwit Bay, heading southeast toward Long Island and the reef where her favorite lake trout frequently schooled. She started to feel frantic and overwhelmed. What if her plan didn't work?

She stopped a moment and turned around in the water as the morning sunlight filtered down the shallow depths and diminished in the deeper water. She glanced over her shoulder, dark hair suspended, and saw a literal glimmer of hope: the dashing glint of silver scales engaged in evasive maneuvers. Her favorite shoal was in their usual spot, and H's gratefulness swelled.

Jayne spoke first, flitting back and forth above her. "Mighty fine morning, there, Mermaid H!"

"We've been searching the seas for you," Zoe blurted out. "Rumor was you had been attacked by Reefers and gone missing."

"We feared you had died! Welcome home." Malcolm swam a circle around her and asked, "To what do we owe the pleasure today, H?"

"The Reefers tried to kill me, and I ended up injured on land," explained H.

"Well, if someone tries to kill you, you should kill them right back," exclaimed Malcolm.

"What did they do to you?" Kaylee asked. Her voice trembled, and her eyes darted toward Simon.

"They wrapped themselves around me and bit my back with their ugly suction mouths until I passed out," answered H.

"They didn't even have the guts to do it to your face?" Malcolm huffed. "That's sleazy."

"They've been feeding around the island—remember those dead whitefish?—and recruiting more of their kind to take over our home. They're coming, and they'll feed on you too. I'm building an army. I need every fish in this lake—every fry, every elder. We're going to Whitefish Bay to build a wall that blocks them from entering the lake. They can't outnumber us if we work together." H lifted her fist in enthusiasm.

"Of course, we can be your living fish fence," Hoban offered. "Where do I enlist?"

"Affirmative," said Zoe. "We will swim with you to protect our water."

"That's exactly what I need," said H. "There's more, though. I need you to sound the alarm. I can't tell all the fish in the lake where to gather; I simply don't have the time. I need you to travel north, south, west, and then east to spread the word. Alert the Council of Fins!"

"The troops need a-rallying," Jayne cheered. "We are finned and furious, baby!"

Inara rotated toward the others. "We need to split up, work fast, and return to the pod. Once everyone's apart, it'll be too easy to get separated." She eyed Malcolm solemnly.

"Dibs on Canada," squealed Kaylee with cheerful enthusiasm, nudging silent Simon with her fin.

"Do you know how you'll know you're in Canadian waters?" Jayne asked.

River eyeballed Jayne. "How?"

"They call it *Eh-2-O*," smirked Jayne, laughing to himself.

"At least he didn't say they put ketchup in it," Kaylee scoffed, rolling her eyes.

"While you all work out the details on who goes where, I'm going to swoosh out of here. I've got one last stop to make before hunting for information on my superpowers," H confirmed, plan falling into place.

River's eyes about exploded. "Your what?"

"I'll explain later," said H as she started to swim away. "Spread the word. Tell every species you see, and tell them to tell their friends. The message must hit everyone! Keep your fins fierce and fabulous." She blew them an underwater kiss, swirled around, and propelled herself eastward with desperate tenacity. "Hey, Malcolm," she added from a distance, "you're not my father!"

She heard him mutter, "Aww, she's gonna leave me suspended!" as she shimmered onward through the water.

H maintained momentum straight past her beloved *Algoma*. Her stomach yearned for Lou's blueberry pancakes and some time to gossip with Frosty, but she persisted. Glorious food could wait, and the fasting would make it even better. H scurried past Rock Harbor Lodge, wondering if Bruce was delighting in tourist mischief.

She turned the corner north like one of Sam's beloved baseball players rounding first. H glided by the *Monarch*, wondering if Betsy the rogue cow was still companion to the ever-kind Jack. Even though H had just made her Isle Royale rounds, she wanted to visit everyone again. There are other ships in the sea, though.

Canoe Rocks welcomed H with open arms, and she honed in on her target. The *Emperor* was nestled cozily in her resting spot, and she could see her favorite navy man, Speed, walking her beloved deck. As H neared the ship, she yelled, "Speed, I really need your help!" Speed looked up from his morning putzing with a look of surprise and delight.

"Oh, dear," muttered Speed. "You best come inside, as we surely know you'll need Wendi's help too."

H nodded and followed Speed into the ship, straight to his lovely captain's quarters. Wendi was sitting in her armchair, reading a book with Penny serenely nestled on her lap. She remained clad in her favorite silk pajamas—a black-and-white floral print—and fluffy house shoes.

Before Wendi could even ask, H blurted it all out: "I was forged by Norse Gods and Anishinaabe Moon Keepers to protect the lake. My full name is Hanging Cloud Astrid. I allegedly possess superpowers relating to lightning and ice, but I do not know exactly what they are or how to use them. If you hadn't yet heard, I was attacked by some of the Reefers and did a stint on shore with a human to recover. The food was amazing—more on that later. The Reefers are plotting an attack on our waters and native species. They're entering from the east, so we're going to cut them off at Whitefish Bay. I'm rounding up as many fish and birds as possible to meet there, hopefully tonight. We're going to build a wall and block their entrance."

"Whoa, darling," trilled Wendi, thirsty for more juicy news regarding her dear friend. "The anxiety from our last visit has been identified!" She threw her arms up in praise. "Thank God it's not a kraken!"

"This is where Speed comes in. I've never gone to war before," said H meekly. "I know I've got heart . . . but I don't have strategic expertise."

Speed nodded and adjusted his ragged ballcap. "In the navy, our goal was always to deter, deny, and defeat our adversaries," started Speed as though he had rattled it off a million times. "Of course, war *at* sea is a little different than war *under* the sea," he continued thoughtfully. "The goal is always to keep your coast free from attack. We did this by destroying the enemy's fleet or shutting down their active ports to prevent ships from setting sail."

H hopped up and gave Speed a giant bear hug. "That's it! That's exactly what we're going for—we need to prevent them from attacking us by disabling them first."

"If you want to go all in, you can block their communication systems." Scratching his beard with one hand, he looked much too pensive for someone wearing flannel. "A competitive edge always exists when you have the stronger, faster fleet. How do you think I got my nickname?"

Wendi cheered, "Operating the ship that out-knotted the others!"

"I have no idea how fast I can even swim," H giggled. "Do you have a device to measure my knots per hour? I'm sure it's competitive after all the water I've covered the past few days."

"The only knots I'm interested in are the pretzel or pastry kind," Wendi admitted, unashamed.

"I would take you up on those in an instant," laughed H. She took a deep breath, returning to her somber pre-battle jitters, and peered back at Speed. "My next task is learning how to use my powers. I was told a cave near Pictured Rocks can help me with that, so I'm going to shake my tail out of here. Sorry for the short visit, and thank you ever so much for the words of wisdom."

"Stop right there," Wendi commanded. "When was the last time you ate? Have you had a single nap in the last twenty-four hours?"

There'd been no time for food, and she hadn't slept since leaving Sam's. "I need to make my way east," she pleaded.

"And you can't spell *east* without E-A-T," Wendi tutted. "Sit. Eat some pastries. Rest your eyes for a moment. You won't win any war on an empty stomach."

"I know. You're right," conceded H. She sat down and grabbed a cinnamon roll. "I'm just anxious."

"We're cheering for you," said Wendi.

It was the last thing H heard before she passed out.

H awoke a few hours later.

"Look at you, refreshed and ready to carry the weight of the world," beamed Wendi.

"Thanks for everything," said H. "I'm ready to find how to use my magic."

"We're always here for you, H," Speed proclaimed. "You've got moxie, and you're gonna leave those knuckleheaded bad guys belly-up." He sprang to his feet. "This might be a cockeyed idea . . ." He didn't bother finishing the thought. "I need to have a chat with my crew of anchor-clankers," he muttered, wandering out to the deck.

H squealed to the hallway after him, "Oh, do I have a story for you about that bear claw!" She made like Speed and got out of there fast because the cave was calling her name, her real name and not the abbreviated version. Tales from the land of the living would have to wait.

"Well, now I'm going to sit and wonder," said Wendi. "How can they both just leave us hanging like that? The anticipation will drive me bonkers."

Penny meowed in agreement. "That must be why they call her *Hanging* Cloud Astrid."

H knew exactly where to go. The turret, which resembled those adorning her favorite Michigan mansion, was a prominent rock formation and tourist attraction.[88] Kayaking was a popular activity near the rocks, and H prayed to the Gods that there

[88] America's first National Lakeshore, the Pictured Rocks are actually forty-two miles of beautiful lakeshore and sandstone formations in the Upper Peninsula of Michigan. Forty-two miles of beauty! That's the same number as the number of degrees that light has to reflect and refract on a raindrop to make a rainbow.

would be no humans paddling nearby while she explored and hunted for the cave. Cliffs lined a fifteen-mile-long portion of the park, nearly two hundred feet high in parts, and fostered glorious waterfalls. Every swish of her stardust-sprinkled tail brought her closer to the sandstone cliffs speckled with pink, yellow, and green coloring.[89]

She wondered if she had hit a distance anywhere close to the orca in Alaska, Lydia, who swam a thousand miles in one day. Birds were still telling the story of her glorious journey, and that news had traveled over three thousand miles in just a few days. The young orca was a legend and inspiration to so many. H hoped to one day have that uplifting effect on others. She vowed to practice her dramatic breaching in the meantime as an act of solidarity.

H dove to the lake floor as soon as the cliffs were within reach. She sped past the unique formations until she reached the area holding the turret.[90] With a seismic gyration, she slowed her body to a pace reasonable for cave searching and wondered how many knots she'd mustered to hit while rage-swimming to the rocks. Speed would surely be proud. She zigzagged upward and downward, from the surface of the water to the seafloor, praying for an opening into the rock face.

H sparkled with excitement from her heart to her tail as she spotted a large yellow archway opening into the sandstone. She could hear the water slapping playfully against the rock. Upon entering, however, she found a small cavern, completely empty, functioning as an echo chamber for the boisterous water.

Defeated, she continued onward. The last two days had felt like an eternity, and the anticipation made her body hum with energy, as though she was ready to explode.

After rounding a corner, H saw a dark spot in the distance a few feet below the water. Her entire body trembled. Nearing the hole in the rock wall, she realized they would have had to crawl through to enter, as it were only a few feet tall. She entered with caution, ready to face whatever, or whomever, lurked within.

[89] Mineral content can change the color of sandstone. Personally, I prefer the pink stuff!

[90] Freezing and thawing in springtime could be fatal to the rocks, as one of the rock turrets collapsed over a decade ago. The birds called it the "big splash heard throughout the lake."

Nothing inside screamed *sacred place of the lake defender.* It was dark, cool, and wet, much like any other cave. Peering up at the dry walls, H poked her head above the waterline to assess the situation. The cavern was a decent size, almost twice as long as it was wide. Thick bands of light-orange sandstone lined the walls.

H popped back under the water. The bottom of the cave had been battered smooth by the lapping waves of time. Frustrated and defeated, H surfaced yet again to get another look. This probably wasn't her cave, and she hadn't prepared herself for how soul-crushing it would be for the cave not to be hers. The sound of air on feathers swooped overhead. H turned to the noise yet saw nothing.

Large droplets of defeat dripped down her forehead, trailing down her chest . . . which had begun to harbor a humble flicker of light. The candlelike glimmer intensified into a dancing beam, escaping her body to illuminate the pitch-black cavern. It bounced from wall to wall, hit the ceiling, and stopped within inches of her face. The light diffused a warm, inviting glow, like a campfire in a cool, dark night. A smooth voice gently filled the space.

"Hanging Cloud Astrid, you have come to harness that which you are made of." The light circled her.

"I have come to learn the ways of lightning and ice," she answered anxiously. Her voice echoed and bounced off the walls. "To harness the power will be my greatest honor."

"The walls of this cavern are decorated in pictographs of a fish woman who bears powers of the elements."

H looked around, first with her head and then with her fish tail spinning. "I don't see a thing but blank sandstone." She reached out to the cool rock and put her hand on it to feel as though it would help her see better.

"To see the whole picture, you must use your power. Remove the heat within the rock. As the rock cools, the drawings will appear. Calm the particles with your touch. Command the atoms of the elements. Reach deep within. Feel the electricity that gives you life, that connects every cell within your body. Feel the thermal energy in the world around you. See the particles that make up every object and being—see them move. Heat exists when the particles move faster. Imagine yourself slowing them down."

"My ancestors had magical thermosensitive cave paints?" H spun around in bewilderment. She placed both hands on the rock in front of her, closing her eyes to focus on their mere existence. Rocks were still and calm by nature with no turmoil. H focused on soothing the minerals and pulling the particles into her own skin. She envisioned an illustration she'd once seen in a textbook—the structure of an atom—thought harder, and mentally pulled the heat out of the rock. Her arms tingled with fuzzy electricity and power.

"Keep going," said the light. "The presence of frost is indicative of the correct conditions for our drawings."

The air in the cave became noticeably cooler. Frost began to accumulate from her hands outward, spreading and crawling across the smooth sandstone. Gently sparkling white frost soon covered the entire cavern. The light glowed at its center, reflecting across the frozen rock and casting glitter over every surface of the cavern.

H marveled at her work and looked down at her hands, stunned. "Where are the drawings?" she asked excitedly.

The light bounced down from the ceiling to the smooth white wall of the cavern. It touched the wall, melted the frost, and began to draw a picture on the freshly made canvas. Forming a circle, the illuminating spirit prophet began with a head, long hair, and a fish tail instead of stick legs. The first arm grasped a lightning bolt. The second arm stretched upward, below a series of levitating snowflakes. "The drawings are what we make them. The canvas is wide open and ready for your next move."

H stared at the quaint drawing on the wall. She had to ask. "So, I was chasing a red herring. In reality, no pictographs exist?" She tried to hide her disappointment. "I have to draw them myself? With my powers?"

"You are welcome to draw whatever you would like to document. With practiced control of the manipulation of thermal energy, the possibilities within your grasp may outnumber that which your imagination can fabricate." The light flickered as it spoke.

"Then how do I harness lightning?"

"Lightning is a form of electricity. The human body, for example, conducts electric currents to function. The cells of the body were built for these behaviors. Think of the chaos that ensues between positive and negative charges."

H lifted her hands, pointing at the back wall of the frost-covered cave. She thought about her heartbeat, about the star burning within, and the blood pumping through her body. She thought about the cells that comprise all living beings, transferring energy and messages throughout. The tips of her fingers warmly tingled as she carried an electric current from her core to down her arms and out of her being. A periwinkle bolt shot from her hands like a firework, and as she concentrated on controlling the energy, it metamorphosed into a full lightning bolt that struck the rock wall in front of her, melting the wallpaper of frost with a delicate sizzle at the entry point.

She paused for a moment and looked down at her hands in disbelief, then back at the wall at the circular spot which melted the icy glaze. She took another go, this time sizzling a large H on the wall.

The light happily spiraled down from the ceiling to meet H's gaze right in front of her face. "You have the skills you need to progress to greatness. Trust the body, and your star will guide you."

The light danced in front of H, a shadow overhead exited the cave, and then the light nestled at the center of her chest, diffusing itself into her skin, making her chest cavity glow like a lantern. The light settled and slowly dimmed from within.

H clasped her hands together, in awe of the star that had just entered her body. The star would shine in the night sky for all to see, but this one chose to shine brightly within her. She felt grateful and magnificent all at the same time for the gift from the elder Woman of

Solstice. She was again very alone in a small dark cavern, but felt the warm, kindred touch of a friend from within.

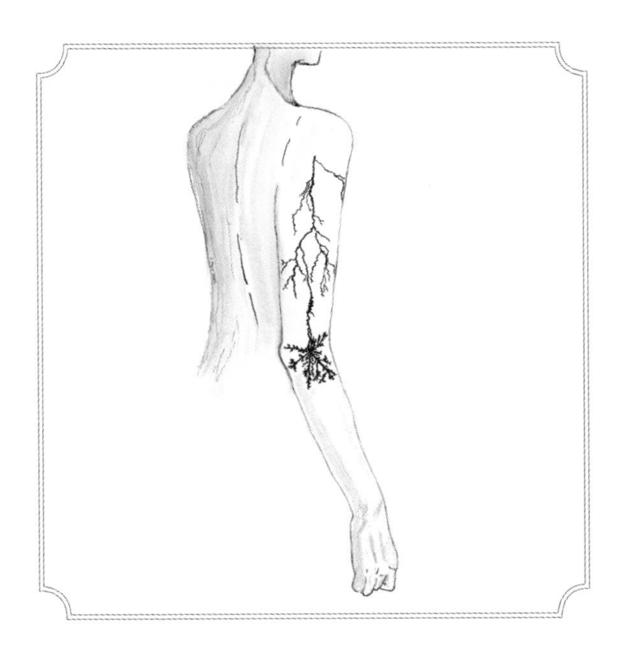

Chapter Sixteen

FEELING LIKE AN ELITE ATHLETE, or maybe a baby skunk that had just learned how to spray its effervescent stink, H continued east toward Whitefish Bay. She rounded the point and slowed down near Paradise to look around.[91]

H considered surfacing again to look for birds but saw the shadows of a few vessels above so chose to stay below the depths of visibility for a bit longer. The watchful sun would be on her merry way soon and, hopefully, all of this would be over. She continued onward, swimming feverishly, oblivious to landmarks she had passed that often were pit stops.

H's mind, occupied and focused, had forgotten about the most famous shipwreck of them all. The SS *Edmund Fitzgerald*'s final resting place was just on the outskirts of Whitefish Bay.[92] She began to hum the song Shirley had taught her about the wreck. Gosh, she had

[91] The shoreline of Whitefish Point wore the crown of most shipwrecks accumulated and was aptly nicknamed the Graveyard of the Great Lakes. I've considered making it a proper landmark sign!

[92] The *Edmund Fitzgerald* sank in 1975 during a wretched hurricane-force storm, killing all twenty-nine crewmen aboard. Her body was found broken in two pieces on the seafloor. She is one of the largest ships claimed by the lake.

really enjoyed Shirley's company and commentary.[93] In her mind, H heard Shirley's voice say, "In her glory days, the *Edmund Fitzgerald* hauled iron ore from Duluth to Detroit and various other ports. The captain was known for blaring music over the loudspeakers while traversing the Soo Locks." H would have loved to hear the music, assuming it was what would now be known as classic rock.

H snapped out of her shipwreck obsession and faux conversation, realizing she hadn't seen any marine life in quite some time. "Hello?" she called out. "Here, fishy-fishy-fishy!" The fry loved that line, but silence answered her calls. Usually, schools gallivanted in these waters, but no fry swam out to tickle her fins. The bay made a quite popular spot for sport fishing and housed a variety of species. The diverse crowd of aquatic dwellers usually met her at the door and welcomed her in. Perch especially loved to swim in a school around her, turning, spinning, and diving as though they were dancing. The fish in these parts were extraordinarily social, shoaling like it was a full-time job, and never attempting anything half-finned.

H popped to the surface. She gasped at the realization that she had met the legendary Thunderbird in the cave where she learned her powers, as it had guided her on how to use her strength.[94] "I heard wings and saw the shadow," she exclaimed to nobody in particular. "The star did all the talking. I'm embarrassed I disregarded those details!" Feeling a sense of calm and confidence with her assumption, she gazed at the heavens. The darkness of the sky away from city lights prominently featured her celestial friends shining brighter than ever. The cosmic woodland creatures twinkled, encouraging her onward, and she channeled their brute force like a beacon through the claw around her neck. She may have been by herself, but she was never completely alone.

As H drew her emotionally weary self near to where Saint Mary's River poured into Whitefish Bay, a distant glow taunted her sapphire eyes. Something shiny was reflecting what little light diffused down to the depths, but she couldn't tell what it was. Adrena-

[93] *smiles*

[94] Thunderbirds are very powerful invisible forces. We'd best leave them to the experts.

line raced through her body as she manipulated the water for more velocity, leaving a trail of miniscule bubbles in her wake.

Nothing could have surprised H more than to realize the glow in the water, illuminating light from the surface, was hundreds of thousands of fish gathered in one place waiting for her. A chill trickled down her spine. It was the most beautiful thing she had ever seen. She paused near the lake bottom to peer up at her esteemed neighbors and friends, suddenly feeling so very small, admiring the majestic mountain of fish that faithfully waited for her.

She looked toward the magnificent gathering and spoke: "I have the strength of those who came before me, and I have the trust of those who fight beside me."

All of the fish paused and one epic bubble of aquatic beings turned all attention down to her, suspended and motionless in the water, waiting to soak up every last word. Had they not been her loyal companions and Sunday swim-mates, the sheer number would have intimidated her.

H's gills flared, and she pumped her fist toward the sky. "We do not open our waters to terrorists, and we will fight to the death for our community and home. An attack on one of us is an attack on all of us. This battle is for those already lost, in hopes that their sacrifice of life has not been made in vain, and it is for our small fry yet to be born. May we always remember the fallen and recognize the fierce grasp of evil before it can flourish in our waters. I am grateful for your presence, your belief in the cause, and I accept your help wholeheartedly. You are my family, and as a member of the bear clan I will protect you with my half-human, half-fish life."

The colossal mass of fish embraced the speech and engaged in silent cheering. They wagged their bodies back and forth, tails shimmying with the motion. Light bounced off every scale, sparkling like an underwater disco ball. A small silver school broke out of the crowd and approached H, which she recognized as her lake trout friends from the Isle Royale reef.

Malcolm was the first to speak. "What's the game plan, lady Commander?"

"Do we need a strategy of attack if these creatures come for us?" asked Zoe, serious as ever.

"I don't wanna die," cried Kaylee. "Fighting's not my strong suit."

"We're not gonna die, Kaylee," answered Malcolm. "We're too pretty to die. God won't let us die because we are just too pretty." He turned to H for assurance.

"I suppose I should alert the nice marine folk to what we are up against," H sighed.

H approached the massive scaled army, who had begun to mumble amongst themselves. "Listen up, freshwater warriors! We are fighting exotic, evolved invasives we've nicknamed *Reefers*. This new lamprey-like species is all black. They are bigger, faster, and they may even be able to jump barriers—we just don't know yet. Their length means they can wrap around your body as you try to wriggle away. They don't hunt solo like they did in the past. They're hunting like a pack of wolves to pin down and annihilate their prey, with teeth just as sharp. The circumference of their mouth is like a freaking crater, so if one attaches it is close to impossible to get free." H surveyed the crowd. Their eyes were dilated with horror, even wider than normal if that was possible. "Be aware they emit a pungent odor—it's like gasoline pumped out a putrid skunk-butt gland near a landfill!"

With the determination of a baby moose standing on wobbly legs for the first time, H continued. "How will we beat them? By working together. Together, we are one fish. We move in unison, and we watch each other's scales. I want you to form your wall blocking the entrance to the lake behind me. Don't give them your broadside—those big mouths need big surfaces, and that's prime real estate. If one lunges for your neighbor, dive and headbutt the bastard! Bite them. Make them bleed. Keep moving around; their eyesight will get confused from all your shimmying. It's harder to hit a moving target.

Hopefully, it won't even come to this. I will stand in front and fight. Things might get weird—don't be afraid if I start shooting things out of my hands. Our bird friends will be above. They'll dive and attack as many Reefers as possible."

"I'll be glad when this Reefer madness is over," admitted Hoban.

Jayne looked H up and down. "*What* about your hands?"

"I'm like a living, breathing security system with star-powered ammunition," said H.

"Shiny," said River.

"Everything the Minong Ojibwe men said has come true," Simon said. "Revna warned you, the bear saved you, and . . ."

"I received guidance from *the* raptor," interrupted H.

H spun around. The fish had assembled into a wall: tiny minnows at the top, aggressive fighters in the middle, and sturdy sturgeon along the bottom. The shiniest fish were scattered in small groups throughout, creating multiple points of visual mayhem. A few muscular muskellunge positioned themselves front and center.

"Imagine the disaster this would be if we were facing an army of cats." H giggled at her own joke as the fish looked at her a bit confused.

The wide shadow of a majestic winged bird filtered through the water's surface. H swelled with excitement. "I should check in with the birds."

H surfaced into a dark world, illuminated by moonlight. It was far too beautiful an evening for impending war. Swiveling, H looked upward, hoping to see the source of the shadow. There was a black cloud hovering ominously overhead—except it wasn't a cloud at all, or a Thunderbird for that matter.

It was Athena's army. They moved together like the hands of an orchestra director, smoothly and effortlessly. Predatory birds flew independently, swooping upward and downward, looking at the lake. If H didn't know any better, she'd think this was either a nightmare or a horror movie. The sheer number was enough to induce fear, that was for sure.

H called for Athena, who appeared in an instant and landed on her outstretched palm. "This is the most impressive gathering of flying beings I've ever seen," gawked H. "They look like a thundercloud."

"We are ready for your guidance," sang Athena. "We understand the fight will mainly be underwater . . . unless you're going to chuck the bad guys into the sky for us to catch?"

A shadow cast from a broad wingspan grew larger as it neared the water. Arne swooped down from the flying mass of dinosaur descendants and plopped himself in the water next to H.

"Anything is possible," said H as her gaze met Arne's. "I need your raptors and divers ready to attack. They are welcome to pluck them from the lake and demolish them at will, even feed on them. Arne, perhaps your family can tell the others when the Reefers are within reach."

Arne nodded, his white head flashing in the darkness.

"It would be like eating a giant sea worm, although they sound like they might be tough and chewy," said Athena. "What's happening under the water?"

"Our fish army has built a wall to back me up," answered H. "I'm hoping I can take the Reefers out or cripple them enough to stop them. Either way, they'll have to get through all of us to get to the lake. If we scare them out of the water, it's all on your winged brethren to take them out."

"The sheer intimidation factor should be enough for them to evacuate their intestines on the spot," chirped Athena.

"The hawks and eagles are ready to hunt," reported Arne with the glint of a glowing moon in his eyes. "For the invaders," he clarified. Resident fish were off-limits in an unspoken truce of warfare.

"I'm leaving you two in charge," said H. "For now, I must return to the depths to watch and wait for our nemesis." Athena took the cue to return to the air and launched off H's hand into flight with an impeccable little hop.

With a splash of her tail, H returned to the troops below.

"As you know, fish are the most patient and easygoing of creatures," started Jayne. "But we might have a few brothers and sisters who are wondering how long it's going to take for the bad guys to get here."

"We're expecting them to make an entrance with full theatrics," said Hoban. "The anticipation might eat us alive before they even get the chance."

"It's gnawing at me right now," said Zoe. "Like a whitefish on a baited hook."

"Just float like a leaf on the wind, honey," said Hoban.

"What's that glowing white cloud in the distance?" asked Inara, motioning west, toward the entire body of water behind the glorious wall of fish.

"I don't know," Kaylee quavered, "but if those are the bad guys, they're coming from the wrong direction."

"What in the living . . . ?" H pushed past her friends, through the crowded wall. She blinked slowly, trying to see what was on the horizon. The glowing white mass was moving fairly fast, and H couldn't get a grasp on what was happening.

"They're not alive," observed River, calmly swimming to H's side. "That's a mass haunting. Those are the ghosts of the lake."

Even the deepest part of the lake was illuminated like a Christmas tree, with a soft glow of hope on a dark winter night. She could just make it out now: a large fleet of ships headed straight for them. After she picked her jaw off the bottom of the lake, H returned to the wall of fish and said, "It looks like we have some backup. Please don't be spooked—they mean you no harm."

Recognized by H immediately, the steel freighter USS *Emperor* lead the cavalry, front and center in all her glory. Adjacent to the *Emperor* was the USS *Essex*, a retired navy ship that was burned near the Duluth Harbor. She could make out the *Algoma*, sweet Glenny, and even the *America* with George smiling at the bow like an ornamental figurehead. The legendary *Edmund Fitzgerald* dwarfed the lot, blasting classic rock anthems to break the silence like the goliath she was. H recognized each and every one—freighters and fishing vessels, paddleboats and steamers. The sight was completely breathtaking, so many sunken dreams culminating into one.

One would expect such a large movement of beings to make noise like a stampede, displacing water and shaking the ground. But the band of ghosts traveled seamlessly through the water without resistance, elegantly and suavely. After all, that was the glory of existing as a supernatural being: gravity never brought you down.

A herd of large mammals ran alongside the fleet with a familiar brown cow front and center. Betsy had obviously made some friends along the way. There were cows, moose, whitetail deer, caribou, and even a couple of bears.

The army of dead ships, around 350 strong, parked themselves right behind the wall of fish. Their glow illuminated the battlefield. Crewmembers began to gather on the decks, holding whatever improvised weaponry they could find aboard. Folks reached for paddles, machetes, pitchforks, and shovels. A couple of men had shiny revolvers.

H swam up to welcome the leader of the pack. "Speed! You sneaky, scheming rascal," she yelled. "You just pulled a move straight from *The Lord of the Rings*!"

"My invitation must have gotten lost in the mail," Speed joked. He had traded his ragged ball cap and flannel for a true white captain's hat and jumpsuit. "We are happy to be of service, and everyone here was enthused to sail again. Each of these vessels and her occupants wanted to be here for you and the lake that is our grave. In fact, those ships without ghosts drove themselves." Wendi waved from the large windows of the captain's quarters, and H blew a kiss back.

"Sure, Speed. We know you are all adrenaline junkies, especially those of you with a history of military service," said H, smiling. "I appreciate that you're here. Thank you." H addressed the whole group. "Thank you all!" She said the words as loud as her gills could muster and was met with polite clapping and a few cheers.

"Well, I guess now we wait for the other army to get here," grumbled Speed. "The waiting is what drives men mad."

"Good thing I'm not a man." H grinned as she held her bear claw in one hand and pumped her fist with the other. She flicked her tail and swam back down to her front line, overwhelmed by the outpouring of support. So many had lost their lives to the lake, yet they now chose to protect its waters.

Something behind the ghost ships shot through the water like a shooting star. "Wait for me!" it wailed.

"Shirley? Is that you?" H strained to see.

"*Holy ship!*" Shirley shrieked upon arrival. "Is that the *Edmun—*"

"No interviews with sailors until after the battle," H hollered.

"*Surely* you won't start a war without my help," said Shirley. She held up her shotgun with a fierce scowl. "I put on slacks for this."

H hugged the old woman with all her might. "Did you look outside?" Shirley asked. "There are so many birds. If they ever get a leader, we're screwed!" Shirley tried to read H's blank face. "Hitchcock? No? Sam didn't give you any vintage culture! How about *The Crows Have Eyes 3*, starring Moira Rose?"

"Nope," H answered. "I suppose you'll have to educate me after the battle."

"It's a date," declared Shirley. "I'm going to join the other ghosts. The one with the knitting needles looks like my kind of gal."

A tiny perch approached H from above, speaking in a high-pitched child's voice. "Lady H, ma'am. A large gray duck dove down to tell us there's a large black mass moving through the Soo Locks right now."

"Thank you, small fry." She gave it an appreciative nod, and it skirted back into place.

H stared up at her planetary body of fish orbiting around her and the glowing nautical ghost army behind them. "Attention finned, humans, machines, and everything in between: we've got a location on the Reefers, and they're in the Locks headed our way."

Butterflies sputtered in H's stomach—or maybe it was the stardust in her heart wanting to jump back into the sky and be at peace with merely existing. She hoped she was prepared to use her powers.

A dark gray cloud appeared in the water emerging from Saint Mary's River. "Dorsal fins up, friends," rallied H as she assumed her position, front and center, against the massive gathering of aquatic dwellers. The enemy approached swiftly and quietly. The lamprey slithered like snakes in the water, eerily riding the motion of the currents. They formed a large, tangled mess of creatures that no one could survive alone. The water turned black with their presence.

H exhaled out her nostrils, and an array of angry bubbles cascaded from her nose like a waterfall. For a demigod with a relatively easy and happy life, she harbored a lot of angst toward the skinny, good-for-nothing, anus-faced grifters.

"Oh, well, would you look at that," said the largest of the Reefers. A pair of growths, like misshapen tentacles, unfurled from his body. "We've got ourselves a welcome party!" The Reefer Prince beamed at the extravagant scene and swam in the middle of his tangled mess of an army.[95]

"Don't think for one Mississippi that you're welcome here," snarled H.

"Reel in the attitude, Madame. We thought you'd had enough of us." His round face lengthened into an evil, toothy grin.

"Turn around and never come back," she demanded. "In fact, don't even look back. And don't let the Locks hit your ass on the way out!"

"You smell delicious when you're angry," hissed a Reefer with a crooked smile, lunging at her tail.

[95] H didn't know the big one's name. She doled out the nickname "Prince of the Reefers." I could hear her from the front line.

H reflexively jumped out of harm's way, clenched fists ready to throw a punch.

"Be careful of that one," said the Prince. "Snaggletooth likes to play with his food."

As if on cue, an eagle broke through the water. Formidable, sharp talons forcefully wrapped tightly around the assumed first victim of the battle. A loon that looked a lot like Lynneh engaged in a swift attack dive.

"Is that how you treat all your guests?" The Prince cocked his body to the side so he could leer at H with his tiny, beady eye. Fully stretched out, he was almost as tall as her.

"Listen, porcupine-balls face," started H, sounding very midwestern mean. "I don't know where you're from, but this lake is already taken. Turn around and leave. We have no vacancies, there is no room in the inn, we are out of beds, you can't sit with us—I'm not sure how else I can put it. Go back to the hell from whence you came. Reefers are not welcome."

One of the smaller Reefers asked, "What if we don't want to?"

"Then I'll send you there myself," growled H, raising her hand. She focused on the energy and rage that flowed through her body. Blazing with starfire, she shot a luminous blue lightning bolt into the army of invaders, sizzling and scorching a few more victims. One Reefer, severed completely in half, sank slowly to the sand below.

Warmth surged through her arms and a comfortable weight settled on her head. Before her eyes, copper wrist guards materialized on her forearms; when she felt her head, she found a helmet shaped like a bear head, ears and all. Her human half suddenly bore a copper breastplate, which protected her heart and wrapped around her back. Thor really did love his theatrics—or maybe knew something she didn't about playing with lightning.

The smaller Reefers jumped behind their leader, startled by the mermaid's barrage of lightning bolts. The Reefer Prince lunged forward toward the mermaid, barely missing the electricity shooting from her hand. She held her free palm out to him, and he tried to wrap his tentacles around her arm. The *thunk* of a musky headbutting a lunging Reefer gave H enough time to grab the little guy by the tail, spin him around, and hurl him toward the surface.

Thoughts of ice surged in H's mind as she held out her free hand and began to slow the water molecules into a solid circular object: a frozen shield, perfectly translucent—much to the confusion of the horrid creatures crashing headlong into it. H held it close to her body as she continued her lightning attack.

As if they were waiting, various diving birds dove as deep as they could to pluck away a few more of their mutual nemeses. The Reefer Prince evaded capture and set a course straight for our mermaid, who continued to shoot blue lighting toward the thick fog of lamprey. From the corner of her frigid blue eyes, she saw a gray log of a fish hurl its body toward the Prince of the lamprey to prevent him from hitting her. The lake shuddered with inner turmoil.

H focused her blasts on the constant charge of smaller grunts, broadening her range by shooting a river of electricity from each finger. She zapped the attackers closest to her, one after another, but the onslaught was never-ending. H held her shield steady and let them hit it, while the sheer impact of it left them stunned and susceptible.

Birds continued to snipe the horrid creatures near the surface while sailors hacked at those near the lake floor. A quick glance down and she saw brothers Dean and Samuel slicing the perpetrators in half with a shovel and a pitchfork while yelling some sort of exorcism. *Was that a jar of table salt?* She'd ask later. The creatures could do no harm to the ghosts, but the Reefers relentlessly continued to strike anyway, hoping their efforts were fruitful.

Vera, clad for battle in a chunky sweater, grabbed and stabbed one Reefer with a long, slender knitting needle. Wadeen was swinging what appeared to be a wooden railing spindle. Speed's crewmen Crockett, Twiggs, and Weasel had taken a lifeboat through the front line; they were in the middle of enemy territory, swashbuckling the

Reefer nest with machetes and curling brooms. Frosty fought with a lace parasol with a sharp tip on the end while kicking those that dropped with her pointy shoes. Lou swung a cast-iron frying pan in one hand and a large kitchen knife in the other. Shirley shot them down like ducks. Hundreds, perhaps thousands of humans that H didn't even recognize were out on the front lines, decimating the enemy's numbers.

Somewhere in the mess of war, the familiar voice of Stanley yelled, "YOU SATANIC DEMONS CAN FUCK RIGHT OFF, ALL THE WAY BACK TO HELL!" Stanley finally had an outlet for his anger. "IT'S THAT GODDAMN MERMAID AND HER BANANA'S FAULT!"

The tangled mess of Reefers was coming undone. Their lunges toward the lake's entrance were quickly opposed, and the dead, scattered below, increased in numbers every second. Desperation kicking in, they tried to yeet themselves at the wall of fish. They were immediately swarmed by small fry, which created a confusing and annoying distraction. A few tried to swim away and were chased down by George, who bit them violently and shook his sweet poodle head in anger. He retrieved a few of the more girthy beasts like a tossed wooden stick to the sailors for destruction.

Electricity crackled through H's copper armor, and futile attacks against her that smacked into the armor created an instant lights-out for the offender. Nobody could touch her, and those that tried were electrocuted and stunned or killed.

H looked upward. She saw a few members of her family floating belly-up. A glance back revealed a whitefish nursing a bite wound. Cisco swarmed the enemy as a diversion while birds lunged. A walleye that looked a lot like Keetaq was fighting a Reefer isolated from their pack, spiky dorsal fins up, with the help of a lake trout.

H let out a monstrous war cry. The scream stopped almost everyone in their tracks, the lake motionless. As the noise traveled, the world slowed to a crawl. A gale of cold air exited her mouth in a forceful stream of hardening slush.

She continued to blast the remaining Reefer mass, letting out another boisterous yell between breaths. The army lost the ability to squirm in the water as ice crystals formed between them and trapped their bodies. "*Frostbite,*" H thought as the message from James finally made sense.

A gray storm cloud formed above H in the water, emitting sharp, projectile ice shards sideways toward the mass of invaders. She shaped her icy breath into clanking shards that fell from the cloud with the frigid tenacity of a storm on Neptune, emitting the scream of wind chimes in a tornado. The sharp projectiles impaled the army and embedded themselves within the giant forming ice chunk. One large mass of ice under the water trapped the creatures with such clarity that you could see the fear in their yellow eyeballs as every part of their bodies became encompassed and immobile.

The ice cube looked like something that had fallen off a calving glacier, and it started to float to the surface akin to the frozen properties of water. Below the ice chunk, a graveyard of parasites covered the entire lake floor. Betsy's mob of mammals headbutted and stomped the creatures to make sure they were truly dead. H dropped her shield and looked upward at the frigid trap. It was possible they could survive the cold, so she'd have to do more than that to make sure none of them could infect her home.

Malcolm dove by as a diversion. "I swear by my pretty dorsal and caudals, I will end you," he yelled at the Prince. The rest of his crew followed.

"H, watch out," yelled a voice from behind. The leader of the lamprey had staged an attack from above. He was scarred from the talons of the birds, with open red wounds throughout his body. He must have been too big for them to carry away. A few lake trout tried to tackle the creature off course, but he was moving full speed toward the mermaid.

"Enough with the antics," said H. "Wave the white flag or take a warrior's death." The creature barreled toward her silently, determined to take her out.

H staggered the positioning of her hands. Her shimmering tail was still and ready for reflexive movement. The bear eyes on her copper helmet glowed like a lighthouse in a storm. About five feet away, the creature hissed, and she unleashed her lightning and let him have it. The storm cloud above her head changed positions to drop ice shards on the Reefer Prince.

Her hand glowed blue from the powerful bolt, which rocked the Reefer Prince's body and jolted him violently back and forth. Each time she let up, he managed to swim nearer. H let him get closer until he was motionless with electricity but within arm's distance. She reached her hand to her side and pulled out her stainless-steel multifunction tool, thumbed the blade open, and stabbed the creature as strongly and deeply as she could. Gratified, she twisted the knife as a mighty roar erupted from her lips.

A yellow lightning bolt jumped from her copper wrist armor and traced her body down every finger to the tight grasp on the knife, meeting the weapon and embracing the conductivity of the metal. The blade easily pierced the thick skin of the dreadful creature, and the electricity that shocked him now flowed within from the knife blade to every square inch of his body. His eyes bulged and mouth opened, revealing a round orifice of sharp teeth. The tongue of the wretched organism went limp, the struggle to wriggle ceased, and the body faltered.[96] H eased her lightning hands and slowly relaxed them to her sides as the creature floated lifelessly to the bottom of the lake, where her ghost friends were ready and waiting to chop it to bits.[97]

H breathed a sigh of relief, chilling the water around her. She eased up on the powers thriving in her demigod body and surging through her veins. The cloud, now above her again, changed from gray to white. Her copper armor and helmet dissolved into nothingness. She felt lighter and clear-minded without all the rage gumming up her body. Her lake trout family immediately congregated to her.

Jayne asked the obvious yet somehow equivocal question: "You brought a knife to a fish fight?"

"Please don't tell me that guy is your father," added Malcolm.

[96] This Reefer was not an easy kill. We postulated it was due to his size and ability to direct the lightning around his skin and protect his vital organs. I'm awaiting autopsy results.

[97] I wrote his obituary. It said, "Rest in pieces, you bastard."

Zoe swam to look H in the eye. "What's the plan for the Reefer popsicle?"

H answered them each in turn. "Technically, it's a multipurpose tool—it even has a screwdriver and teeny-tiny scissors. Those creatures had no place in our earth family. And I'm not entirely sure how to eliminate the iceberg full of ass-faced mother-reefers."

"Language," exclaimed Malcolm sarcastically.

"You could have the birds peck them to pieces to make sure they're dead as it melts," said River.

"That's a vile thing for a human to find," said Inara. "What if they try to resurrect the monsters without knowing?"

"I think they are beyond the point of saving," answered Simon.

"Next time we do this, your dead humans need to have more spears," added Hoban.

"I think they made do just fine with their primitive weapons," argued Jayne. "Minus the frying pan. May I never see one of *those* again."

"I need to check on our friends of flight," said H, exasperated, with a fist up as she glided toward the surface.

The moment her ears left the water, H heard an extravagant racket. Swallows sang and swooped in pure joy. Loons yodeled, gulls were giddy, and ducks paddled with glee. Eagles sat atop the floating iceberg, pecking hungrily at the horrors within.

H noticed the white cloud had followed her above the water; a gentle breath upward released it into the sky. She squinted across the inlet toward Michigan, trying to make out the scene in the darkness. Birds circled the treetops in large flocks. Black bears waded in the shallows while moose and deer stomped the shoreline, rabbits and squirrels hopping around their hooves. A wolverine darted back into the forest right next to a giant slinking cougar. H's heart swelled. Baby lynx played and rolled in the sand while a herd of skunks exited stage right, as all the furry brethren cleared a large open path for them to pass. A pack of wolves howled in the distance. A dark shadow, possibly biped, disappeared into the forest.

Athena swooped down from above and found her place on H's outstretched hand. "Holy Ishpeming, H." Her body shook with excitement, wings trembling with every spoken word. "The ghosts' glow gave us a clear view of everything—there was a bam and a slash, a strike and a dodge, a war cry and a zippy-zap! Evasive maneuvers! The ice was a brilliant way to make them freeze, literally!"

"Your diving cavalry saved us more than a few times," said H, loud enough for those nearby to hear. A small crowd of avian swimmers had gathered around.

"You made your own storm cloud," Athena exclaimed. "You lived up to your name!"

Lynneh the loon swam by elegantly singing, blood still dripping from her pointy beak. She looked at H and said, "You should have seen the show from above! It looked like a patchwork quilt—yellow eyes, black shadows, blue lightning."

"The forest creatures wanted to know what was happening," Athena continued, "so we had Schwan Swan relay live commentary north to Canada and Michigan. A few times, the eagles dropped some Reefers for the bears to devour. Then the wolves got jealous and wanted in on the action."

Arne glanced over from the floating piece of ice, a lamprey tail hanging from his golden beak. "What's your plan here? I'm not sure this will melt by morning. Your supernatural ice could have supercooling properties."

"I was hoping I could use my powers to make it explode," H announced, snapping a few quick photos.

Some of the ducks quacked with laughter. Athena took to the air.

"I'm being serious, guys. I'm not ducking around," explained H. The raft of ducks quieted.

"By all means, give it a shot," encouraged Arne. "The less evidence we can leave behind, the better!" He motioned with his large brown wing for others to clear the ice.

"You might want to give me some room," said H. "I don't want to hit anyone in the face with Reefer guts."

H stared at the chunk of frozen water and held her hands with palms facing each other. She fired up her lightning hands and bounced the power into a ball between her palms. The ball started off yellow and changed to an icy blue as it formed. She hurled the lightning ball into the iceberg, focused, squinted, bit her lip, and released. Thunder echoed with a giant kaboom as the ice cube disintegrated into tiny pieces of ice, which quickly melted in the lake water.

"Wow," trumpeted Arne. "I hereby relinquish my job as official symbol of the United States."

"I appreciate you all," announced H. "Thank you from the bottom of my star-filled heart." She waved goodbye to all the animals flying above and those still watching from the land, then retreated back to the sea.

Epilogue

"I AM GRATEFUL FOR ALL that was accomplished here tonight, as our family has joined fins and feathers in solidarity to defeat those that would destroy our home." H spoke with her head bowed. "To my ships and eternally living, may you rest in peace knowing your haunting ground remains unscathed by evil. I thank you all. And I will continue to keep this lake safe from this day forward. I will defend the glory of nature until the day I die."

Nigig reached out a paw to shut Blue's gaping mouth. Gabby grinned at H in silence from her seat on a picnic blanket. Sam, who had barely touched her pie, tried to hide that she was wiping away a tear with a tissue.

"And that's why I'm never eating lutefisk again," Shirley uttered. "Fish are friends, not 'fisk."

Sam crimpled up her nose in disgust. "Eww, Shirley. Nobody should *ever* eat 'fisk. Nasty." She shuddered.

H continued, "After thanking everyone, I noticed some of the fish were fixated on the seafloor. I rushed through the crowd to lay eyes on the subject that was gathering so much attention. Her lifeless body was battered and resting amongst the fallen. Nancy Sturgeon had hurled herself at the Reefers to protect me. She took a direct hit from their prince. We bowed to her honor and prayed to the Gods to bless her soul. We covered her in rocks at her final resting place as a memorial to her long life. Some of her close friends said words in remembrance. She had a large family."

Tears welled up in the eyes of her audience, and Sam sniffled.

"And then we cheered, swam, danced, and ate food that Lou prepared. Laughter and smiles filled the air—er, water. The fish swam in intricate patterns to reflect the glow of the ships and create a light show. The ghost ships glowed away in the night, returning to their resting places. The fish shoaled back up and went to their respective homes, and I came here," H added with a smile.

"Lou's blueberry cobbler really was delicious!" Shirley exclaimed.

"Show me the picture of the ducks and the iceberg again," begged Nigig, twitching his little nose curiously.

"He wants you to give him the bill," joked Blue, wrapping his striped tail around his feet.

"I like the selfie with Athena on your hand and the ice and eagles in the background," chimed in Sam. "That's classic Hanging Cloud Astrid right there."

Nigig stood upright. "Can we see the drunk chipmunks one more time? And the house with the ghost in the window? Maybe we could try photographing Shirley!" H leaned over to pet his furry brown head. She had really missed her friends.

"It was an honor to battle with you," Shirley declared. "I brought my shotgun, but I also wield a mean filet knife."

H laughed. "I think that would have scared the wrong crowd." She leaned on the rocky shore, dripping wet. "I did discover one pretty cool thing." She picked up her phone, opened the case, pointed her finger near the bottom, and shot a small lightning beam at the charging port. "I can charge my phone without help!"

Sam smiled. "It was nice to feel needed for a moment there. Promise me you'll still write! Also, you should have checked in with us more. One of us was worried." Sam shot a telling glance over at Nigig.

"Tell us again how you shot lasers out of your bear helmet!" Blue pleaded.

H laughed. "That's not exactly what I said, Fluffy. The eyes *glowed*."

Nigig joined in. "Can you freeze something for us? I want to see more mermaid demigod magic in action!"

H looked around and found a divot on the rock that was full of water. She pointed, thought her magic, and froze the water. It had become much easier with practice. When she looked up, she was met with wide-eyed stares.

"When do you get to meet Thor?" Blue hopped up and down. "He's my favorite Avenger."

"Easy there, Fluffy boy. You have been watching far too many movies with Dan," warned Sam.

"It's all Shirley's fault," Nigig insisted. "Her commentary is hilarious, and she thinks he's dreamy."

"Can we at least try on your bear helmet?" Blue asked with giant pleading eyes.

"I can't just conjure it for fun. I have to be in battle, you know. Safety first."

"We could throw rocks at you and see what happens," offered Nigig.

Gabby, lifetime member of the Clean Plate Club, looked up from licking her bowl of blueberry pie. "Throw balls and Frisbees, not rocks. Silly otter."

"Watch it, doggo! I'll itch that spot on your back hindquarters that renders you useless!" Nigig pumped his little fist in the air in feigned victory. Gabby smiled, wagged, and slurped a wet kiss across the otter's face.

"Next time we have a movie night, you're making us slushies," cheered Blue.

"Anything for you, my little marshmallow Fluffy."

"Anything but sharing your armor," Nigig clarified. "The handsome sidekick gets first dibs."

Sam scrunched her eyebrows with concern. "Did they ever figure out where the Reefers came from?"

"Athena sent word to the east, since they had to travel those waterways to hit the lake. The large mass was spotted near a tributary to Lake Huron. The birds have been talking to the local fauna, discussing possible river contamination by a chemical company." H frowned at the thought of dirty water for profits. Some humans had such appallingly low standards and utter disregard for their home. "Some of the frogs there have deformities, extra legs . . ."

"I hope prescription drugs aren't involved. Excreted hormones and drug metabolites could do nasty things to fragile creatures, making them hostile and drastically changing their build over time," worried Sam.

"Perhaps the Reefers were also possessed by evil spirits. They're exploring every possibility," reassured H.

"I could see them being demons," grumbled Shirley. "It was in their eyes. If they come back, I'll be on them like ketchup on a tater tot."

"Easy, Shirley. You're getting a little salty for this body," chuckled H, motioning toward the lake.

H didn't know what her next adversary would be, but she was going to do everything she could to prepare. Lake Superior continued to warm at an alarming rate, according to her most astute residents, and the science backed it up. Of course, mermaids didn't need scientists when they had temperature-sensitive fish and algae blooms, but the validation that they were correct was encouraging.

What if the lake was trying to take the stress off the living organisms? Perhaps her noble sacrifice had unintended consequences. H wished there was a way to communicate with the water herself, but she was a large living being with a lot going on inside of her—like Fury's mom, minus the elusive, quiet streak. H silently swore her next mission would be to meet that famous cougar and get all her stories about tramping around the upper Midwest.

Perhaps the turmoil of the lake was a blessing *and* a curse. If she used her powers to still the waters, perhaps the kinetic energy would decrease and the lake would cool. She could calm the individual molecules of water, for they had seen a lot over their existence. She set forth a plan to gift the waters a blessing of serenity and a release of the microscopically stored kinetic energy of the particles that exist with heat.

She was attending her first real physics class—online, of course—courtesy of Michigan Tech, that beautiful university by the Keweenaw Waterway. While H was away slaying dragons, Sam had discovered their online classes and made up a resume and a name for H to enroll, footing the bill and all. Delighted to listen to the academics speak, H also wanted to enjoy lectures in the field of biology. Their fish biology course sounded especially interesting, although she probably knew it all already. Indigenous knowledge is science, after all.

Sam asked, "Did you check out that link I sent you?"

"Yes, thank you. I will definitely be studying that and exploring the language of my ancestors," said H, referring to an online virtual language program. "For some reason, I can understand it but I struggle to speak it fluently, although my powers translate for me. I've been around too many Minnesotans to fully understand how vowels work."

"It doesn't make you any less Indigenous to not know the dialect," whimpered Nigig with concern.

"Yeah, but it just doesn't feel right not having that connection to our storied past," answered H. "Besides, you should talk, skinny boy. Your name literally means *river otter*."

"My mother was blessed with the gift of Gitchi-Gami vernacular," shrugged Nigig. "Don't hate me 'cause I'm beautiful." He put his little paws on his chest and struck a pose, head pointing to the sky.

"I'm going to visit the Agawa Rock Pictographs near Ontario, also. They've always resonated with me, but now I might be able to see more," shared H with a sapphire sparkle in her eyes.

"Be sure to send lots of photos," said Sam excitedly. "You know I've loved the feeling of adventuring right alongside you."

"Send me a postcard," demanded Shirley. "I'd settle for an email to Sam."

"I hate to cut my visit short, but I need to get to Isle Royale by nightfall," announced H. "The sky is clear, and I've been promised one heck of an aurora dance party with a very rad red squirrel."

Blue's whiskers twitched as he tilted his head to the side. "How do you know there will be aurora?"

"I checked the Twitter app for the account that gives aurora forecasts," H confessed with a cheesy grin that rolled her eyeballs upward. "Conditions are in our favor."

"You just made an expression like a girl in a GIF. Dear God, for the love of all that is holy, don't let social media rot H's brain!" Sam pleaded with her hands in prayer position.

H reached her arms upward toward Sam. "I love you, friend. You know I'll be back. Maybe you could send Dan away for another week so we can hang."

Sam embraced the wet mermaid hug. "Please be careful out there. I'm so glad you're OK. I love you, too, friend!"

Blue looked around innocently. "So now that all the besties have professed their love, when do we get more pie?"

Nigig scampered to H for a hug of his own, as did Blue and

Gabby. Gabby jumped in the lake and doggy-paddled with H a bit, and then H swam off on another journey.

H rolled up to Isle Royale ready to be free of the problems plaguing the planet for just one night. Joy filled her heart as she swam into Malone Bay and saw her favorite beavers. By now, Howard had probably heard how he'd helped her save the world, and she would hear about that assist for years to come. Upon closer examination, she spotted all her friends, predator and prey alike, awaiting her arrival. The lights in the night sky began to dance, and the woodland creatures followed in gleeful harmony.

The mermaid closed her eyes and imagined her ancestors by her side, guiding her path. This was the life she chose and also the path she was given. She was truly blessed. The lake clapped her waves gently on the shore as if to acknowledge her appreciation. Hanging Cloud Astrid opened her eyes, looked toward the sky, and spoke.

"I am your water defender, and this is the home of a warrior."

Afterword

Hello again, friend!

Is it alright if I call you that? We've been through so much together! I've been enjoying freedom and exploring the waters a bit. H brought me to the *Algoma* for blueberry pancakes. I even made it back to the Little Spirit Cedar Tree a few times. I'd like to thank Vera for the sketches to help tell my story. Not to be a gossip gull, but I've seen a few things you should probably know about . . .

In the meantime, I would love for you to send me postcards from your adventures around the lake. Sam says she'll post pictures of them on the Twitter so H can read them too. Something about "hashbrown postcards for Shirley." I'm not sure why we are talking about breakfast. All we do at home is eat! H also called me an instant Gram. Well, yeah you betcha! I can be a Gram to all these furred and finned misfits.

All my love,

Shirley

P.S. Blue says it's #PostcardsForShirley. It's a pound sign, not a hashbrown. I can't tell if he's being sincere or just messing with an old lady.

P.S.S. You can find H on the social medias at @hthemermaid. My CB handle is Old Brown Skunk, and you can find me on channel 19. Breaker, breaker one-nine, over and out.

Teaser from the Next Book in the Heart of Stardust Series

A DIM LIGHT GLOWED IN an underwater cave. A large, intricately designed copper throne sat against the back wall of the room. A large, circular woven rug lined the floor, while traditional cave paintings decorated the walls with records of history. In the middle of the room was a rectangular wooden table, on which sat a large game board of sorts. The board resembled a map of the lake with accurate topography, with tiny, copper-cast miniature figurines of every creature living in the lake. Shipwrecks were marked on the map, and small moving copper dots tracked schools of fish. The game pieces that represented living beings moved in real time as though tracking every movement. Trippehjay swam in and peered down at their beloved live-action lake board, debating on picking up one of the twenty-sided dice from the table and making things interesting. Moose were quite active sprawling across Minong, and the schooling fish danced across the board like shooting stars.

Weary from all the excitement, Trippehjay had felt responsible for the safety of the Mermaid created to protect the lake all these years; lo and behold, she had superpowers that could probably rival their own. The battle of the Reefers would live as a legend for eons to come and was quite possibly was the most exciting thing to ever happen under these waters. They watched the tiny copper mermaid swim toward Isle Royale while preparing the paints to document the invasive species death extravaganza. Hanging Cloud Astrid had relatable qualities, after all. They were both hybrid creatures of sorts. Perhaps coming out of hiding and creating a little chaos or befriending her would be reasonable.

A voice spoke in the darkness, snapping the river of thoughts pouring through their brain. "It's your roll," said Thundy, handing them the dice with his large wings. "We are still playing, right?"

Betsy's eyes slammed open so hard that her eyelashes created their own water currents. She jolted up in her king-size feather bed. She mooed, "Jack! I had another drea—nightmare?"

Team Mermaid Recognition

I can't express enough gratitude to the folks at Beaver's Pond Press for taking a chance on the quirky woman in Alaska. Lily welcomed me to the pond, and I felt like I was back home in Minnesota. Never in my life had I considered writing, so having a tour guide to the industry helped immensely.

My project manager, Laurie, intuitively knew the only course of action was to assemble a team of badass women, lovingly deemed Team Mermaid. My editor, Paige, the true MVP, challenged me in ways that made my ideas truly come alive. She worked with my strengths and mentored me to perfection. When I first met my designer, Laura, I was starstruck—I couldn't believe this accomplished woman was a member of my squad. How did I get so lucky?

Jill Myer is more than just an artist—she's an inspiration. She's my brown-bear-viewing wilderness buddy and roller derby mentor. She didn't hate me for leaving a trail of glitter across her apartment the first time I visited (dressed as a mermaid, I might add).

Thanks to the strong women in my life who inspired characters, especially my roller derby gang and Alaska friends. Special thanks to Niketah, my beautiful derby wife who inspires me every day. I'm blessed to have met your kind soul, and your presence makes me a better human. Special thanks to Lorelei Killmore, the hardcore librarian genius who could take over the world.

I'm grateful to have had the best high school English teachers who encouraged my writing. Hyland taught me to be efficient, Richardson taught me to use words with purpose, and Hornseth always encouraged me to embrace my creativity. Their influence has stayed with me all these years. My biology professors at Michigan Tech fueled my love for nature and the world around me.

Thank you to the most glorious woman of them all, Valette. She's a photographer who takes the best portraits.

Thank you to Lee for the encouragement and Jedi Master level guidance in the early stages of this project.

Thanks to tech support, also known as my husband. You're the best.

Mom, I wrote this book with you in mind. Your love of books borders on hoarding and I can't wait to be in your collection. You're amazing for taking me to the library as a child and reading the same bunny books to me over and over. Thank you for teaching me how to swear. Now the whole world knows.

Thank you, Dad, for taking me fishing by Isle Royale. The trip gave me the vision of the setting for this romp through the wilderness. The boat ride almost killed me, but here we are.

Thanks to Grandma Joan, for teaching me kindness, patience, and how to raid a candy drawer. You made this project possible, and I can feel you smile down from heaven when I get sassy.

About the Author

Aurora Lothbrok was born and raised in Northern Minnesota. She began her lightsaber training at Michigan Tech, where she studied biology, and continued onward to the University of Iowa to study pharmacy. Her love of the outdoors and penchant for adventure took her north to Alaska, where she currently resides on Dena'ina Elnena land. She's been told that she looks like she belongs on the set of *The Big Bang Theory*. Inside Aurora are two wolves—one is a hobbit who wants second breakfast and the other wants a real-life Jurassic Park on the island of Adak. Her favorite recreational activities include roller derby, photography, and sci-fi marathons with her husband and pets. In fact, it's a miracle this book was even written, as the dogs occupy important lap real estate and make using a computer quite difficult. Aurora loves bears and sparkles, and she swoons with affection for a strong female lead. Fermented tea may be her one true weakness.

About the Artist

Jill Myer has lived on the Oregon coast since 2019, and when she isn't in her garage/studio making art, she spends as much time as possible walking in the woods and on the beach. Myer works in many mediums, but her current focus is on encaustic wax and watercolor. Myer draws inspiration from the ever-changing weather on the coast and the natural landscape. You can often find her taking inspirational photos during a rainstorm on the beach or post-rain in the forest, attempting to capture the freshness in the air. She repeatedly paints the ocean and sky, trying to capture the dramatic movement and power. Myer's current work can be found in the For Artsake Gallery in Historic Nye Beach in Newport.